THE FIREMAGE'S VENGEANCE

A BOOK OF UNDERREALM

GARRETT ROBINSON

THE FIREMAGE'S VENGEANCE
Garrett Robinson

The author greatly appreciates you taking the time to read his work. Please leave a review wherever you bought the book or on Goodreads.com.

Interior Design: Legacy Books, Inc.
Publisher: Legacy Books, Inc.
Editors: Karen Conlin, Cassie Dean
Cover Artist: Sarayu Ruangvesh

1. Fantasy - Epic 2. Fantasy - Dark 3. Fantasy - New Adult

Second Edition

Published by Legacy Books

To my family
Who make everything I do better

To Johnny, Sean and Dave
Who told me to write

To Amy
Who is endlessly patient (though I don't deserve it)

And to everyone who followed me
from the Birchwood to the Academy

You have made my life epic.

I hope I can enrich yours.

GET MORE

Legacy Books is home to the very best that fantasy has to offer.

Join our email alerts list, and we'll send word whenever we release a new book. You'll receive exclusive updates and see behind the scenes as we create them.

(You'll also learn the secrets that make great fantasy books, *great*.)

Interested? Visit this link:

Underrealm.net/Join

For maps of the locations in this book, visit:

Underrealm.net/maps

THE BOOKS OF UNDERREALM

THE NIGHTBLADE EPIC
NIGHTBLADE
MYSTIC
DARKFIRE
SHADEBORN
WEREMAGE
YERRIN

THE ACADEMY JOURNALS
THE ALCHEMIST'S TOUCH
THE MINDMAGE'S WRATH
THE FIREMAGE'S VENGEANCE

CHRONOLOGICAL ORDER
NIGHTBLADE
MYSTIC
DARKFIRE
SHADEBORN
THE ALCHEMIST'S TOUCH
THE MINDMAGE'S WRATH
WEREMAGE
THE FIREMAGE'S VENGEANCE
YERRIN

THE FIREMAGE'S VENGEANCE

A BOOK OF UNDERREALM

GARRETT ROBINSON

ONE

THE SNOW THAT FELL IN THOSE MIDDLE DAYS OF MARTIS did nothing to chill the air—nothing, that is, when compared to the ice in Ebon's heart. The frost inside him was made of fear and dread, and if asked, he would have called it more frigid than the winds and snow that blew in his face, for the winter within kept him from noticing the winter without.

He led Kalem and Theren through the streets of the High King's Seat. His friends felt the same, he knew. Theren huddled deeper under her hood. She had not bothered to dye her hair in some time, and her dark roots showed through the blonde, though that hardly mattered since her head was rarely uncovered these days. Kalem wrapped his arms tight about himself, pale cheeks glowing red as his hair against winter's gales, and his spindly limbs shook whenever he stayed in one place too long. Yet Ebon guessed that neither of them were any more aware of the weather than he was. They had greater troubles, ones that plagued them day and night. Their studies suffered, and in the midst of conversation their thoughts drifted away. They were left staring at nothing in the middle of the dining hall, and their worries kept them lying awake in their beds late into the night.

The first was Dasko, the instructor they held in bondage, though they did not wish to. The second was Erin, the dean's son who was captive or dead. And the third was his captor, Isra, who had vanished from all sight and knowledge, a trail of corpses in her wake.

"This is a fool's errand," said Theren, bringing Ebon's mind back to the present.

"It is no errand at all," said Ebon. "We are invited."

"And why did we accept? What if something happens to Das—what if something happens back at the Academy while we are gone?"

"We cannot watch him every hour of every day, Theren." Kalem's voice held a note of careful reproach. "Indeed, we do not spend much time with him as it is."

"Yet we are always near," Theren insisted. "If our control should slip . . ."

"If we are discovered, we will be discovered," said Ebon. "Kalem is right. We cannot spend our every hour sitting on our hands, half in hope and half in fear."

"You say that more easily than I would," Theren muttered. Ebon could not tell if she had meant for him to hear it or not, but he did not blame her either way. She had the most to fear in all this untenable situation.

At long last, the black iron gate of the Drayden family's manor loomed before them. Once the guards spied the three Academy students making their way through the snow drifts, they hastened to draw the gate open. Ebon shook out his boots on the cobblestones of the courtyard, which was better swept than the streets had been. He had never spent winter in the northern lands; at home in Idris, winters were colder, but drier, and snow was an Elf-tale. To him, this type of winter seemed a deadly danger, though Theren assured him it was in fact very mild this year.

A happy shout preceded a short, plump figure bounding towards them, and Ebon recognized his sister, Albi, beneath a furred hood. She hugged him first, and he grinned as he hoisted her up off the ground. But then she embraced Kalem just as warmly, and Ebon's mouth soured. Theren she gave a more customary greeting; both hands clasped at once, she bowed. Theren rolled her eyes, but returned the greeting without complaint.

"I thought the three of you would never come," Albi said. Her voice seemed uncommonly loud after the dead quiet of the snow-covered streets, and after the anxious, hushed words Ebon had shared with his friends. "But then, it seems much later than it is, for the sky is so dark and grey. Come inside. Halab eagerly awaits you."

"We will, and gladly," said Ebon, forcing a smile. "Northern winters suit me ill."

Albi laughed and led them in. Both hearths burned in the wide front hall, and Ebon sighed in relief at the warmth of them. He cast back his hood and bent to remove his boots. They were gifts Halab had sent only recently—black to follow the Academy's rules, but lined with grey fur and laced up to just below the knee. Theren and Kalem, too, had received their own pairs, but Theren almost forgot to remove hers, and had to be reminded by a sharp word from Kalem.

Unshod, they climbed the stairs to the lounge where Halab awaited them. She rose at once and came forwards with a smile. Her dress was ochre and white, like fine-spun gold dusted with snow. Though all faces were paler now in the waning sunlight, Ebon thought she had never looked lovelier.

"Dearest nephew," she said, reaching for him. He kissed her cheeks, and then she bowed to Kalem and Theren. Kalem flushed, and Ebon knew the boy was thinking of the first time they had met, when he had kissed Halab's cheeks. Theren, for her part, did not roll her eyes so hard as she had with Albi. Ebon knew the high estimation in which she held his aunt.

"Our heartfelt thanks for your hospitality, especially in the depths of winter's chill," said Kalem.

"But that is when hospitality is needed the most," said Halab with a smile.

Dinner had been prepared already, and was brought from the kitchens to be uncovered for them. They ate ravenously, for all three of them felt their appetites could hardly be sated these days. Halab laughed as she saw them devour their meals, and quipped that the three of them must be growing. Ebon thought to himself that the likelier explanation was the oppressive cold. When snow made walking a chore, even after a small distance, he seemed to need thrice as much food just to remain upright.

After, she took them back to the lounge, where they sat and talked of small things—their classes, and their friends (only Kalem had any of these outside of present company), and the little bits of news Halab thought they might enjoy hearing. But, as happened so often in the Academy itself these days, Ebon often found his mind wandering, and he saw the same in his friends. Halab noticed it as well. Often he found her looking at the three of them, a question in her eyes, her lips pursed. At last he leaned forwards and grimaced in apology.

"I am sorry, dearest aunt. The three of us have made terrible guests, I fear."

Halab shook her head at once. "It is I who should apologize. I have taken little consideration for the troubles the three of you bear. I have heard of the Academy's rogue student, and the dean's son who she stole away. No doubt such dark thoughts are what trouble you."

Ebon studied his fingernails, not wishing to meet her eyes. She was right about Isra, of course, but she did not know just how intimately the matter concerned Ebon, nor how often he heard Erin's screams as the boy was dragged away. Mako, it seemed clear, had not told her of what transpired in Xain's home.

Kalem spoke, as Ebon did not seem to wish to. "It is a dark time for the school indeed," he said quietly. "In one sense, the danger that plagued us is gone, for everyone believes that Isra has fled the Seat. But the darkness she left behind her is not so easily cast aside."

The room fell to silence as Ebon and his friends stared at the floor. When he glanced at Albi, Ebon was surprised to see that she looked bored. But Halab wore a vaguely mournful look. She sat straighter and put her wine goblet on a side table.

"If it is not too great a request, I should like a word alone with my nephew."

Theren and Kalem straightened at once. "Not at all," said Theren, ducking her head in a sort of sitting bow. "We have troubled you long enough as it is."

"I have enjoyed your company," said Halab with a smile. "This is only a little matter, and afterwards I must leave for the High King's palace. Albi, will you please . . .?"

Albi looked burningly curious, but she sighed and led Ebon's friends away. "Come, young master Konnel," she said, holding out her arm. "Our gardens are nearly frozen over, but you and I can keep each other warm regardless." Ebon glowered as she took them towards the staircase down.

Halab gave a soft chuckle after they had gone from view. "Your sister seems very taken with young Kalem."

"I have noticed," said Ebon, mouth puckered.

Again Halab laughed, and heartier this time. "You should not worry. She is only having some amusement. Albi knows full well that Kalem's parents will never accept her as a bride."

The words came from nowhere, and Ebon sat a bit straighter in his seat. "Why not?"

"It is nothing to do with Albi herself. She will make a fine wife someday, if she meets someone who knows not to get in her way. But the royalty are . . . reluctant, shall we say, to allow us *merchants* any more power than they think we deserve." She smirked as though at some hidden joke just remembered.

Ebon frowned. "I am not sure I understand."

Halab sighed. "That is just as well. It is a complicated matter, and more so as time goes on. But Albi knows enough of it to keep her heart safe. She means only to have a little fun with Kalem. Nothing more."

In truth, Ebon was more worried about Kalem than

about Albi. It seemed clear to him that Albi saw Kalem as a plaything, but Kalem did not look upon her the same way. The royal boy had had many conversations with Ebon on the subjects of love, and intimacy, and other things besides . . .

But he pushed these thoughts aside, for he doubted that Halab wished to speak with him on matters of love or matchmaking. Now she straightened and placed her feet on the floor, rather than draped along the seat, and patted the spot beside her. Ebon rose and went to her, just as she reached into a nearby drawer. From it she pulled a small iron trinket in the shape of an ankh. This she placed into his open palm.

"Here," she said. "This is for you."

Ebon was taken aback. "Thank you, dearest aunt." He looked at it curiously. The ankh was the symbol of their house, and was featured upon their crest. Yet he wondered exactly why she would give him this, for it seemed to bear little purpose. She had to know they were allowed to keep few possessions in the Academy.

Halab must have seen some of his confusion in his eyes, for she smiled and took it from him. "It is not only a trinket. Watch." She pressed the handle into the spars, and with a small *skrrtch*, sparks sprang out from the tip.

"A firestriker," said Ebon. He took it back, a bit more eagerly. "That is most cleverly made."

"Specially crafted when I was a child," she said. "It is of Calentin make. Among craftsmen, their artisans have no equal."

"Thank you," he said, and this time he meant it. "I will keep it with me always."

"That would please me," she said. Then she sighed and took his hands in hers. "This brings me to the next matter. You must know by now that your father has no intention of letting you keep your inheritance. That will pass to Albi."

Ebon stared at his lap. "She let something of that slip," he muttered.

"And I am sure you at least half-guessed it before. You have always been a wise boy. That means you will never get your mark."

The mark of their house was scarified on the skin of those who entered the family's service, on the wrist of the right arm. Father had his, and Ebon's brother Momen had had one as well. Ebon had long anticipated receiving his own mark, though the prospect lost more of its luster the older he grew.

But he forced a smile and looked at her. "Well, that is no great loss. I will be a wizard, after all. How many of our kin can say the same?"

Halab gave him a sad smile. "I want you to know," she said softly, "that if any but a parent could grant the mark, I would give it to you myself. And for those who obey me, this firestriker will serve just as well as a symbol upon your skin. You will never want for help from my house while you bear it."

His eyes stung. "Thank you, Halab. I am an even poorer guest now, for I have no gift in return."

"It is the joy of the old to provide for the young." She leaned back and took her wine goblet again. "Until very recently, I half thought I should give you a dagger. The Academy has not been a place free from peril, though it seems that danger has now passed."

Ebon's mood fell, for her words drew his thoughts back to Erin and Dasko. "I suppose it no longer plagues me, nor my friends," he said carefully. "But that does not mean there is no danger at all."

"You speak of the dean's son, yes? Erin of the family Forredar, is it not?"

"Yes. The rogue student, Isra—she took him, and no one knows where."

"Odd that she should escape both the High King's guards and the constables. I have heard even the Mystics lend their eyes to the search."

Ebon stared at his feet, fearful she would see the torment within him if he looked at her. "They say his father, Xain—the Academy's dean—is favored by the High King. I met him once. The boy, Erin, I mean. Briefly, only, yet I would not see him come to harm." He heard again Erin's cries for help as the boy was pulled into the streets. Unconsciously, his lips twisted in imitation of Isra's snarl.

"Xain Forredar has always been . . . difficult," said Halab. There was no mistaking the irritation in her voice. "To our family, I mean. Cyrus in particular earned his ire, as did your uncle Matami."

At that, the room fell to swift silence. Ebon's gaze

darted about, seeking somewhere to rest. His own wine goblet sat unattended, and he took it to refill, all the while avoiding Halab's watchful attention.

The last time Ebon had seen his uncle, it had been when Mako killed him slow in the sewers beneath the city. Ebon still remembered the empty gap where Matami's eye had been, the bloodied stumps of his fingers . . .

He drank deep from his goblet and filled it once more. When at last he looked to Halab, her face was stony. But her eyes glinted with tears expertly held back. Mako had said that Halab would know, or guess, at what happened to Matami. But he had said also that she would not mention it.

Sometimes it was easier that way. That the truth be known, but unspoken.

Halab rustled her shoulders, and it was as if she shook off a cloak that had kept her mood solemn. She graced Ebon with a smile that hardly seemed forced and put her hands upon his shoulders.

"I want you to know, Ebon, that you are the closest thing to my own son, and I could want for nothing more. The pain and danger you have suffered of late weigh upon me, and I am glad such suffering has passed you by. If ever you need something from me—anything at all—you have only to ask."

Ebon's throat seized up. He had never heard such soft words from his own parents. Forgetting his manners, he seized Halab in a tight hug. "How could I ask anything of you, when already you have been my one bright light in dark times?"

She let him hold her for a moment, and then gently urged him away. "Go now, dearest nephew. I must leave, so rejoin your friends and your sister. The shadow has passed—enjoy the daylight while it remains."

He smiled in answer, and held it until she left the room. Then his face fell, and he put a hand to his forehead, remembering Matami's empty eye socket.

TWO

THE GARDEN WAS LIKE A STAGE PLAY, FOR IT WAS HUSHED and fresh, the white snow forming a platform waiting for its actors to arrive. The quiet of winter's air was like the audience standing in the pit below, breath held eagerly in anticipation, hearts thrumming with promise. Ebon stepped into it, and for a moment he paused there in the door. He closed his eyes, breathing deep to take in the smell.

Then, far off, he heard Albi's bright laugh. He opened his eyes with a sigh and set off down the path to find her.

She and Kalem and Theren were among the hedges, walking aimlessly along winding paths. He could see from their footprints that they had walked in many circles already. Albi still held tight to Kalem's arm, and Kalem was pressed against her side—though he flushed and parted from her slightly when he saw Ebon. Behind them, Theren had a long-suffering look on her face, and her relief at Ebon's arrival was obvious.

"You and Halab must have shared heartfelt words," said Albi, smiling at him. "I can see your eyes clouded in thought."

"We did," Ebon said quietly. "And she gave me this." From his pocket he withdrew the firestriker and held it up.

Albi tilted her head. "Why . . . why, that was Uncle Matami's. I saw him use it on the road we took here from Idris. Sometimes he would strike it absentmindedly as we drove, his thoughts wandering elsewhere, and his hands seeking something to do."

That put a sick feeling in the pit of Ebon's stomach. He looked at the firestriker anew. It had to be a message. Had Halab simply meant to tell Ebon that she knew of Matami's death? Or was it a token of forgiveness, absolving him of blame for his part in the murder?

He had been silent too long, and they were staring at him. "What have the three of you been speaking of?"

"I was telling Kalem of the caravan I will soon

lead," said Albi. "I will take the wagons back home to Idris—though not directly, for that would bring us far too close to Dulmun, and there is a war on, after all. First we will sail to Selvan, there to take the King's road until it reaches the Dragon's Tail river. We will sail upon those waters until they reach the king's road again, and then drive east until we are home. I am most excited about the whole thing."

But Ebon was gaping at her. "*You* will lead the caravan? But . . . but your age."

He could almost see her hackles rise. She released Kalem's arm to put her hands on her hips, and her plump, rosy cheeks grew redder for a moment. "You think me a child? I am fourteen, Ebon—very nearly a woman grown. Our father was my age when he led his first caravan, and Halab was even younger."

Theren smirked as she looked at him over Albi's head. Kalem's eyes were wide, and he looked as though he would rather be elsewhere. "I-I meant no offense," stammered Ebon. "I was only surprised, that is all."

A thought tickled his mind: Albi would lead this caravan, not because that was what the family wished, but because Matami was no longer there to do it himself.

She lifted her chin haughtily, but some of the spark of anger died in her eyes. "Well. I suppose surprise is warranted. I half died myself, when Halab told me. But the more I have thought upon it, the more excited I have become."

"Will you not grow bored?" he said, smiling to soften the words.

Albi stuck her tongue out at him. "I will have plenty and more to do. We are not only driving the carts. We will be trading wherever we stop. That, of course, will be managed by others—I will have some oversight, but this trip is as much for me to learn as anything else. Come now, though. I am nearly frozen through. Let us go inside, and I will tell you more."

They followed her back to the manor, where they tramped the snow off their boots and removed them. She then led them upstairs to a sitting room, smaller than the one where they often met with Halab. A servant at the door stepped forwards, but Theren spoke before he could even open his mouth.

"Yes, wine, please. Something fine." She blinked and looked at Ebon as if it were an afterthought. "That is, if you do not mind. I never learned my noble graces."

"Not at all," said Ebon. With all of the news Albi had told them, he thought he could rather use a drink.

As they waited for the wine, Albi took a table and put it in the center of the couches. Then she leaned over, putting objects and trinkets at various places, naming them for the cities she would visit upon her route. And Ebon noticed that whenever she leaned forwards or back, she brushed against Kalem's arm.

"Here is Garsec, where we will land first. Then we follow the road west until it turns south and reaches Cabrus. We will stay there a little while; there is no better place to find steel in all of Selvan. Then it is a journey of many days to Redbrook, with little on the road to entertain, and that sits upon the Dragon's Tail. In each city, and mayhap some of the towns, we will stay a short while in order to trade some goods for others, or for coin. And, of course, to find new guards, if we should need them."

The wine came, and Theren drained her cup at once before handing it back to the servant. The man refilled it and then left the bottle for them. "Why should you need to find new guards?" said Theren.

"Why, if anyone should die, of course," said Albi simply. "A caravan should always travel with at least half again as many wagoners and guards as it needs. The roads are not safe in these days of war, and if some of our men should be waylaid, or shit themselves to death from foreign water, who will keep our goods moving safely?"

Ebon balked, and Kalem spit up the little sip of wine he had just taken. To hear Albi speak so plainly of men's deaths . . . it made Ebon feel suddenly lightheaded, as though he had found himself in a dream. Who was this young woman who sat before him? Where was young Albi whose eyes would shine when he told her his dreams of the Academy? It seemed impossible she had changed so much in the short time he had been here upon the Seat. Yet the only other explanation was that she had ceased to be a little girl some time ago, and he was only just beginning to realize it.

Theren laughed at her frank words, while Kalem turned red. Albi saw his reaction and giggled, putting a hand on his arm.

"Do I shock you, dear Kalem? You must understand, I spent two months on wagons traveling here from Idris, and wagoners have bawdy tongues. I would guess I could teach you a thing or two of language." Then her eyes brightened, and she gently slapped his arm. "Kalem, you must make me a promise. Once you have finished your studies in the Academy, you must let me take you upon a trip. Some caravan on a long route across the nine lands. Mayhap not even to Idris. I think we might have more fun other places."

Her eyes flashed, while Kalem's grew wide and starry. But Ebon scowled in disgust. Albi's relentless flirting seemed harmless enough, most of the time, but she never left well enough alone.

Ebon stood quickly. "We should leave."

Albi frowned at him. "What? But the day is young."

"It was Halab's invitation that brought us here in the first place, yet she is gone, and we continue to take her hospitality. Besides, I have an appointment at the Academy." And that, in fact, was true. Astrea waited for him there, the way she did every day, their visits born half from Ebon's desire to help and half from his own guilt.

"Then why do you not go yourself, and leave your friends here?" said Albi.

Kalem looked like he might agree, but Ebon took

him by the arm and lifted him up at once. "I am not the only one with duties at the citadel," he said, and fixed Theren with a meaningful look.

Her eyes darkened, and she rose as well. "You are right. I had hoped you would accompany me in my chores this evening, Kalem."

Kalem's mouth turned in a frown, and he lowered his eyes. In the manor, it was easy to forget about Erin, and Isra, and Dasko, but now Ebon had brought memory back to the fore. "Of course," he said quietly. "It was my pleasure to see you again, Lady Drayden."

"Albi, I beg of you. Lady Drayden sounds ever too formal for such a dear heart as yourself." She held his hand tightly in hers, until at last he kissed her fingers. Ebon gave her a brusque hug, and Theren clasped her wrists, before he could finally usher his friends out the door and back into the snowy streets.

THREE

"THAT SEEMED A BIT RUSHED," SAID KALEM AS THEY trudged on.

"I had forgotten about the time, and remembered all at once," said Ebon. It was a lie, and likely Kalem could hear it in his voice. But just now, he did not care overmuch.

They said little else before they reached the Academy. Its iron doors stood closed against the chill, but they opened easily. Without thinking, they made for one of the side halls—but a shrill cry stopped them all in their tracks.

"*Snow!*" cried Mellie. The little old doorguard thrust a spindly finger at their boots and held it there quivering. Her eyes glowed with madness, almost like magelight.

"Yes, Mellie," the three muttered in unison. They went to the side of the front door where an iron grate lay over a pit and tramped the snow off of their feet. Mellie paced behind them like a sellsword general before her troops. When they were done they stepped away—but Mellie snatched Ebon's arm and held him still, then lifted his boot up to inspect it as though he were a horse and she about to shoe him.

"Fine, fine," she muttered. "Snow! It gets everywhere, it does. Everything wet. Ugh!"

They slipped away as quick as they could, making for the stairs to the dormitories. But once again they were brought up short—this time by Jia. The instructor stepped suddenly in front of them, sandy hair pulled into its usual tight bun.

"Ebon, Kalem," she said briskly. "I must see you in the dining hall this evening. Nine o'clock. Do not be late."

That made them pause. Ebon looked to Kalem, and Kalem back at him, but each was as confused as the other. "Of course, Instructor," said Ebon. "But may I ask . . ."

But she had moved on as soon as he had agreed, and the question died on his lips.

"What could she want?" said Kalem.

"You do not think . . ." Theren let the words hang.

"She cannot know about . . . about our friend," said Ebon firmly, meaning Dasko. "If she did—if anyone did—we would be greeted by an assembly intent on capturing us. We would not be summoned to a late-night meeting. But come, we are almost late. Our 'friend' needs tending to."

"I know that," said Theren, scowling. "See to your own affairs."

"Until the morrow, then." Kalem set off towards the grounds.

But Theren did not follow him at once. "Go. I will be there in a moment." Once Kalem obeyed, she turned to Ebon. "You should not think so harshly of him."

Ebon blinked. "Harshly? What do you mean?"

"He is young, and likely cannot help the way he feels about your sister."

A moment passed before he understood, and when he did he scowled. "You think I am upset with *Kalem?* You misunderstand me. It is my sister who behaves foolishly."

Theren cocked her head. "But she is scarcely older than he is. It is the same thing."

He shook his head quickly. "I might once have thought so, but no longer. She is growing up a bit too fast, and while she has a good heart, I see too much of my family in her. She plays with him and with his affection. I am only trying to keep him from pain."

She gave him a sad smile. "That will not work for-

ever. But do as you will. I only wanted to mention it."
Then she turned and left him.

Ebon glowered as he made his way up the stairs to
Astrea's dormitory. It was all well and good for Theren
to dismiss the matter brewing between Kalem and
Albi. If the two of them were to have a falling out,
Theren would not be the one caught between a sibling
and a best friend who would not speak to each other.
Then again, the thought of the two of them avoiding
each other had much more appeal than the present situation. Mayhap he would let things play out after all.

He had reached the door he sought, so he pushed
his thoughts aside and stepped in. Among the many
chairs in the common room beyond, he spied little
Astrea where she sat by the fireplace. It burned low,
and Ebon threw a new log upon the flames before he
turned and sat in the chair beside hers. She did not so
much as lift her gaze.

"Good eve," Ebon said quietly. "How do you fare?"

"The same," she murmured.

He swallowed. "I do not have as much time as I
wish," he said. "Jia needs me for something this evening, though I know not what."

Her brow creased, and she folded her arms across
her chest. "Very well. You do not need to come and see
me if you are busy."

"I would not leave you alone. Not after . . ."

Her eyes flashed as she looked at him. He fell silent. She did not like talk of Isra, who had been like a

sister to her. Ebon supposed he could not blame her. He decided to change tack.

"Why do we not take a walk upon the grounds?" he said, sitting up in his armchair. "It is cold, but in a bracing sort of way. The air might do you good. You hardly ever leave the citadel."

"I do not want to," said Astrea.

"It is not good to stay cooped up. Now more than ever. Come with me. It will be only a little walk."

She rolled her eyes, and for a moment reminded him strikingly of Albi, though the two of them could not have looked more different. "All right." She rose and followed him from the room, but he could not miss the morose stoop in her shoulders.

Outside, the air was bracing indeed. It made him gasp as it first splashed across his face, and Astrea huddled closer under her cloak. But after a few minutes of walking, the blood began to flow, and his breath did not come quite so shaky. Astrea, despite the deep scowl she kept upon her face, began to move more easily as well. After a time she even threw back her hood. The night was dark now, but the Academy's grounds were lit by many lanterns hanging from the walls.

"How have you been feeling?" said Ebon after a while.

"I am fine," she grated. "Except that everyone keeps asking me that, or some other version of it. It is as though they think some lever will turn, and one day I will be happy again."

"My apologies," said Ebon. "It is only . . . we worry for you."

"Why should you? You see me every day in class."

"Is . . ." Ebon tried to remember how Halab had spoken to him before, so kind and gentle. "Is there any way I can help? Do you need anything?"

She looked away to hide her eyes. "I want Isra to return. I want this all to be a terrible dream."

After a moment he saw her shoulders quivering. He put out an awkward arm to drape across them. "I know she was like a sister," he said quietly. "I cannot imagine what I would feel if my own sister were taken from me this way."

"Of course you cannot imagine it," said Astrea sharply. But immediately she ducked her head. "I am sorry. I did not mean that."

"It is all right."

When she looked at him again, her eyes were wet. "She always looked after me. In our orphanage, sometimes food would be scarce. She would share hers with me so I would not get so hungry. Some other children liked to bully me, but Isra never let them get away with it. She could tumble anyone, even children larger than her. I have often become lonely here at the Academy. I have often wished I had parents to write home to, or who would come and visit me. But during the day I could always go . . . go and see Isra and she would . . . she would . . ."

She began to cry in earnest, burying her face in the

front of Ebon's robes. He held her tightly, awkwardly. With one hand he gently patted her hair.

Her words echoed in his mind, giving him a feeling of vague unease. The girl Astrea spoke so highly of was nothing like the Isra he had known. He still had dreams, sometimes waking, sometimes in his sleep, of Isra's mad eyes as she tried to kill him. He still saw Vali, his neck snapped on the stone wall, and Oren, pierced by dozens of knives in the dining hall.

How could the monster who did those deeds have been so loved by this innocent, sweet girl? It seemed even the worst sort of people had some good in them. If that was so, the reverse must also be true. And so he said, not as a comfort, but as a lesson, "Even the best people have some evil in them."

Astrea pulled away from him and kept walking. "But some people do worse things, and no one calls them evil. If Isra were rich like Lilith, I think some people would help her. People might not call her a villain."

"Lilith received no special privilege because of her wealth," said Ebon. "I saw her while she was under the knives of the Mystics. It was horrible. She was like a broken creature."

The girl shook her head. Not a rejection, but a refusal to hear. Ebon almost pressed the point, but then the Academy's bell began to ring. Nine times it called out.

"Blast," said Ebon. "I am late. Jia requested me. I will come and see you again tomorrow. I swear it."

Astrea only shrugged. "Every day," she muttered. "Every day the same."

He put an arm around her shoulders and ushered her back inside through one of the white cedar doors.

FOUR

Once Astrea was on her way up the stairs, Ebon ran for the dining hall. When he reached its wide oak doors, he nearly ran full-on into Kalem, who had come from the other direction.

"At least I will not be the only one who is late," said Ebon.

"I lost track of the hour," said Kalem, wheezing hard. He had never been athletic, even for a noble-born son. "After she visited our 'friend,' Theren required some consolation."

Ebon frowned. "Is everything all right?"

Kalem's brows shot for the ceiling. "Of course not, Ebon. How can you even ask that?"

He grimaced. "Later."

They pushed open the doors and entered the dining hall. But both of them froze in the doorway, for they found they were not the only ones present. Many other students had been called, and all of them were sitting at a few tables near the entrance. Some looked up curiously to see them standing there, but most kept their eyes on Jia.

The instructor stood at the head of the little group, watching them all with a keen eye. She seemed ready to give a speech, but it did not appear she had started yet. As soon as she saw Ebon and Kalem, she waved them to the benches at once.

"Come, come. Sit, sit," she said. "There we are. Excellent. Now, I believe we may begin."

The other students began to quiet down. But Kalem whispered quickly in Ebon's ear, "Why are we here, but not Theren? What is this?" Ebon shrugged.

Jia lifted her chin. "This," she began, "is a dangerous time. Not only for the Academy, nor for the Seat, but for all of Underrealm. The High King is beset on all sides, and she requires the help of every one of us to preserve the nine kingdoms."

She paused for a moment. The dining hall settled to silence. Ebon and Kalem stared at each other. Ebon was even more mystified than before.

Suddenly Jia shook her head as if she had remembered something. "Yes, she requires our help," she went on. "But some may help more than others. Some have greater strength of arms—or spells, in our case. Some have larger armies, and some have deeper pockets. These must aid her according to their means—but it begins at the very roots, with each one of us, and not with the grand schemes of the kingdoms. Who better to defend Underrealm against its enemies than the noble families of which you are a part? A short time ago, Lilith had the wise idea to form a group of you for just such a purpose. The Goldbag Society, I believe she called it, though it is an uncouth name."

Ebon's blood ran cold. He looked at Kalem. The boy's face had gone Elf-white. A quick glance around the room confirmed it: Ebon saw no one there but the children of merchants and royalty. These were the same children Lilith had called together when she was under Isra's mindwyrd.

Jia spoke on, but Ebon could scarcely hear the words. He leaned over to whisper in Kalem's ear. "She is here."

"She cannot be," said Kalem. "How could . . .?"

"No time for wondering now," said Ebon. "Go and fetch Theren, as quickly as ever you can. And tell her to bring Kekhit's amulet."

Kalem nodded, but then gave Jia a wary look. Slowly he stood from his bench. Jia seemed to take no notice, but only continued her speech. Step by step Kalem backed away, edging towards the door of the dining hall. Some students caught the motion and stared, but Jia droned on regardless. It was as though she did not even see him. Ebon's stomach did a flip-flop. Kalem turned and ran, vanishing into the Academy's hallways.

Ebon looked about him carefully. Other than the few tables near the front, the dining hall was nearly empty. But there, at the back of the hall, he spied the doorways leading into the kitchens, which were now dark and looked abandoned.

One of the doors was ajar.

He stood from his bench and walked towards it. Jia took no more notice of him than she had of Kalem, though some of the students watched him go. He hesitated on the threshold of the kitchens for a long moment, trying to let his eyes adjust to the darkness. But when at last he could see inside, no one was in sight.

Heart thundering in his ears, he stepped into the darkness.

The dish room was empty. An oak door in the corner opened into the kitchens proper—and Ebon saw that it, too, was ajar. He crept carefully forwards, muffling each footstep as best he could.

It was darker still inside. No lanterns were lit here, and no windows let in the moonlight. He longed to reach for his power so that his eyes might help light the way, but then he might be seen. So he crept forwards, avoiding the tables around him, which might send dishes clattering to the floor if he bumped them. The air smelled of meat left out too long.

He thought he could hear a murmuring drawing near. And then, from the next room, he caught a faint glow. But something was . . . wrong about it. In its light he could see shapes, but not their color or distance. It was like an awareness rather than true sight. His mind hurt, and his eyes kept shuddering away from it.

He stepped into the doorway.

It was a storeroom, and here at last there was moonslight from a window high in the wall. There were barrels and sacks in great piles all around the place and crates stacked in its center.

In one corner sat a girl in the robes of an Academy student—only they were filthy and threadbare, and Ebon thought he could smell them from where he stood. Her hair was just as dirty, and hung lank around her shoulders.

It was Isra. The glow that shone from her eyes sent a lance of pain through Ebon's head. She was facing away from him, but it leaked around her edges like a malicious, oozing thing, a poison that sought the mouth and nose to slither in and choke the breath.

At first he could not force himself to move, or even to think. When at last he did, he grew curious what it was that she was doing. She remained hunched over, her back to him, and the feverish rasping of her voice bounced harsh off the stone walls into his ears. He took one step forwards—every moment a skipping of the heart, a fearsome clenching in his gut.

A few paces in from the door, he could at last see

what it was she held in her hand. It was a lantern. At first he thought that was where the black glow was coming from—but then, looking again, he realized it was coming from her eyes.

He remembered something . . . something Kalem and Theren had told him about a black glow in the eyes. Then it came to him in a flash: *magestones.*

At once he realized what must have happened. Jia had called the assembly in the dining hall under Isra's control. Somehow the girl had got her hands on magestones, and she was using the power of mindwyrd once again.

Ebon realized he could do no good here. Quickly he backed away. He was almost to the door.

He did not think he had made a noise, but Isra stopped chanting. Her head jerked up, and then she turned around.

"Drayden," she growled.

An unseen force snatched him up. He flew through the air and into a shelf of pots, and now made up for all the clatter he had avoided while sneaking in. The dishes scattered everywhere, and after his hushed entrance it sounded like the breaking of the world. But was it loud enough for the other students to hear from the dining hall?

Isra's magic clutched him around the throat. She hoisted him up until his feet dangled helplessly above the stone floor. He gasped for breath as stars burst in his vision.

"This is a gift beyond reckoning," said Isra, walking towards him. The black glow in her eyes had increased. Now Ebon thought the sight of it might drive him mad. "I could not have planned for you to be the first to die tonight. Yet here you are, delivered as though upon a platter."

A flash of silver in the moonslight caught his eye. In Isra's hand, she still held the silver lantern over which she had been chanting. He could see something inside it: some faint and twisting light, pale and green, spinning in and around itself like the threads of a tapestry, over and over again without end. But he could hardly spare a thought for it while he hung in Isra's grip.

Then from nowhere, a blast of power rocked the kitchens, and Isra flew through the air. She crashed into another shelf of dishes, sending them flying in all directions. They were wood, and none broke, but the clatter was deafening. The magic holding Ebon vanished, but he was unprepared for it and landed hard on his hands and knees with a cry of pain.

Isra tried to find her feet, but the magic struck her again, and she flipped over backwards. Ebon heard the *crack* of her shoulder on a carving table. He looked in the direction he had come.

There stood Theren, and beside her was Kalem. The boy's eyes were alight as he touched his magic, though Ebon knew not what he hoped to do. Beside him, there was no glow in Theren's eyes at all—yet she held her hands aloft, and Ebon knew it was she who had attacked Isra. He could not see it, but he knew that beneath her robes was Kekhit's amulet, which gave her magic the strength to match Isra's.

Across the kitchen, Isra snarled as she fought her way to standing at last. Darklight flared in her eyes, and she threw a contemptuous hand through the air. Yet if she hoped to bat Theren away like some child, she was disappointed. Theren's magic met her, and it matched her. Then Ebon saw a ripple in the air, forming a wall that swept around Isra like a cage. Isra gritted her teeth as she blasted it, but the rippling air held firm.

"Are you whole, Ebon?" said Theren, though she spoke through a clenched jaw herself.

"I am." He went to stand by her. "Can you hold her? Shall we fetch an instructor?"

"She is—" But the words were cut off. Isra screamed, and Ebon felt the room shudder as Theren's barrier was cast aside. Before he could blink, Isra flung the silver lantern she had been holding at them. It clattered to the ground at their feet, but its glass did not break. Then Isra ran into the storeroom and leaped. Magic lifted her towards the ceiling, and she vanished through the high window onto the grounds beyond.

Theren made to go after her. But Ebon looked at the lamp on the ground. He saw the light within it—it was spinning faster and faster now, and blazing with a fury like the sun. Now the kitchen shone as if it were daylight.

"Down!" he cried, and snatching Kalem's collar, he tackled Theren behind the storeroom's crates.

THOOM

The air was wracked by an explosion. There were no flames, no heat. Instead it was as though an unseen battering ram struck everything in the room at once. Crates from the pile rained down atop them, but Theren batted them away with her magic. All around, sacks of flour and barrels of grain burst, coating the room in white dust and small brown kernels of wheat.

All fell silent. Slowly, Ebon got to his feet. But Theren did not hesitate. The moment she had shoved off the last crate, she jumped up and leaped through the window where Isra had vanished.

Ebon hauled Kalem up and ran through the kitchens. There was a door leading outside, and they burst through it together. Winter's air blasted them, and Kalem huddled against him on instinct. They met Theren outside, where she stood with hands raised.

But the grounds were empty. Fresh snow fell from the sky, covering everything. No one was there. No figure in a black robe could be spotted against the white. Isra had escaped.

"Darkness take me," said Theren, kicking a great fountain of snow into the air. "I thought we had her for certain."

"What is she doing here?" said Kalem. "I thought she left the Seat."

"We all did," said Theren. "It would have been the

wise thing to do. I do not know what she hopes to achieve by being here."

"Do you not?" said Ebon. "She called all the gold-bags together. Every merchant's child. Every royal son and daughter." He shuddered as he remembered Lilith's cold, lifeless voice saying the words, prodded by Isra's mindwyrd. "But where is Erin?" he said suddenly, as the thought struck him. "If she is here, Erin must be nearby."

"Or dead," muttered Theren.

Ebon was about to respond, but Kalem raised a hand to point. "Look," he said quietly.

His quivering voice silenced them both. Going to either side of him, Ebon and Theren followed his outstretched finger. Yet Ebon saw nothing untoward.

"What is it, Kalem?"

"The window. She jumped out the window. And yet . . ."

It took another moment. Then Theren gave a sharp hissing gasp, and Ebon saw it in the same instant.

There was only one set of tracks in the snow, and they led right to Theren. Isra had leaped through the high window above, and then had vanished without so much as a footprint.

FIVE

"WE MUST TELL THE INSTRUCTORS AT ONCE," SAID Kalem. He took two quick steps, running back towards the Academy's white cedar doors. But Theren snatched his collar and hauled him back around like a mother with an unruly kitten.

"We must do nothing of the sort," she snapped. "We *can* do nothing of the sort. I hold the amulet, Kalem, or had you forgotten? How do you mean to explain that to them?"

Kalem blinked. His mouth opened and then shut without releasing words. But in another heartbeat he shook his head. "No. We *must* tell them, Theren. Everyone thinks Isra has left the Seat, but she remains here. She infiltrated the Academy itself. If they do not know they are in danger, they can do nothing to protect themselves."

"Those words come easily to you—it will not be your neck upon the chopping block if the amulet is found. We cannot afford any attention now, not while we still hold a magical artifact beyond the King's law. Not to mention that we hold Dasko in mindwyrd."

Ebon caught Kalem's uneasy look. "Theren, we cannot simply ignore this."

"What do you mean to do, then?" Theren's shout was sudden and loud, and it looked like it surprised even her. "Shall we run inside and find Perrin and say, 'Instructor Perrin! We saw Isra, Instructor Perrin, and her eyes glowed black. But I defeated her, for I wore Kekhit's amulet and used my strength of magestones against hers. Oh, yes, I should likely have mentioned that Kekhit's amulet is not in fact missing, but is about my neck.' The High King has declared martial law, Ebon. I will not receive mercy. The constables will execute me if the Mystics do not get their hands on me first."

Kalem spread his hands. "Ebon. Do you really mean to let everyone carry on in ignorance?"

It seemed an impossible question. Ebon looked back and forth between his friends but found no words to speak. In the end he shrugged. "I cannot go against

Theren in this Kalem. She has the most to lose if we tell the whole truth. But Theren, neither do I think we can keep this only to ourselves."

Theren's jaw clenched. She looked up at the window, and then at the snow where no footprints showed Isra's passage. Then, all at once, the fight went out of her. Her shoulders sagged, and her head drooped. "I know," she said. "I know it. Damn her. Damn her for coming back."

Ebon put a hand on her shoulder. "We will not tell them about the amulet. Of course not. Only . . . only we must find the right lie to tell."

Kalem's mouth soured at that, but he held his peace. Theren did not seem wholly convinced. "We could tell Jia . . . mayhap we could tell her we came upon Isra by surprise—"

"Not Jia," said Ebon quickly. "She is the one under mindwyrd. We must tell someone else. Perrin, as you said. Though not the words you said, of course."

"Yes," said Kalem. Still he looked unhappy, but he gave a grudging nod. "Yes, Perrin might believe us. Especially you, Ebon."

"Then let us make our story."

Quickly they built the lie, and then they ran into the Academy and through the halls to Perrin's classroom. They found her at the front of the room, sitting at her desk. She stood at once as they burst through the door.

"What is this?"

"Instructor Perrin!" said Ebon, trying to fill his voice with panic. "We saw her. We saw Isra."

Perrin's eyes sharpened at once. "What? Where?"

"In the kitchens. She was doing . . . something, I am not sure what. We had grown hungry, and I thought to sneak in for a snack. I know that is not allowed, and I am sorry."

"Never mind that," said Perrin. She started for the door. "Where is she now?"

Ebon put up his hands to stop her, though it felt like a mouse trying to stop a bear. "She is gone. Whatever she was doing, we startled her."

"She attacked us with spells," said Theren. "I fought her off, but barely. She fled after throwing this at us."

She held aloft the silver lantern. Perrin snatched it from her hand like a venomous serpent. She went to a high cupboard, gingerly placed the lantern inside, and then locked it.

"What happened when she threw it at you?" said Perrin. "How are you . . .?"

Ebon nodded. "The explosion. I saw a light brewing within it, and something told me to run. We barely got out of the way in time." He felt a glimmer of relief—it was much easier to tell that part of the story, for it was true.

"Very well," said Perrin. "I will fetch some of the others. The three of you must go to your dormitories, immediately." She pushed past them into the hallway.

Kalem put a hand on her arm. "Instructor. There

is one more thing. I . . ." he looked anxiously back and forth down the hallway. A pair of anxious tears leaked from the corners of his eyes, and Ebon marveled at his ability to act—though considering the circumstances, he likely did not have to reach far to summon the terror in his expression. "I know I should not know of this. But . . . but Theren said Isra was more powerful than she had been before, and . . . and her eyes glowed black, Instructor."

Perrin's ruddy features went pale. Carefully she removed Kalem's hand from where it rested, and then pointed at the three of them. "Into bed with all of you. Now. Do not leave for any reason. And tell *no one* of what you have seen. Do you understand?"

"But what about Jia?" said Ebon. "She is in the dining hall speaking to some other students. And she will not answer when anyone tries to speak to her. Something is wrong with her."

"Mindwyrd," Perrin whispered, almost too soft for them to hear. Then she roared, "Bed! Now!" They all jumped and hurried off as she thundered down the hallway in the other direction.

Ebon looked to his friends as they walked. "Do you think it will work?"

"The die is cast," murmured Theren. "We have no choice now but to see where it will fall."

Ebon did not follow Perrin's instructions at once, and

went to his common room rather than straight to bed. There he waited a while, until the door opened again and some other students came in. He saw Nella among them and jumped up from his seat to catch her eye.

"What happened?" he said.

She stopped short and regarded him carefully. As one of Lilith's friends, Nella had never been exactly friendly with Ebon. But after the two of them fought beside each other on the day the High King's Seat was attacked, Ebon had always felt a sort of mutual, grudging respect between them.

"Several instructors interrupted the meeting," said Nella. "They took Instructor Jia away with them."

"Was she all right?"

"She fought them." Her eyes shifted away from his face. "I have never quite seen the like of it. First she screamed, and then she thrashed in their arms. She even tried to turn herself—with weremagic, I mean—but Perrin dispelled it. By the time they removed her, she was speaking nonsense. Then they told us to come straight to bed."

Her gaze fell away, and she pushed past him into her dormitory. After the door shut behind her, Ebon stared at it for a long time before his mind returned to the present. He shook himself and returned to an armchair before the hearth.

Since the moment he and Kalem had begun to suspect something was wrong, he had hardly had any time to think. Now he watched the flickering, writhing orange and red of the fire, his mind racing, unable to banish the memory of the black glow in Isra's eyes.

Why would she still be here? Wisdom would have commanded her to leave the Seat as quickly as she could. But clearly wisdom did not rule her mind now. Ebon knew little of the madness that magestones could bring, but he thought he knew enough.

Then he shot up straight in the armchair. Did this mean that Erin, the dean's son, also remained on the Seat? It would make sense.

He got up and very nearly ran from the common room. But with his hand on the door, he paused. If he had only just come to this conclusion, Dean Forredar certainly would have thought of it already. It would do no one any good for Ebon to come running to the instructors and tell them, and it might call more attention down upon him—mayhap even suspicion.

Damn the suspicion, he thought. He saw in his mind Erin's terrified eyes as Isra dragged the boy away. But another moment passed, and he let his hand fall from the door. Though it made his gut clench in self-loathing, he feared to draw any more attention than they already had.

He returned to the armchair, and there he remained until dawn's light shone through the windows. Once it did, he washed himself and made his way to the dining hall. Theren and Kalem were not there yet, and so he filled three bowls with porridge for them and himself. As each appeared, he flagged them down with a wave, and soon they sat eating quietly.

"Have you heard—" Kalem began.

"No one has heard anything yet, Kalem," said Theren.

They fell to silence again.

At last, when most of the students had assembled in the hall, the faculty came in. Ebon studied them carefully. All looked haggard, and he doubted any of them had slept a wink. At their head was Dean Forredar. His eyes looked haunted, troubled in a way Ebon could not define. It sent a shiver through Ebon's limbs. When the instructors had settled themselves into their seats, Xain tapped his cup on the table for silence. He hardly needed to; the dining hall had fallen to a quiet murmur the second the faculty had appeared.

"Students," Xain began. "Last night, there was an attack, though not a fatal one—and thank the sky for that. In recent weeks, we have tried hard to keep the rumor from your ears, but I do not doubt that you have all heard it: Isra, once a student here, is the Academy killer."

He paused for a moment, and Ebon saw his jaw twitching. What he had not said, and likely would not say, was that Isra had taken his son, Erin, as well.

When he had composed himself, he went on. "We, along with the constables and Mystics who searched for her, thought that she had fled the Seat. But last night she returned."

A hushed gasp rippled through the students. Xain did not try to shush it, but instead regarded them all carefully.

"Yes. She was here. And she tried to kill three . . . students, who came upon her in the kitchens. By sheer luck, they survived. The next time, we might not be so fortunate." Ebon heard the word twist in Xain's mouth, and it made his heart skip a beat. But Xain went on steadily. "There is something else. Another thing you should all know. What I am about to tell you goes against the ruling of past deans for many, many long years. But I was once a student here, as you are now. I know we have all heard things of which it is forbidden to speak aloud. But I will speak them aloud now, for I believe that it is more dangerous to remain silent. Isra is an abomination—an eater of magestones."

The hall burst into tumult. Some students stood from their benches in fear, while others simply sat in place and cowered. Ebon felt stunned. It had seemed dangerous enough last night when Kalem had said the word to Instructor Perrin. Now it felt as though Xain had stood before them all and spouted curses like a common dockhand. He hardly knew what to think.

Xain let the noise continue for a moment, but then he raised his hands. "Silence. *Silence!* I do not tell you this to frighten you—any more than you should be frightened, at any rate, though that may be a fair bit. I tell you this so that you know: Isra is not to be approached. She is not to be regarded with anything but fear. If you should catch sight of her, you *must not* try to fight her or capture her. She can command you with a whispered word, and you will have no choice but to obey."

"But then there is no hope!" In the middle of the hall, one student rose from her bench with a cry. Her pale skin was even paler now with fright. "We should leave. All of us should leave. How can you hope to stop her?"

"If you were to leave, no one could blame you," said Xain. "That is one reason I tell you this now. If you wish to leave the Academy for your own safety, or if you family wishes to withdraw you, I would not call it an unwise choice, and you should make it with both eyes open. But as for Isra—I said that *you* all must not fight her. I did not say that *we* would not. For mage-stones make a wizard powerful—but not all-powerful. Even an abomination can be stopped. Sometimes they can even be saved."

That silenced them. The girl who had spoken slowly sank back into her seat. To either side of the dean, instructors looked uncomfortably at their hands. Only Perrin kept her gaze upon him, unflinching at his words, though they bordered on blasphemy. Ebon noted that Dasko hardly seemed to be listening to the speech. His eyes were far away, and every so often his shoulder twitched as though he were flinching from something.

Xain leaned forwards, his knuckles pressed into the wooden table. "Yes. It is true. Since the time of the Wizard Kings, generations of deans have forbidden you who study here from having this knowledge. In times past, I might have understood why. But now things are different. Underrealm is at war, and mage-stones, though still beyond the King's law, are more common than they have been in a long while. Only knowledge can save us now. Knowledge of the good and the evil alike.

"We here, the instructors and I, will keep you safe to the best of our ability. But we cannot do it without your help. You must be ever wary and ever vigilant. You must come to us at once if you see anything odd going on—a friend acting out of sorts, or an instructor whose mind goes vacant and wandering. We can stop Isra, but not by hiding in the dark from truths that have been kept from us too long."

The dining hall was dead quiet. Someone nearby shifted their feet on the floor, and it seemed to Ebon as loud as a breaking branch.

"That is all," Xain said. "If you have questions or wish to speak to anyone of this, please see your instructors in class."

He turned and left the dining hall. The moment the door swung shut behind him, whispers burst out in the hall. But when Ebon and his friends looked to each other, none of them uttered a word.

SIX

Xain's speech was not the last time Isra and her magestones were mentioned that day. In Perrin's class just after breakfast, she spoke of it again and invited questions from the students. None were asked—the students were second-years, and most were timid, and likely few of them knew anything of magestones at all. Ebon withheld his tongue because he knew more about magestones than he wished to, and he did not want to draw any attention to himself after the events of the night before. In the library that afternoon, Kalem and Theren told him that their classes had been much the same—except in those cases, many questions had been asked. And Ebon was chilled to hear that one student had asked if they could not use magestones *against* Isra—to procure their own supply, and thus defeat her. That idea had been immediately shouted down. But the fact that it had been voiced at all . . . Ebon shuddered to think of such an idea being put into action.

Well he remembered the days after the attack on the High King's Seat, when everyone had been fearful and solemn. Now that mood had returned again, only worse. Then, they had been afraid of some enemy from far lands. Now a foe was in their very midst, and she had once broken bread with them all. She had slept beneath the same roof. And worse, no one knew where she had gone or where she might be. The weight of that terror was heavy upon them all.

"I do not understand," said Ebon. "How could she have vanished?"

"No one knows," said Theren. "They only know that she did."

"They say the Academy was searched from top to bottom," said Kalem. "But she was not found in any room. They searched in teams, and all kept careful watch to make sure that she would not trick them with mindwyrd. But they saw no trace of her."

They studied in worried silence after that. It seemed an eternity before the final study bell rang. Ebon rose from his armchair with a sigh of relief. He joined his friends in the dining hall, but found he had no appetite.

He had an appointment that evening in the city. The events of the night before had made him reconsider going out, for Isra might be anywhere. But in the end Ebon decided that Isra would hardly expect him to be out in plain sight on the streets, and would not know where he was going in any case. He would only encounter her by the most terrible of luck, and even he did not think that poorly of his own fortune. So, with blood rising to his cheeks, he excused himself and left the hall. Kalem and Theren were too preoccupied to notice his embarrassment.

Winter ran its persistent fingers up and down his skin as he stepped through the Academy's front door. He quickened his steps to get the blood flowing and headed west towards the blue door, as he had so often before—only now, he did not mean to pass through it. His heart skipped a beat, though the day's worries plagued his thoughts, and they were reluctant to leave him. He swore silently to himself that he would not spend the evening voicing such concerns to Adara. This night was about the two of them, not him alone.

When at last he reached the blue door, Adara gave him a smile and a nod. The snow dusting her mantle told the tale of how long she had spent waiting. She had chosen to wear his family's color, a golden dress with a cloak that was a few shades darker. The hood was lined with fur, which she blew into to warm herself. The moment she saw Ebon, her face lit like a kindled lantern. But then the light was doused at once, and she gave him a nervous smile. It pleased him a bit, the thought that mayhap she was as anxious as he was.

"My love," she murmured.

He took her in his arms. "Your love? I would argue that you are mine."

Her smile broadened. Then she put his arm in hers and led him away. He expected another lengthy walk—but after only two blocks, she stopped before a wooden door, this one unpainted. It stood between a tavern on one side and a building on the other that looked like a cobbler's shop. The buildings were pressed tight together so that it seemed they crowded the door to Adara's home.

"Here it is," she said breathlessly. "Would you like . . .?"

The words trailed off. She waved at the handle. Ebon tried to speak, but his throat was suddenly bone-dry, and so he gave it up.

The handle turned easily under his fingers. The hinges gently squeaked as they swung open.

There was a short staircase—short, but steep. He tramped the snow off before he climbed its steps, thankful he had remembered it and not made a slob of himself. A little railing helped him make the climb.

And then, there he was. Adara's home.

It was small, but not cramped. He guessed she did not want for more space, since many of her needs were seen to by the guild of lovers. The windows at the front of the room drew attention at once. Ebon guessed that each looked out over the front door of the tavern and the cobbler's, respectively. The evening light they admitted illuminated the room so that it did not yet need lamps. Tucked in one corner was her bed. It was nothing so ornate as the silk-sheeted thing behind the blue door, though Ebon noted with a blush that it seemed just as sturdy. On the other side of the room was a bureau, as well as a closet that stood out from the wall. Finally, before one of the windows was a small table with two chairs, behind which was a low cabinet that looked like it might hold wine (or, Ebon realized, mead, for Adara favored it). Where there was color—sashes over the windows, the bureau's trim, the bedspread—it was deep, muted blue, the perfect contrast to the dress and cloak she now wore.

Adara stood behind him now, hands clasped before her, fingers rubbing against each other anxiously. Her eyes were wide as they remained on him. It was so utterly unlike the Adara he was accustomed to. She smiled as he looked at her, though it seemed somewhat forced.

"Well? I know it is nothing so grand as my room at the guild, nor, certainly, your family's—"

"It is wonderful. It is just like you," he said quietly. Then he realized how that might sound, so he spoke hastily to correct himself. "I mean only that it is . . . it is warm, and beautiful, and does not seem to try too hard to be beautiful. Only that is not what I mean either, not at all. I . . ."

He put his hand to his forehead. She must think him an utter fool—or a caustic-tongued ass. But she smiled and took his hand, and then gently kissed the back of its fingers. "There is my Ebon. I feared to see something different in your eyes—haughtiness, or disdain, once you saw how I lived. But you are just as tongue-tied as I feel."

Ebon laughed. "That is no compliment, yet I am glad to hear it from you."

She studied his eyes. "Is it only our meeting that occupies your thoughts? I have heard some dark whispers concerning the Academy."

He sighed. "They cannot be darker than the truth." She waved him to the table before the window, and he sat. While she moved to fetch wine for him and mead for herself, he went on. "You remember what I told you of Isra. She has returned. We saw her within the Academy—Kalem and Theren and I, that is."

She froze in the middle of pouring his wine. He had to tip the bottle up to keep her from spilling it. "*In* the Academy, you say? Does that mean you are in danger?"

"I certainly do not feel safe," said Ebon, forcing a laugh. "That, along with our situation with Dasko . . ."

"Have you thought of no way out of that?" said Adara. "It must weigh terribly on Theren."

"More and more every day," said Ebon, lowering his gaze. "She will hardly even speak of it, and when she does she is short-tempered and irritable."

"Would you not be the same?"

"I do not criticize her," said Ebon. "I wish there was a way I could help her. But if she releases him from mindwyrd, it will wear off. Then we do not know what would happen. He might remember us and what we did. We know for certain that he would suffer, for the process of weaning off mindwyrd is very painful."

"Will it not get worse the longer she keeps him under control?" said Adara softly.

"It will. But we know not what else to do." Ebon's eyes began to smart, and he swiped at them, trying to make it look as though he were scratching an itch. "Forgive me. This is a happy evening, and one for celebration. Yet I have spent most of it talking about myself, as I do too often. I even told myself not to do so, just before I saw you."

"Do not trouble yourself over that," said Adara, giving him a little smile. "That is why you and I met in the first place, is it not? So that you might ease your burdens?"

A slow grin spread across his face. "I suppose that was part of the reason." But then he took her hands and grew solemn. "But now we are something more. The fact that I am here is proof of that. This is not for gold, and I do not want it to be. Tonight is not for me, but for us—or so I hope."

Her thumb rubbed the back of his palm. "So I hope as well."

He smiled and took a sip of his wine. But his eyes

widened as soon as it touched his tongue, and he tilted the cup to look inside. "Stars and sky. Where did you get this?"

She waved a hand airily. "Somewhere. Sometimes I receive gifts, and sometimes those gifts are wine, for my clients do not often ask me what I prefer to drink." She gave him a secret smile, and he blushed. For a long while he, too, had assumed she liked wine, until he learned of her love for mead. "When that is the case, and when they do not wish to drink it with me immediately, I bring it here to save for a special occasion. Tonight is the first time I have opened one of the bottles I have saved."

"You must have a fine store, then."

She laughed and slapped his wrist. "You will be well sated, you drunkard."

Though he chuckled, Ebon soon fixed her with a look. "Adara . . . there is something I meant to ask you tonight, ever since you first invited me here. Only I do not wish to give offense."

"Oh?" Her eyes grew careful. "Then is it wise to ask your question at all?"

"I hope so," he said. "If I am wrong, forgive me. But . . . understand, I am overjoyed to be here. I can scarcely tell you how honored I am that you wished to bring me into your life. But . . . why? Why me, in particular?"

She softened at once. "Because I love you, Ebon. Do you not believe that?"

"You have said so, and I *do* believe you," he said. "And yet . . . I wonder why. I am nothing special. No, do not look at me like that, nor argue. I do not say this to earn words of praise. I am *not* special. I am no great man. There is little about me that is remarkable, other than my family, who few hold in very high regard."

Adara did not answer him at once, but leaned back in her chair and gave him an appraising look. Then she stood and came to him, and sat so that she was side-saddle in his lap. "A boy who is usually foolish, and sometimes wise, said that love often springs forth unbidden."

He blushed, for he remembered those words. He and Adara had whispered them often enough since he first uttered them. "But honestly," he pressed. "Have you never thought upon it?"

"I have," she said, so quickly that it surprised him. "Here is the truth. And you have begged me not to take offense at your question, so I will ask you to do the same with my answer. I did not love you from the moment I set my eyes upon you, Ebon. I think your love for me may have begun that night, but to me, you were a guest like any other. Though I saw at once that you were an uncommonly sweet one—and you were a reminder of Idris, of home, which lent you some slight favor. But when you came to see me the second time, I gave you a lover's words, as I would have done for anybody else."

She leaned in then, and pressed herself against him,

and kissed him deep. "And then the Seat was attacked," she murmured. "You were an utter fool to come after me when you saw Cyrus escorting me through the streets. Yet that foolishness endeared you to me. And then you risked your life to save me after I learned of Cyrus' evil. I could not love a boy only because he was sweet. I could not love a boy only because affection made him foolish. And I could not love a boy only because he would give his life for mine. But you were all three at once, and in the same person. And love sprang forth unbidden, for you never spoke lovers' words to me."

It was hard for him to speak for a moment, and so he only held her. "But that is because I am not a lover," he finally said.

Adara shook her head. "That is not what I mean. Lovers' words go two ways. A lover tells a guest what they want to hear. But guests also lie to their lovers. The guest will speak of their lover's endless beauty, and say they wish they could be wed, and say they would buy the lover a palace if they could. But if given the chance to fulfill such whispered promises, most guests would refuse. And that is no evil thing; a lover delivers not only the pleasures of the flesh, but the pleasure of dreaming a perfect romance together, a love greater than true life will permit. Lover and guest both know that dream will never come true, but it is a precious dream nonetheless.

"The day the Seat was attacked, I realized you had never spoken a lover's word to me. You loved me in truth. I do not know when after that I knew I loved you in return. One day, I simply did."

He smiled at her. "And that has never happened before? You have never fallen in love?"

Everything about her changed at once—her posture, the look on her face, and her smile—and he saw it. Inside, he winced. Adara stood and returned to her seat. "Before I answer that, I would ask you something. Would it bother you if I had?"

Quickly he shook his head. "I am sorry," he said. "That was wrong of me to ask. I never meant to throw doubt on your feelings for me. I only . . ."

"You thought to stoke your own pride," she said with a wry smile. "To prove to yourself that you were the only one. Well, puff up your chest, my love—you are the first guest who has ever stepped into my dwelling."

He hung his head. He had made an ass of himself after all. "I am sorry, my love. You deserve someone with a smoother tongue than mine, for it trips over itself no matter my intent."

A moment's silence stretched as she drank deep from her mead. Her eyes glinted. "Your tongue is not so bad as all that."

His heart leaped—until the moment was shattered by a pounding at the door below.

Ebon was on his feet in an instant, but no faster than Adara. Their eyes met. He shook his head. "I am expecting no one," he whispered.

"Nor I."

The pounding sounded at the door again.

He ran to the left window. The sash was drawn, and he pulled it aside, trying to look down. But the angle was bad, and he could not see the street just before the door. Adara went to the other window, but from the look on her face it was clear she could see nothing more than he could.

"Hide yourself," he hissed. "I will see who it is."

"Do not be an idiot." She went to her cupboard. From its bottom drawer she pulled a long knife. "This is my home."

Before he could even try to stop her, she had pounded down the stairs and thrown open the door. Ebon was a half-step behind her as she thrust the knife out into the street.

Mako looked down at the blade and arched an eyebrow.

Ebon felt thunderstruck. For a moment he could not so much as speak. Fortunately he did not have to, for Adara did instead. "Who are you?" she said. "What do you want?"

For a moment, Mako did not answer. Then he moved, making Ebon flinch—but he only took a step back so that he did not impale himself on Adara's dagger when he gave a deep bow.

"I beg your every pardon, my lady, for this intrusion. To disturb you was my last wish. I only sought my master, Ebon, of the family Drayden. He is the boy standing there just behind you."

Ebon gawked. Adara glanced back at him. He nodded, and slowly she withdrew her dagger. Mako, seeing the motion, straightened from his bow—and then he fixed Ebon with a hard stare.

"Come with me, little goldshitter. There is work to be done."

SEVEN

AFTER BIDDING ADARA A HASTY FAREWELL AND promising to return as soon as he could, Ebon followed Mako into the streets. The moment they had turned a corner, he seized the bodyguard's arm to pull him around. Mako gave the hand on his elbow a hard look, but Ebon did not care.

"How did you know I was there? I have not even seen you since we fought with Isra. Where have you been?"

"You have never been curious about my whereabouts before," said Mako. "I thought it was because you did not wish to know. Nor have you ever asked how I knew where you were. It is a sort of assumed truth between us, is it not?"

Mako turned and stalked off. Ebon's nostrils flared, and his hand curled to a fist at his side. But what could he do? Striking Mako would do no good—even if the bodyguard did not strike back, which seemed doubtful. He hurried to trot after Mako's retreating back.

In truth, he was terrified that Mako knew where Adara lived. But then, as he thought of it, it seemed likely that Mako had had that knowledge for some time. In fact, it would not surprise Ebon if Mako knew the dwelling of every denizen on the Seat and their families across the nine kingdoms besides. That was, after all, part of his duty. Not only as a Drayden bodyguard and messenger, but also as their assassin.

Something of Ebon's thoughts must have shown in his face, for Mako laughed at him. "You may unclench yourself, little Ebon. Your lover is in no danger from me."

"Oh? And what about from Shay?"

Mako's mouth soured in an instant. "From what we have learned of your father, I certainly will not be reporting anything to him—about Adara, or anything else."

Rather than bringing comfort, the words further darkened Ebon's mood—except instead of anger, he felt a cold fear. He saw Matami's gaping eye socket, heard his uncle's screams.

And then he remembered their fight against Isra, when the girl struck with her magic. But Mako stood untouched and leaped forwards with his dagger. Her magic had been powerless against him, and Ebon still did not know why.

"You are very silent, Ebon," said Mako. "Come. Speak. What do you wish to tell me?"

"I . . ." Ebon swallowed hard. Something, some urgent voice in the back of his mind, told him not to speak of what he had seen during the fight. "You mentioned my father. It brought an unpleasant memory to the fore."

"Does Matami still plague your thoughts? If everyone were so naive as you, there would be no more war in Underrealm."

"Never mind that now," said Ebon. "I must tell you something about Isra. Last night, in the Academy—"

"She appeared," said Mako. "I know it, boy. That is why I have come to see you in the first place. Did you think I sought to converse for my pleasure? I do not think either of us have enjoyed ourselves so far."

Ebon looked around. He did not recognize the streets they passed through. A twinge of nerves struck him. "Where are we going, exactly? You cannot know where she is already."

Mako snorted. "Of course not. You are more craven than that old instructor of yours, Ebon, and it suits you ill. I wish we *were* going to see her now, so that I could end the little girl once and for all."

"Then where?"

"You would do well to learn patience."

The next few streets passed in silence. Ebon knew only that they were somewhere in the southwest end of the city. Little construction had made its way there, and many buildings were burned or fallen to ruin. This was where the Shades had brought the full strength of their assault, and few who lived here had survived the attack. It seemed the High King did not see fit to rebuild where no one would live afterwards.

At last they came to a wrought iron fence that surrounded a wide house of nobility—wide, but not so tall as the Drayden family's manor, nor as resplendent in its design. Here and there the fence had been bent and broken, so that there were many gaps to slip through. Mako paused, fixing Ebon with a look.

"One more thing before we enter. With Isra about, you may have need of me, and your lover's messages cannot reach me quickly enough. Do you remember when I snuck you out of the Academy?"

Ebon frowned. "Of course."

"There is a piece of alabaster on the ground near that place. You cannot miss it. If ever you must tell me something, or need my help, write a note and leave it beneath the alabaster. I will come as quickly as I may."

"Very well," said Ebon. "But do you think I am in danger?"

Mako spread his hands and grinned. "A rogue mindmage is on the loose, and she has the strength of magestones within her. Do you think anyone in the Academy is safe?"

That seemed a fair point. Ebon looked up at the manor before them. "What is this place?"

"It once belonged to the family Skard." Mako looked the place over, his lip curling slightly. "They are one of—"

"A merchant family from Dulmun," said Ebon. "I know the name."

"They left the Seat just before it was attacked—and now it may be guessed that they knew of Dulmun's treachery before it happened. They have not returned since."

The sky was already darkening above them. Ebon gave a weary sigh. "What is this all about, Mako? Curfew is not far off, and I cannot be out this late."

"This will not be a long engagement," said Mako. "And besides, if you are late in returning, you will not be the only one."

He ducked in through a gap in the fence, crossed the courtyard, and entered the manor through its front door. Ebon swallowed hard, wondering what the bodyguard had meant by that comment, before he finally mustered the courage to follow.

From the street, the manor looked nowhere near as impressive as the home of Ebon's family. But when he crossed the threshold, the sight of the main hall froze him in place and robbed his breath. Far it stretched, thirty paces at least, and lined with hearths to either side. At its head was the greatest fireplace of all, where a fine mantel of marble was likely meant to hold treasures and goblets of silver and gold. The shelf lay bare now—what the invaders had not taken, looters would have stolen since. That is, if the family Skard had not taken their valuables with them when they fled.

Running the hall's length was a mammoth wooden table, wider than Ebon was tall, and a long bench to either side of it. Where the Drayden manor had little dining rooms in which the family could take their meals in privacy and comfort, this was a place for feasts, banquets for an entire clan at once, where merchants and servants alike could be seated by station, while their children and the dogs played and tussled on the rugs in the corners. Some of these still remained: those too grease-stained or ratty to be stolen. Though all the hearths lay cold, and the place was lit only by the fading daylight coming through the door, Ebon could imagine the hall filled with proud Dulmun warriors, the air ringing with their ululating songs.

Then he caught a motion at the other end of the hall, and his breath caught in his throat. But peering deeper, he saw it was Mako—and beside the bodyguard, to Ebon's great shock, were Theren and Kalem.

"What . . . Mako, what are they doing here?"

Theren glowered at him, and then at Mako. "We were summoned. Mako told us you were in great peril, and to meet him here at once so that you might be rescued."

"And look how quickly they came, boy." Mako's smile was cruel. "We should all be so lucky to have such loyal friends."

"Ebon, what is going on?" said Kalem. Ebon could see the fear in the boy's eyes. Kalem eyed Mako's cruel knife, and Ebon knew he was thinking of the time the bodyguard had drawn blood from Ebon's throat with the tip of it.

"This sack of dung has lied to us," said Theren. "We are not your lackeys, bodyguard, to be dragged across the Seat at your whim."

Mako flicked his fingers in the air. "Isra is on the loose, and we must find her. Do you not want that? You may spurn my aid if you wish, but then you must capture her yourself."

"Do you think me incapable of it?" Theren drew up to her full height, which was only a pair of fingers shorter than Mako. "I would stand a better chance against her—one wizard against another."

"You think I have never killed a mindmage before," Mako's voice had taken on a dangerous growl. "That is the trouble with you wizards. You are used to being more powerful than everyone you meet, and so you grow overconfident. That is when someone like me ar-rives to slit your throats."

Theren glared back at him. But Ebon remembered Isra, and how she had blasted Mako with her magic, only to leave him unharmed. A shiver of fear ran through him.

Before Mako or Theren could utter another word, Kalem stepped between them. He held his hands out to either side, though it was ludicrous to imagine he could stop them with his diminutive frame.

"If the two of you have taken sufficient measure of each other, mayhap we could speak of whatever Mako has summoned us for? I would rather not miss curfew."

Mako's countenance shifted at once to a kindly smile. "An excellent idea, child. Here is the matter at hand: ever since last we saw Isra, something has been brewing upon the Seat, and I have not been able to wrap my fingers around it."

Theren scoffed. "Something? What does that mean? *What* is brewing?"

"If I knew that, do you think I would require your help? I am aware of how desperate I seem, coming to the three of you. But the spies I have tucked into the city's dark corners tell me nothing. When someone gets up to dark business, it sends out ripples. There have been many such ripples of late, but I cannot follow them back to the center. I thought it must have to do with smuggling Isra from the island, but now we know that she is still here."

"You are telling us, then, that you were wrong?" said Theren, arching an eyebrow.

Mako's nose flared. "Not all information is a clear as the words on one of your scrolls."

Theren nodded. "Of course not. It is easy to imagine how you might have been misled."

Ebon feared that Mako might strike her. But with great effort, he went on. "In any case, now we know she is here, and she seems to have no intention of leaving. I am bringing you into the fold on the slight chance that you may be able to help. Am I wise to do so?"

"We will do what we can, of course," said Ebon. "But I fear we know nothing more than you."

"That may be true," said Mako. "But then, you may know something *without* knowing it. Whatever buzzes within the city, it has something to do with the family Yerrin—an odd thing, for recently they have been on their best behavior."

That raised Kalem's eyebrows. "Yerrin keeping their noses clean? That is a wonder."

"They were implicated in the attack," said Mako. "The High King had half a mind to purge them from the land, and they only barely avoided that fate. They have been good little children since—but now they have begun to lurk again."

"You think they are working with Isra, then?" said Ebon.

"That is entirely possible, though not certain."

Ebon thought of Lilith. Surely if Yerrin were involved with Isra's doings, then Lilith could be of help one way or another. But even as he opened his mouth to speak, Theren caught his eye. She looked anxious, or frightened, and gave him a quick shake of her head. Ebon closed his mouth again.

The silence in the hall had stretched a moment too long, and Mako was peering at them. Theren spoke up quickly. "Yerrin, working with Isra? It seems unlikely. Her schemes brought them great suffering. Oren was murdered. Lilith was tortured, and would have been executed."

Mako shrugged. "That is hardly out of character for the Yerrins. Their thoughts and schemes stretch for years, and they are willing to prune some dead branches to ensure a healthy growth."

But Ebon was not so sure. He remembered Oren's mutilated body and the madness in Lilith's eyes. Surely even the cruelest plan could not stand by such actions. He saw the same doubt in Kalem's face.

Their hesitation seemed to annoy Mako, for he gave a little growl. "Very well, then. Let us leave the Yerrins alone for now. But to search for Isra, I must start in the right place. Tell me what happened when I left you in Xain's home—and I mean all that happened, with no detail added or left out."

Ebon stiffened in fear and saw it reflected in the faces of his friends as well. Mako saw it, and he smiled as he settled down on one of the benches at the head of the table.

"This must be an interesting tale indeed."

"As she fled, I tried to stop her," said Ebon. "I missed her, but I got hold of the amulet. Kekhit's amulet, the one she used to cast mindwyrd, and also to hide her magic."

"I remember it," said Mako. "What next?"

"When we ourselves tried to leave, she was there. She had Xain's son, and she took him prisoner." Ebon shuddered as he remembered the fear in the boy's eyes, his whimpering cries as Isra dragged him away. "She tried to kill Kalem and me, but Theren recovered and saved us."

Mako's eyes narrowed. "Why did you not give Theren the amulet? She could have stopped Isra, could she not?"

"I had not yet thought of that," said Ebon sharply. Then he stopped, and his eyes went wide.

"Yet," said Mako, his smile widening. "You had not *yet* thought of it. But you did think of it."

Theren shook. "Darkness take you, Ebon."

"He is trying to help," Ebon told her. "We will do ourselves no favors by holding back. Yes, Mako, I thought of using mindwyrd. For when Isra fled, Dasko arrived. He is an instructor at—"

"I know the man," said Mako. "And I think that now I know the rest of your tale. He found you before you could get out of Xain's home, and you were holding the amulet. You thought he would expose you—and you were right to think it. So you gave the amulet to Theren, and she used her mindwyrd to make him forget you had been there."

"Yes," said Ebon. "You have it."

Theren turned to hide her face. Kalem's head drooped, and carefully he took a seat at the table opposite Mako. Ebon sighed. To speak the truth so plainly . . . it was a relief, and yet he wished it had been to someone other than Mako.

The bodyguard was studying his fingernails. He drew his knife and began to pick under one of them. "I am no wizard. Yet it seems I have heard something of mindwyrd—that if it is not maintained, it produces a sort of mind-sickness in the victim."

No one answered him. Theren met Ebon's eyes, and he saw how haunted her expression had become.

"I take it that your silence means I am right," said Mako. "If that is so, you did not use mindwyrd upon Dasko once, and then let him be. You have been using it ever since."

"We have," said Ebon quietly. Theren turned away again.

"That is excellent," said Mako. "Your new Dean Forredar has some knowledge of Yerrin. And Dasko will be close in Xain's counsel, for he is a wise man and well respected at the Academy. Mayhap we can use Dasko to use Xain."

"What?" said Kalem, straightening at once. "We will not use mindwyrd on Dasko to control him, but only to make him forget. Keeping his memory empty is one thing. Using him to accomplish our own ends . . ."

"I will not do it," said Theren. She stormed up to the table and slammed her hands down on it. The heavy *THOOM* of the blow echoed around the hall, flitting about its many pillars. "I will not, and that is the end of it. He is like a puppet on strings, and I feel more of a monster every time I jerk them. Mayhap I do not suffer from magestone sickness, but this is its own kind of torture."

"We will not use him for evil," said Mako. His tone was gentle, as though he were persuading a wounded animal. "We will only collect information we cannot get ourselves. And that information could do great good. It could even save the life of the boy, Erin."

"Erin could already be dead," said Ebon. "He likely is. It has been more than a week."

"I know something of these matters," said Mako. "One does not take a hostage if one does not intend to use them. And through Dasko, we could learn something that—"

"Stop saying that!" cried Theren. "Stop saying 'we,' when you mean me. We are not committing a crime—I am. We will not be put to death if this scheme is discovered—I will."

"We are with you to the end, Theren," said Ebon quietly. "We have been there every step of the way. If the King's law learns of our dealings, we will not abandon you to die alone. And if you refuse this scheme, I for one will not argue against you."

"We cannot do it," said Kalem. "If we do, we are little better than those we hope to expose. Evil cannot defeat evil, but only strengthens it."

Mako stood suddenly from the table, and his eyes had grown hard again. "This is not a council. My duty is to see to Ebon's safety—and if you call him your friend, girl, then your duty is the same. The next time you use your power on Dasko, have him tell you what Xain knows of Yerrin, as well as anything he knows about where Isra went. I assure you, Dean Forredar will have been most earnest in his searching."

Theren did not answer him for a moment, but looked to Ebon. He gave her a little shrug. "It is your choice."

She sighed. "Very well. I will ask him—but I will not command him to go digging any further."

Mako smiled. "Good enough, I suppose—for now. In that case, the three of you had better scuttle off back home. I have heard that curfew draws near."

EIGHT

The streets had grown colder still, for the sun was almost gone. They hurried between the snow-drifts, moving quickly for warmth as well as for the lateness of the hour. Ebon waited until they had left the manor a few streets behind before he spoke to Theren.

"When I almost spoke of Lilith, you stopped me. Why?"

She gave a nervous look over her shoulder. "I wish you would not speak of her even now. I feel like that man has ears everywhere, even among us."

"He is nowhere in sight, and I am no traitor," said Kalem.

Theren sighed, and the frost of it whipped around her face as they hurried on. "I fear that if Mako knew of our closeness—well, *my* closeness—to Lilith, he might think of her as a target. Especially now that he is so interested in the doings of the family Yerrin. And I think that we have already put her through enough. We pursued her when she was innocent, and she was put to the question because of it. I wish to cause her no more harm."

"I see that," said Ebon. "Yet if Yerrin is truly a threat, and if they are behind Isra's crimes, Lilith could be most helpful. She might even help us save Erin's life."

"You sound too much like your bodyguard," Theren spat. "I thought you had no wish to be like the rest of your family, yet I hear their echoes in your words."

"Leave Mako out of it, then," said Ebon. "But we must stop Isra as quickly as we can. I have not forgotten the sight of Oren's corpse—nor Credell's, nor poor little Vali's."

"And do you think I have?" Her eyes flashed. "She has left a longer trail of bodies than that, though how can I blame you for remembering only the goldbags among them?"

Ebon stopped walking and squared his shoulders, looking her in the eye. "That is not fair."

She glared back for a moment, but then she sagged. "I am sorry. I know you do not think of it that way. It is only . . . Ebon, I am frightened."

"We all are," said Kalem. He put an awkward hand on her arm. "Who knows when Isra will appear again?"

Theren shrugged. "Who cares for Isra? I am afraid for Dasko, and for the mindwyrd I keep him under. I am afraid for all of us, and what will happen if we are discovered. And I am afraid to use the mindwyrd to pry information from Dasko's mind. I never wanted this power, and now I cannot stop using it."

They stood a moment in silence. Then Ebon tossed his head. "Come. Time stops for no one." They fell into step beside him. "I feel your fear as well. But we could at least speak with Lilith. Mayhap she can help, and mayhap not. If not, we can leave it alone, and it will never reach Mako's ears at all."

She sighed. "Mayhap. Let me think upon it. It is no decision to make lightly."

"Of course."

They reached the Academy a little while later, and no sooner had they passed through the front door than the curfew bell rang. Theren redoubled her pace, making for the white cedar doors that led out to the grounds.

"I am almost late. I will see you both on the morrow."

But Ebon increased his pace to keep up with her. "I will come with you."

"And I as well," said Kalem, who scampered along with them.

Theren did not stop moving, but she tried to wave them off. "There is no need. I can do it myself easily enough—I have the practice, certainly."

"I told you, Theren. We are in this together."

He caught the faintest quiver in her chin. "Very well," she said, her voice wavering. "Thank you both."

The grounds were as cold as the streets had been, but better lit, for the groundskeepers had already been around to kindle the lanterns. They went for the place in the hedges where they always met Dasko. He was there when they arrived, sitting by himself on a stone bench. Kalem waited at the entrance to the sitting area, standing just out of view where he could keep watch.

Dasko stood as soon as he saw them. Ebon stopped short. He had not been so close to the man in some time, a week at least. Something about him seemed . . . off. It was not just his face, which had grown a touch gaunter, nor the grey at his temples, which seemed to have spread some little way into the rest of his hair. It was a weariness, a thinness, as though the instructor were only half there, and half an Elf-dream. But mayhap Ebon was only imagining that. So far as he knew, no one else had remarked on Dasko acting strange.

Theren reached into a pocket of her robe, and Ebon knew she was holding the amulet of Kekhit. "You will not remember that you have seen us here tonight," she began. "You will return here tomorrow just before curfew and remain until I come to see you. If anyone asks, you will not tell them why you are here waiting, but will invent some excuse."

"Yes," said Dasko, nodding. Ebon shuddered at the lifeless monotone in his voice.

Kalem and Theren had explained a bit to him in the days since they had first placed Dasko under control. Theren had thoroughly erased his memories of these meetings. If they released Dasko from mindwyrd, the danger was that he might remember them. Even if he did not, there might be gaps in his memory, and he would start showing withdrawal from the control. That would prompt an investigation by the faculty, and that could lead to Ebon and his friends.

Their position seemed untenable. Often Ebon felt that they were drawing a blanket over an ever-widening hole in the floor and hoping they would not get in trouble when some unwitting child fell into it and broke their neck.

Theren gave him an uneasy look. Ebon nodded at her. "It is your choice," he said quietly.

She sighed and turned to Dasko. "Tell me what the Academy faculty knows of Isra's reappearance."

"We know nothing," said Dasko. Again his voice made Ebon shudder. It was like hearing a corpse speak.

Theren shook her head. "Tell me what the Academy faculty suspects of Isra's reappearance."

"Most think Isra must be getting help from inside

the Academy," he said. "There will be an investigation to unearth anyone she may be using. We will look for anyone who shows signs of being under mindwyrd."

Theren stiffened. Ebon's heart leaped to his throat, and he spoke. "How would you find someone being held in mindwyrd?"

Dasko said nothing. Theren gave an exasperated sigh. "Tell me how you would find someone being held in mindwyrd."

"There are sometimes gaps in the memory, for Isra would not want the victim to remember seeing her," he said. "Therefore she would command them to forget the meeting."

Ebon and Theren looked at each other. "If they question him, he could lead them to us," said Ebon.

"Yes," said Dasko, surprising them both by speaking without being prompted. "In fact Dean Forredar already strongly suspects you, Ebon."

"Tell us who else suspects us," said Theren.

"No one," said Dasko. "Jia thinks Xain's suspicion is paranoia, born of his hatred for Ebon's family."

"Still, we should do what we can to hide the effects of mindwyrd," said Ebon.

Theren nodded. "I think I know how. Dasko, when you leave here tonight, you will remember being out upon the grounds, but you will remember it as if you were alone. You will not remember speaking to anyone, and you will not remember hearing anyone speak to you. You will remember all of our previous visits the same way—you have been visiting the grounds alone each night, on your own, and speaking to no one."

"Yes," said Dasko.

"Leave us now. Enter the Academy, and then forget."

"Yes." He left them, slipping out through the gap in the hedge.

Theren sank down onto the bench, her whole body going limp as though she had just run a league. Ebon quickly took a seat beside her and put a hand on her shoulder. Kalem came in a moment later, his eyes filled with concern.

"I am sorry, Theren," said Ebon. She looked exhausted. But when she lifted her head to look at him, he saw the weariness was in her eyes—a bone-sunk debility of the soul.

"It is wrong, Ebon," she whispered. "This is wrong. I know it is, and yet I cannot stop. How can I go on, committing a new evil every night?"

"We are only keeping ourselves safe for now," he said. "And we *will* come to a solution. I promise you. We will not rest until this is over."

"Of course we will not rest," she said. "I can barely even sleep these days."

Ebon stood and held out his hand. She took it and allowed him to pull her to her feet. They made their way towards the Academy with arms over each other's shoulders—not to remain upright, but merely for comfort.

Then they opened the white cedar door and nearly ran into Dean Forredar.

Xain stopped short just before they hit him, and though the children took a hasty step back, he did not move. He had eyes only for Ebon, and disgust burned in his gaze.

"Dean Forredar," murmured Kalem.

"What were you doing out upon the grounds?" said Xain. "Curfew has been called."

"It is not against the rules," said Theren. But some of her usual fire had left her voice.

"It is cold out," said Xain. "After an encounter like you all had last night, most students would wish to remain inside, where the danger seems less."

"Are we in danger upon the Academy grounds?" said Ebon, meeting Xain's stare. He was growing more and more fed up with the man's unreasoning hatred of him. "Is it not your job to protect us? I seem to remember that you made such a pledge when you first came here."

"It is my job to protect the Academy," said Xain. "From threats within, as well as without. Sometimes it is hard to tell the difference—other times it is quite clear."

Kalem quailed, but Theren drew herself up. "You have been wrong about such things before, Dean. Mayhap you see threats when none exist."

Xain stared her down. For a moment Ebon feared they might come to blows, the way they had when

Xain had attacked him in the dining hall. Then, without a word, the dean stalked away.

"Darkness take him," muttered Theren.

"He is a suspicious man," said Kalem, shaking his head. "Yet who can blame him? These are dark times, and his son is missing. Come. I am weary, and I suspect the two of you feel much the same."

They made for the stairs and then up to their dormitories to sleep.

NINE

In the library the next day, they reunited in their favorite spot on the third floor. The place was even darker than usual. That part of the library had never been very well kept, and now the faculty had suffered losses, so that many of the lanterns stayed unlit. Kalem took one from the wall out in the main area and set it on the table beside them so that they could read by its fiery glow.

But reading did not come easy. Ebon struggled to keep his mind upon the book in his hands, a weighty tome entitled *The Conquering of Idris: A Telling of the*

Fall of the Tomb-Kings. Idris was his home, and he had thought the subject might hold his attention. But too often he caught himself staring off at nothing. It did not help that the book was written in a dry and informational style, with no attempt to make the events more interesting. Not that they needed much embellishment—the magic of the Tomb-Kings of old was well renowned, and well feared. His distraction was aided by weariness, and often his head drooped towards his lap. He had spent another sleepless night in the common room of his dormitory, dozing off only in little fits and starts.

After they had sat there for mayhap an hour, Theren gave a frustrated little growl and slammed her book shut. "Enough of this. I am through pretending to study when all of us know we are doing nothing of the sort."

Kalem looked up blinking from his book, shaking his head as though he had forgotten they were there. "Hm?"

"Well, except for Kalem, I suppose." Theren folded her arms across her chest. "But I cannot even see the words on the page. Do neither of you wonder what she is waiting for?"

"Who?" said Kalem, eyes still foggy.

"Isra, of course, you idiot," Theren snapped. "It has been two days since we saw her. Why has she not struck again?"

"I had not wondered, for I have been thinking

about Erin," said Ebon. "Where on all the Seat could she be hiding him?"

"There are many abandoned buildings upon the Seat after the attack," said Kalem. "Why, Mako himself took us to one of them."

"But that is just it," said Ebon, leaning forwards. "He must have searched out all such places by now. They would be the easiest to search. If Erin were in one of them, Mako would know something of it. Isra must be staying in some place where there are other people, and she can rely upon their secrecy to conceal her."

"Then let us catch her and throw her to the Mystics so they may put her to the question," said Theren with a glower. "Only that leaves the same mystery as before—what is she waiting for?"

Ebon shrugged. "It has been nearly two weeks since we fought her in Xain's home. She took her time to plan the attack in the dining hall. Now that we foiled it, she will likely be even more careful in her plotting—especially now that she has revealed herself."

"That will take more time that we do not have," said Theren. "Mayhap the story I planted in Dasko's mind will hold. Mayhap not. I have never had to hide—" Theren stopped short, looking about to make sure no one was close enough to hear. "I have never had to hide mindwyrd before. What if I did it wrong? What if they find us? I should throw the amulet into the Great Bay and have done with it."

Kalem's eyebrows raised. "That may be a fair idea

now. Dasko would show mindwyrd sickness, but the faculty might ascribe it to Isra's doing. I would still rather we told the truth of what happened, but this is a good half-measure."

But Ebon frowned. "And what if Isra returns? She has the strength of magestones in her, and no one can resist her without the amulet. Mayhap we should leave it somewhere for the faculty to find instead. We could slide it beneath Jia's door when no one was looking. Then Xain would have it, and *he* could use it to stop Isra."

"He would not," said Kalem sadly. "The faculty would never use its powers. That would be a crime against the King's law, and punishable by death."

"I know it is!" Theren burst out, before quickly lowering her voice again. "That is why I hate this, why all my waking hours are a torment, and yet I cannot sleep. I know full well what awaits me at the end of this journey, but I cannot stop walking the road." Her arms and legs were shaking, and her knuckles were white from their grip on the arms of her chair.

Ebon looked away, for he felt her pain as if it were his own. And then, suddenly, an idea struck him. He looked at his friends, wondering that he had not thought of it at once.

"What if we find her ourselves?"

Theren and Kalem stared at him. "What do you mean?" said Kalem.

"Well, either ourselves, or with Mako's help," said Ebon. "If we capture her, and subdue her, and then *put* the amulet upon her before we turn her over to the faculty, then our problem is solved. They will assume she had it all along. Xain will have no choice but to accept that we are innocent."

Kalem frowned, and even Theren looked doubtful. Yet he watched them think on it, and saw the spark of the idea blossom to flame within their minds.

"I would still have to keep the amulet," said Theren. "At least for now."

"Yet you could release Dasko from your control, immediately," said Ebon. "You no longer need to hold him under mindwyrd."

"If she were discovered . . ." said Kalem.

"How could that happen?" said Ebon. "You have a good hiding place for it, Theren—or so I assume, since you do not carry it with you everywhere. And we can finally put this dark chapter behind us."

Theren spread her hands. "Let us say that is true. We must still find Isra, but we have no idea how."

"I think we must start with Yerrin," said Ebon. "Even Mako thinks they may know something."

Her eyes hardened. "You mean to bring Lilith into this."

He leaned forwards, counting the steps on his fingers. "If we do, everything falls into place. We release Dasko from our control. With Lilith's help—help, I say, not coercion—we track down who in her family is helping Isra. We know they must be—it is where she is getting her magestones. We capture Isra. And then we turn her over to the King's law with the amulet in her pocket. And everything will be over."

Theren looked desperately hopeful. But Kalem sat deep in thought. After a moment, he shook his head. "It is a lie, and a great risk as well. We have other resources, more than Mako, I mean. Ebon, you could ask Adara. The guild of lovers has a thousand ears, and they are always listening."

"I have hope for Mako, and I already mean to speak with Adara—this very night, in fact," said Ebon. "But Lilith may best them all, for she is closest to the source of the magestones. Yes, it means we must lie. But I am willing to bear that burden, for you and I have the least to lose as things stand. This plan helps Theren more than you or me, Kalem."

Theren studied her fingernails, and then put one in her mouth to tear at it with her teeth. Kalem and Ebon watched her.

"Let us try it, then," Theren muttered. "It cannot be worse than living this way."

"Then we must take the first step," said Ebon. "We must speak with Lilith."

"But she is still . . . Lilith," said Kalem. He shivered. "I have had difficulties enough with her in the past. Now that I am one of those who helped throw her to the Mystics' knives, I suspect she will be even less kind than before."

"We have no choice," said Ebon. "We must bring her to Mako so that she can help him in his search."

"No," Theren snapped. "Not Mako. I will not bring him anywhere near Lilith, nor will you."

"But Theren, he is the best chance we have at—"

She held up a hand to cut him off. "No. Remember your uncle Matami."

He fell silent at once, seeing Matami's brutalized corpse in his mind.

"Think on it," said Theren. "What if Mako decides that Lilith knows more than she is telling? Will he drag her down into the sewers to do to her what he did to your uncle? She is not even his kin. Do you think he will be more reluctant to kill her than another Drayden?"

"Lilith is a youth, like us," said Ebon, but the words sounded weak even in his own ears.

"I do not believe for a moment that that will save her. If we mean to work with Lilith, we will do it on our own. Mako will only put her in greater danger."

Kalem nodded in agreement, and so Ebon shrugged. "Very well."

But even as he said it, he thought of how helpful it would be to have Mako's counsel in this. He did not trust the bodyguard, exactly, or even like him very much. Yet Mako had proven his worth time and again, and had saved the children's lives more than once.

"If we mean to speak with Lilith, why wait?" said Kalem. He put his book aside and stood from the armchair. "Let us find her. Her schedule is the same as ours, and she should be in the library somewhere."

They rose together and set out to find her. Quickly they scanned the shelves of the whole third floor, but there were few students scattered among them, and Lilith was not there. The second and first floors took longer to search, for they were much more crowded, and Ebon and his friends earned several curious looks as they poked their heads in between bookshelves. But in the end they stood together on the bottom floor, and Lilith was nowhere to be seen.

"Has she returned to her dormitory?" said Kalem. "I know she has been granted special permissions to rest, if she wishes, after what she suffered."

"She has not," said Theren. In her voice was a sorrow Ebon could not place. "Come. We will have to sneak out of the library. I know where she is."

TEN

JIA HAD NOT RETURNED TO DUTY AFTER BEING PLACED under mindwyrd the day before last. Another instructor had replaced her in the library's afternoon study period. Her name was Uma, and she was short and plump, with eyes that seemed too large to work properly, and they were always blinking. One by one Ebon and his friends excused themselves to use the privies and then met each other in the hallways outside. Theren took them around a wide, looping route through the Academy's less traveled passages. At one point they climbed to the second floor, creeping among the younger children's dormitories where the space rang hollow and empty.

"Where are you taking us?" Kalem whispered.

"Hush, and you shall find out soon enough," said Theren.

They descended to the first floor again. Now they were in a part of the Academy where Ebon had seldom been. He knew some of the doors must lead to teacher's offices, and these they flew by in a rush. At last Theren stopped before a thick oaken door. It had a lock, and the keyhole was very large.

Theren tried the handle. "Locked," she said with a sigh of relief. "That means that Carog is not here."

"Who is Carog?" said Ebon.

"The bell-keeper," said Kalem, looking at Theren with awe. "Is this the bell tower?"

"It is," said Theren. "It is . . . well, it is where we will find Lilith."

"How can you know?" said Ebon. But she only gave him a steely look and did not answer.

Kneeling, she peered into the lock and extended a finger. From behind her he saw the glow of her eyes. A soft *click* came from within the lock, and the knob twisted in her hand. Quickly they all filed in through the door, and Theren locked it again behind them.

They stood in the base of a wide round tower with a stairwell that ran around the outer wall to the roof far above. Many windows pierced the walls, letting in shafts of light that crisscrossed each other in the air, illuminated by the dust motes that danced within them so that looking up from the ground was like seeing a honeycomb made of the sun's glow. At the very top they could see the Academy's great bell. Ebon had only viewed it from the streets of the city, where it seemed much like any other bell. From here, however, it seemed a massive thing, at least as large as a house, and its bronze glow in the sunlight nearly blinded them.

"Come," said Theren. "We should climb as fast as we may, for there is no place to hide down here if Carog should return."

"I have heard she is half blind, anyway," said Kalem.

"That may be, but she has ears like a cat. Quickly!"

She leaped up the stairs two at a time. Ebon and Kalem hastened to follow. But after only a few flights they both wheezed and gasped as they clutched at the stone handrail. Theren hardly slowed at all. When they had almost lost sight of her, she stopped and turned to look at them in disgust.

"Honestly, how do the two of you survive? Most noble children are not so frail."

"Most noble children learn to be warriors, especially firstborn," said Kalem. "They are not bookish."

"You claim that word as though it is something prideful," said Theren, arching an eyebrow.

"To some, it is."

She slowed her pace, though she kept prodding and urging them to go faster. But Ebon grew more and more uncomfortable the higher they climbed. Soon he had to press himself against the wall to their left, for he thought he might vomit if he caught sight of the floor far, far below them. He had never been overly fond of heights.

It seemed an eternity before they reached the top. When they did, Ebon and Kalem collapsed to the floor, wheezing. Ebon scooted quickly away from the edge, for though the railing between him and the open air was thick and strong, still it made him nervous. But the other direction hardly seemed better, for about five paces away was the edge of the tower, and the railing there was made of thin wooden poles. His stomach turned again, and he pressed his fingers hard against the wooden floor, as though he could catch it in his grip and hold on to it.

Theren stood there before them, dwarfed by the mammoth bell beside her, looking all around. There were a few boxes and crates of things about, though Ebon could not guess what they held, as well as many coils of rope stacked in the corners. Theren inspected them, eyes narrowed.

"Lilith?" she said softly. "It is Theren. I know you are here."

The tower was silent. Kalem looked to Ebon uncertainly—Ebon only tried not to look at the tower's edge. But after a moment they heard shuffling footsteps. Lilith stepped out from behind the coils of rope, a deep scowl embedded in her features.

Ebon was startled at the sight of her. He had not seen her plainly in some time. Even against the darkness of her skin he could see the fading remnants of bruises where she had been beaten. Her Academy robes covered most of them, but the fabric did not hide her face. And while her sleeves covered most of her hands, he spotted the pale pink of scars on the tips of her fingers, which were thin and wasted like a starving child's. And her eyes—her eyes were an animal's, filled with the futile indignation of a fox brought to bay, showing its teeth without hope.

"What are you doing here?" she snapped.

"I needed to speak with you," said Theren.

"What are *they* doing here?"

She turned eyes of fury on Ebon and Kalem, who had, without realizing it, retreated halfway behind Theren. Ebon steeled himself and stepped forwards to stand at Theren's shoulder.

"We need your help, Lilith."

Lilith ignored him, looking only at Theren. "I *never* brought Oren or Nella into the bell tower. Never."

Theren looked as though she had been slapped. "I . . . I did not know that. But I would have brought them even if I did know. Isra has returned, and she has magestones. We think she is getting them from your family."

For a moment, whistling wind was the only sound. Then Lilith's eyes widened, and her lips twisted to a snarl.

"You think *I* have something to do with it?" she screamed. "You think I would set eyes on Isra without catching her in a blaze? She *killed* Oren. She did *this.*"

She held up her hands before her face so that the sleeves of her robe fell to her elbows. Beneath were tight underclothes of wool, proof against the cold, which she dragged down to reveal her skin.

Kalem gasped, and Ebon's stomach lurched. The scars on her fingers were not the half of the harm that had been done to her. Pink lines of torn flesh raced down the length of her arms, crisscrossing each other over and over. Some looked to still be healing.

Theren's mouth worked, but she said nothing. Ebon saw tears spring to her eyes, threatening to flood forth. He stepped forwards, drawing Lilith's baleful gaze away from Theren and onto himself.

"I am sorry," he said. "We all are. You deserved none of what you received, and Isra was not alone in the blame for it. We were just as guilty."

For a moment he wondered if she had even heard him, for her expression did not change. Finally she turned, stalking away to the other side of the bell tower.

"Go away," she said over her shoulder. "I want nothing to do with any of you."

Ebon let loose a *whoosh* of breath and heard Kalem do the same. But Theren, unmoving, only watched Lilith go.

"It was wrong of us to ask this of her," Theren murmured.

He wondered if she was right. But then he remembered Isra in the kitchens, and felt again the blast of the artifact she had tried to use to kill them. Ebon squared his shoulders, and then he took Theren and Kalem's arms.

"We are not done yet," he said quietly. "Come."

They set off along the platform after her. She had gone to sit on the edge of the tower, her feet hanging off the lip while she held on to the thin wooden railing. Ebon's stomach did a turn at that. She did not look up, even as their feet scuffed to a stop behind her.

"I do not blame you for wanting to turn us away," said Ebon. "Indeed, Kalem had no wish to come to you, for you have never been kind to him, and Theren felt the same, for we have been far too cruel to you already. I cringe at the thought of trusting you in this after the way we met. But Theren has spoken to me of you, and of the nobility she still sees in your heart. And her belief has convinced me."

Lilith turned. Her gaze locked with Theren's, and Ebon saw her expression soften at the same time he felt Theren tense beside him. But it lasted only a moment before Lilith looked away again.

"I only want to be left alone," she said, but this time softly and without malice.

Theren went forth and sat on the stone edge beside her. Ebon's gut wrenched even worse—but from the ease with which she sat there, he guessed that Theren had done this many times before.

"What was it like when Isra had you under mindwyrd?" said Theren.

Lilith shuddered beside her, and she bowed her head. "It was horrible," she said in a low voice. "Still my mind reels when I try too hard to remember it. Some things I can recall, but it is like I watched it happen to someone else. When I entered the vaults, or when Vali . . ." She stopped, remaining silent through several deep breaths. Her scarred, ruined fingers crept up to scratch at her temples. "Other things I have forgotten entirely—and there are still other memories which come and go, and when they have gone I cannot remember having remembered them. It is . . . it is like a madness."

Ebon waited a moment. Then he took a step forwards—only one, for he was still terrified of the tower's edge—and said, "That is what Jia suffers even now. Isra has had her under control. Mayhap she has others. They will all suffer the same way. I would not ask you to face Isra again. But will you help us find her, so that we may?"

Lilith glared at him over her shoulder for a moment and then turned her face out again.

"You are fools if you think my family could have done this. Oren's death and my torture prove their innocence."

"Can you be so certain?" said Theren. "From what we have heard, some scion of your house had a hand in the Shades' attack. Mayhap they are also the ones who helped Isra—and may be helping her still."

"I know of whom you speak, but she could not

have acted alone," said Lilith quickly. "You are saying that others helped spit Oren like a pig. That others left me to scream as the Mystics dug their knives into my flesh."

Theren hung her head. "These are dark days, filled with dark deeds. Say, for a moment, that we are right. Would you let such deeds go unpunished?"

Lilith closed her eyes, taking a deep breath of the chilled air before letting it out in a rush.

"Very well," she said quietly. "I will ask about and see what may be learned. But I will not risk my neck for the three of you. It has been squeezed tight enough already."

"Of course," said Theren. She put a hand on Lilith's shoulder. The girl jerked away as if by instinct, but subsided almost at once. "Thank you, Lilith."

She rose to rejoin Ebon and Kalem, and they set off for the stairs leading down. Just before they rounded the edge of the bell and lost sight of Lilith, Ebon glanced back. She had not moved. Not even to watch them go.

ELEVEN

AFTER STUDIES ENDED THAT EVENING, EBON MADE for the streets and turned his steps towards the blue door in the west. Mako had begun his search, and now they had enlisted Lilith's aid as well. Only one more resource remained to them: Adara, with her fealty to the guild of lovers. And besides that, Ebon had not been able to spend much time with her the previous night, and hoped to make up for it.

The evening was even icier than normal, and he pounded his hands against his arms. He thought at once that he should have brought a second cloak, and considered going back for one. But just when he had made up his mind to do so, he heard the scrape of a boot on stone.

Ebon froze. He had ducked into an alley, a shortcut between two busy thoroughfares, and it had appeared empty. But the sound had been very distinct, though he could see no sign of anyone behind him now.

He took one careful step forwards, and then another. Then he pressed on at a regular pace, trying to convince himself that he had imagined the sound, or that it had been an echo of the noise of his own walking. But such thoughts did nothing to still his heart, which had begun to race.

His steps quickened, though he told himself it was only to warm his limbs, and every few paces he glanced back over his shoulder casually, as though he was just looking about to see the sights of the city. Soon he had reached a main street again, and that relaxed him considerably. There were too many people around, constables and Mystics and soldiers of all the nine kingdoms, for him to worry very much about an attack in the open. The black robes of an Academy student were distinctive, and wearers of such were known to be under the High King's protection.

But the busy street did not last forever, and eventually Ebon had to turn. He reached the street and balked. Far down it he could see one trader's cart plodding its way forwards through the snow, but between him and the cart was a great stretch of empty space with no one in sight. He skipped the turn and made for the next street, but it was even more barren, with not a soul to be seen from where he stood to where it vanished in a turn behind the corner of an inn.

Ebon glanced back along the thoroughfare down which he had come. He saw nothing untoward among the crowds. No one spared him a second glance.

He swallowed hard and stepped into the street. Now his footfalls, though muffled, could be heard bouncing from the buildings again. He listened hard, but he heard no steps other than his own. And he could not be sure if he was imagining the feeling of eyes upon his back, or if they were there in truth.

At last he reached the corner of the inn behind which the street turned. Without slowing, he stopped on the spot and whirled to look behind him.

The street was empty. Or . . . or had he in fact seen the corner of a grey cloak whipping behind the edge of a nearby building?

He passed the inn, and now he made no pretense of calm. He ran. The snow clutched at his boots, dragging at him. He imagined fingers beneath its surface, like the water-wurts that dragged sailors down to their deaths. Soon he was panting like a horse on the edge of collapse. His breath clouded around his head as if he were casting mists.

Mists. Ebon, you fool. He had utterly forgotten his magic. Now he darted for the closed mouth of an alley, dark and forbidding—but small, mayhap only a pace wider than his shoulders. Ebon flung himself into its mouth and reached for his power. The alley, which at first had been pitch-black to his sight, lightened considerably as his eyes began to glow. He focused on the air touching his skin. He *saw* it. And he spun mist within it.

It sprang from him, flooding out to fill the tiny width of the alley. He was nowhere near as proficient as Kalem, but he still managed to extend it a few paces in every direction. It was thick as a stew, so that no one could see through it—but it blocked Ebon's sight not at all, for it was born of his magic. He could see the alley's walls clearly, and when it branched off in two directions he made the turn without pausing. But he left the mist where it was, moving through it while it remained at the fork. He could only hold it a moment, but by the time it dissipated, he had already turned the next corner, and the fork was out of sight.

He would have laughed if he were not afraid of being heard. Anyone behind him would be lost now. And just ahead he could see the next main street, where many carts and travelers on horseback crossed the alley's—

A blast of air struck him in the chest, flinging him backwards and robbing his lungs of breath. He tried to cry out, but only a thin wheeze emerged. Strong, wiry hands clutched his collar and dragged him upright, around the corner and out of sight of the street. The hands slammed him up against the alley's wall.

Ebon stared into the eyes of Xain, dean of the Academy.

"Good eve, Drayden. Where are you off to in such a hurry?"

Xain's voice was carefully controlled, but Ebon could hear the fury within it. He tried to answer, but Xain's hand pressed against his throat. Hot breath washed over Ebon's face, and he smelled wine.

"Ah-ah-ah. Speak not. You are a student. Listening should be your primary concern. I wanted to tell you . . ." His lip curled. "I wanted to tell you that I received your family's note."

Ebon blinked. "What?" He barely managed to croak the word.

"I will not tell them where she is," Xain growled. "I would die first. I would not let Erin die for her, but then, I do not believe you mean to release him no matter what I do. I know the note's true purpose. It is supposed to make me lash out at your family—mayhap even at you yourself—so that the Draydens will have leverage. Then they can persuade the High King to remove me. Did you think this was a clever plan? Did you think I would not see through it? You were wrong."

"I know not—"

"Do not speak," hissed Xain. He did not squeeze, but the venom in his words silenced Ebon anyway. "You are fools if you think to dupe me with the same ruse as before. Drystan played this game, and it worked for him then. It will not work again. I am wiser now—

wise enough to see what you are doing. You may tell your family they have made a mistake. I will find my son. I will prove you took him. And then your names will be purged across the nine kingdoms. And if Erin has been harmed, I will not be gentle in the purging."

He snatched his hand back. Ebon fell to the ground, clutching his throat and coughing. Xain looked down on him with malice, his fingers twitching as though he longed to fill them with fire.

"Tell your kin, Drayden. Tell them they have but one hope. They may return Erin to me. Bring him to the Academy, and leave him at the front door. If it is done, I will cease my efforts to destroy them. If it is not, I will not rest until you all burn. Tell them."

Ebon raised his head to look Xain in the eyes, and despite his fear he did not waver. "I know not what you speak of," said Ebon. "I have nothing to do with your son. Isra took him. She tried to kill *me* only two nights ago. If you think we are in league with her, you are mad yourself."

Xain snarled, and blue fire sprang into his palm. He snatched Ebon's collar and pressed him to the wall again, and the blue flames swung back. Ebon flinched and cried out, pressing back against the wall as though he could sink through it and escape.

But then Xain stopped. His gaze locked with Ebon's. Slowly the magelight died in his eyes—and when they were clear, Ebon saw no fury at all. Instead he saw only a trace of doubt.

"Either you are lying, in which case, darkness take you—or you are telling the truth, and you are ignorant of your family's deeds. If that is true, then you are their sacrificial lamb. Either way, you are a walking corpse. Tell them what I have said. Tell them quick, lest they use you like bait on the end of a hook."

His eyes filled with light, and wind sprang from nowhere. It flung snow up to fill the air, thicker than mist, and Ebon had to shield his eyes against the stinging gale. When the wind died down and the snow settled back to the street, Xain had gone.

TWELVE

For a little while he stood there, every limb shaking, afraid to move, for he thought his legs might give out if he tried. But then he realized he was still in the alley and still out of sight of the street. So he forced his frozen legs to walk, and soon he was in a crowd again. He had drawn closer to the blue door, and when he saw it at last he began to shake again—though this time from relief.

The door opened easily under his hand, and the matron in the front room looked up expectantly. When she saw Ebon, her eyes filled with surprise.

"Good eve, young sir," she said. "Adara is in her room, and unoccupied."

Ebon fumbled for his coin purse, but the matron held up a hand with her palm out.

"That is not necessary. She has informed us of your new arrangement, and you no longer need bring any gold to visit her here."

Ebon pulled out a gold weight and placed it in her hand, where her fingers closed around it after only a moment's hesitation. "Take it regardless," he said. "Tonight I do not visit only for love."

He let himself through the door and made his way down the hall. His careful knock produced only silence for a moment. Then he heard her hesitant voice, almost a question. "Come in."

When he opened the door, she looked even more surprised than the matron had. "Ebon," she said. "I thought not to see you so soon."

"I thought not to visit tonight," said Ebon. "But things . . . plans have been altered, and I must speak with you."

"Has it something to do with Isra?"

Ebon looked behind him, but the hallway remained empty. Still, he closed the door and turned the lock. "It does," he said quietly.

"Come."

She patted the space on the bed beside her. He sat, and at once her hand covered his own, stilling his fidgeting fingers. He smiled up at her.

"You are shaking," she said. "What has happened?"

He remembered the fury in Xain's eyes, the wine that filled the dean's breath. But he had not come here to speak of Xain.

"I need . . . I had thought to ask you for a favor."

"If I may grant it without dishonor, then consider it done," she said. "Only, Ebon, you must tell me what is wrong."

"I . . ." But something overcame him, and he swiped at his eyes with the back of his hand. Now that he was in her presence, the whole encounter with Xain seemed at once distant and forgotten, and yet somehow more real and terrifying. But the last thing he wanted was to weep in Adara's presence, for their time together should be joyous.

Adara leaned back with an appraising look, and he flinched, thinking she scorned him. But she stood quickly and took his hands, drawing him up after her.

"Come," she said softly. "Let us retire to my home."

He had no chance to answer, let alone argue, for she led him out and down the hall at once. The matron asked no questions, but bid them farewell with a nod. It was not long before they were situated in Adara's little room again. As before, she seated Ebon at her table by the window, but she did not sit with him. Instead she went to her cupboard and drew forth two glass goblets—no, not glass, Ebon quickly saw. Crystal. Each was wrapped with a narrow gold band, and the crystal was carved in intricate, rippled diamond shapes. He marveled at them while she drew wine and mead from a cupboard.

"These must have cost a fortune," he said, distracted from his fears for the moment.

She shrugged. "I did not buy them. Another gift from a happy guest—and a wealthy one, I wager."

Ebon grew solemn. "I did not mean to take much of your time tonight, nor reduce the coin you might have earned. I can be brief, and mayhap another time we—"

Adara stopped short, and one of her fingers rose from the neck of the bottle it held. "No. It is my evening, and I will choose how to spend it. Your concern for my work is touching, but I do not lack for coin."

He smirked at his goblet. That was something he did not doubt. She came to the table with the bottles and filled both their cups.

"What do we drink to?" he said, raising his cup.

She did not raise her own, but only met his gaze for a moment. In her eyes he saw a fresh anxiety. It was the same look she had worn when first she invited him here—another wall coming down. He leaned forwards.

"To knowing more of each other," she said.

Ebon smirked. "I hardly think we could know more of each other than we do."

That earned him a wicked smile, but it quickly subsided, and her voice grew even more solemn. "I should like to get drunk with you, Ebon of the family Drayden."

He blinked, looking at the cup of wine in his hand. "I . . . I do not understand."

"Drunk. Inebriated. Overfilled with wine until our brains are addled. You cannot be a stranger to the concept."

Ebon tried to frown, but the sardonic twist of her lips softened him. "You know that is not what I meant. *Why* do you want to get drunk?"

"I have meant to ask you this for some time," she said. With a fingernail she picked at the table, scraping up a bit of its lacquer. "Even before you and I . . . before we told each other how we felt. In fact, that was how I first thought I would hear true words of love pass your lips. I thought for certain that they would never pass mine any other way."

His hand covered hers, stopping her from scratching the table further. "Adara, you need not get me drunk to hear that I love you. Have I not said it enough? A thousand times will I repeat it, and learn to say it in all the tongues of Underrealm if you wish. I will find the imps and the wurts and the satyrs in their homes, and even the centaurs where they have vanished in Spineridge, and learn to speak their words as well, if that is what you want."

"It is not," she said, rolling her eyes. "And you are a fool. Charming, but a fool. It is not the words I hoped to draw from you, for I told you that lovers' words do not only come from lovers' lips. I thought, once, that you said pleasant things we both wanted to hear, and that I might hear the truth if you were . . . disarmed, shall we say. And I feared to tell you how I myself had begun to feel, and thought mead might make the confession come more easily."

Ebon leaned back. "I see. But you know now that I speak true."

"You know the same of me," she said. "And yet."

He looked down at his hands, for he had guessed at her mind. Not long ago, he had been shocked to learn she once lived in Dulmun. Yet how could that have surprised him? He had learned nothing else of her life, and she knew little enough of his, beyond his deeds since he had come to the High King's Seat.

"To your life and mine," said Ebon. He raised his glass and looked into her eyes, suddenly aware that those sounded far too similar to wedding words. But he did not flinch.

She met his look and raised her goblet in turn. "To your life and mine," she said. "Let them be laid bare, and we the better for it."

They both drained their cups. Adara reached at once for the mead to fill hers again—but Ebon stopped her and took the bottle to pour it for her. She smiled and poured his cup in turn.

"Can you tell me now what brought you to my door?" she said. "Or must I force another goblet down your throat?"

Ebon tried to smile, but his thoughts turned dark again. "It was a little matter."

Her eyes said she did not believe him. She put her hand over his. "Tell me something else, then. A thing of yourself you have withheld until now."

"Withheld from you?"

"Yes. Whatever you wish. Something new."

He looked down at her hand, for he had thought of something at once. But even now he hated the thought of telling her, for it stung his eyes and put a lump in his throat. She lowered her head a bit, trying to catch his eye.

"That, Ebon. Remember. Your life and mine."

"I thought of my brother, Momen," Ebon murmured. He was afraid if he raised his voice at all, it would break. "I thought of when he died."

She waited a moment. When he did not go on, she spoke softly. "What about when he died?"

"When I heard the news, I locked myself in my room and did not come out for days. I let no one in. I know they all thought I wept. The truth is, I could not. Tears would not come, no matter how badly I wanted them to, and I was ashamed. I thought I was a monster for not weeping at my brother's death, for I loved him dearly. And I never told anyone about those days locked in my room. I know they all think I shed tears in private, but I never did."

By the time he finished speaking, his head had already begun to fog. The wine must have been strong, or else it was the effect of drinking it so quickly. Adara took her hand from his and leaned back, nodding slowly. When she answered him, her words ran together.

"I left Idris when I was only a little girl," she said. "My parents brought me to Feldemar with them, for my father had a cousin who promised him a position upon a merchant's caravan. He joined it, and was often gone on long journeys. Years he worked for the same merchant and spent more time away than at home. One day I found out my mother had taken a lover in secret, betraying him. The next time he came home, she told him what she had done and that she no longer loved him. He told her that he, too, had found another. He had met her while journeying in Selvan years before. They screamed at each other for hours, until finally I rose from my bed, slipped out my window, and ran from the house. I have not seen them since."

Ebon was frozen in his seat. He could scarcely imagine anything worse. Certainly if that had happened to his parents, he would have cared little—his father had never had love for him, and he had always thought his mother would be happier with another. But in Adara's voice he heard an aching, bone-deep sadness, and he knew at once that she had loved her father and mother both.

"Is that when you left for Dulmun?" he said quietly.

Adara shook her head. "That is another tale. And another cup. We have both told one, now. Drink."

She followed her own advice, raising her goblet and beginning to drink. Ebon drank from his as well, though not half so eagerly as last time. He could feel the drink seeping in at the back of his mind now, like a soundless ringing in his ears, an ecstasy longing to be acted upon. He refilled Adara's cup, and she filled his.

"Xain attacked me tonight," said Ebon. "Well, I say attacked . . . he did not harm me. Though I suppose he did, after all, did he not? But not greatly. Not if there is no small red mark here."

He pointed to his neck, where he vividly remembered Xain's thumb pressing into his jugular. Adara leaned forwards, blinking twice.

"There is not."

"Then he did not harm me greatly," said Ebon. "But he . . . he threatened me. He told me my family sent him a note."

"What kind of note?"

"Am I telling the story?" he said, but he grinned to soften the words. "He said . . . a note about his son. Erin, his name is. His son, not Xain—Xain's name is Xain. He said he would not tell us where she was."

Adara frowned, looking out the window. "Where who was?"

Ebon spread his hands helplessly, almost spilling his goblet. He put it back on the table, reflecting that he probably should not have held it when he gestured so. "I do not know. But he would not tell me the information he seemed to think I desired, that much was certain. And he said that if we harmed Erin, he would destroy us. All of us."

"But you do not have Erin."

Ebon shrugged. "I have told him that—or rather, I told him that tonight. I have just realized that I never told him that before. I likely should have. Not that it would have been a comfort, for he would not have believed me. And it might have sounded suspicious, defending against an accusation that had not yet been leveled."

"But if you do not have Erin, why would your family have sent him a note?"

"That troubles me. Of course, anyone could have put our name on a scrap of paper. Or left it blank, and Xain would have guessed it came from us, for his hatred knows no limits."

She looked at him in silence for a moment, and through the fog of wine he saw her eyes glint with appraisal. "You do not think Mako would have done it? Even without Erin in hand, if he thought he could gain something from provoking Xain . . ."

"The thought had not crossed my mind . . . yet you are not wrong." He scowled into his goblet. "I mean to speak to him tomorrow, for in any case I should tell him what happened with Xain. I will ask him then."

Adara nodded sagely at that, as though it were a great wisdom. Then she held up a finger. "Your last truth was a truth of the past, and I answered in kind. But the truth you have just told me is a truth of the present. So I will answer with my own. Tonight, a boy behind the blue door told me I was a fool for falling in love with you. He said you were a merchant's son, a goldbag, and that you had tricked me into giving you my services without asking for coin in return."

Ebon frowned. "But that . . . that is a lie. I—"

She stopped him with a sharply-raised hand. "I did not ask for your answer. That is the purpose of . . . this." Adara waved a hand in the general direction of the goblets and the bottles. "And besides, I gave him my answer already. I told him he was a wool-headed steer, that I had heard complaints from many of his clients about his woeful lack of expertise in our trade, and that he likely received only half of the usual rate for his work. He broke down weeping and fled through the blue door. I hope he never returns. And now we have each told another truth."

They both took their time now, sipping gingerly at their cups. But they spoke no words, only met each other's eyes. Ebon became aware of her foot atop his under the table. He twitched his leg. She moved her own in response.

"Mayhap we should finish these goblets upon the bed," he suggested.

"Are you certain?" She gave him a coy smile. "We both know wine can trouble your performance."

"That is why I suggest we move quickly," he said, standing from his chair. "Because you have never seen me well and truly drunk, Adara, and so I suggest you make use of me while you may."

She laughed easily and took his proffered hand to rise. Cups forgotten, they undressed each other piece by piece. Again she cared for him, and he for her. Then they took their cups and brought them to the bedside tables, huddling together under the warm fur blanket. But they did nothing else.

"You did not come here to speak to me of Xain," she whispered in his ear. Her hand traced the almost-absent lines of his thin, youthful chest. "He found you on your way. Why did you come to see me again so soon?"

He sighed. "I came to ask a favor, though I have no great wish to do so."

Her hand slid lower. "I am amenable to favors. What do you need?"

"We . . . I mean Kalem and Theren and I . . . and Lilith. Oh, yes. We have befriended Lilith. Not befriended, that is wrong. We are . . . in league with her. I suppose that is a poor way to put it as well. In any case, we need to know where Isra has gone. She is here on the Seat. There must be a trace of her. And you are a lover."

"Of course. I have many lovers I can turn to. Not—" She giggled, and Ebon snorted a bark of laughter. "Not lovers. That is not what I meant. Other lovers. Lovers like me, I mean."

He kissed her deeply. "There are no lovers like you."

"Be silent, flatterer. I will ask them. But I do not understand. Why were you reluctant to ask me this? It is hardly any trouble at all."

That sobered him, for the answer had been troubling him greatly. "At first my mind was taken by Xain and his threats. And then . . . I still fear for your safety, and more so the further you are drawn into all this. If Isra knew of your existence, I do not doubt that she would come for you just to hurt me. And between the amulet and our mindwyrd of Dasko, and now our investigation of Yerrin, I feel as though peril haunts my every step. And I walk well outside of the King's law now, though I hate to do it."

"But you *do* hate to do it," she said. "And that makes the difference. Now you have told me something of the future. I will do the same. One day—not soon, mayhap, but one day—I want you take me back to Feldemar, where I have not returned since I left."

He ran a finger through the hair on her temple. "Of course. I know not when, or how. But I vow that I will do it."

Her eyes shone with tears. "Dear, dear Ebon. Was that a truth? You do not owe me another one."

Ebon kissed her. "I will give you all of my truth, whenever you wish it."

To his shock, the tears broke, trickling down her cheeks. "One day I, too, may be able to do the same. I cannot yet. Not even now." Then she pushed him gently back towards the side table. "Now drink."

THIRTEEN

EBON SCARCELY REMEMBERED STUMBLING HOME LATER that night. He had one vivid picture of vomiting into a gutter in the streets of the city. And the next day, he did not receive punishment for staying out late, so he guessed that he must have returned before curfew. But his next clear memory was waking in his bed with a terrible headache and a stomach that felt ready to spill itself onto the stone floor. He threw on his robe and ran to the privy as quickly as he could, where he spilled his guts again. Then he simply sat there for a while, leaning to the side so that his head was pressed against the frigid stone wall.

A bell rang at last, signaling the end of breakfast and the beginning of the day's classes, and so he stumbled out and down the hall. But he made one quick diversion on his way to Perrin's room. He stepped outside and went to the place in the citadel wall where he knew Mako's secret door stood. There he found the stone of alabaster, and under it he placed a scribbled note on a scrap of parchment from his pocket.

Morning's class was slow and painful. Perrin often gave him a disapproving look. Next to him, little Astrea kept leaning away. Ebon guessed he must smell like wine, and mayhap vomit. But he managed to keep some level of composure. After years beneath his father's roof, he was no stranger to drinking. And so his class passed without comment.

The moment the lunch bell rang, he was out of his seat and hurrying through the halls again. He found a bench near the secret door and sat, leaning back against the cool citadel wall. He did not have to wait long before he heard a rustle in the hedges beside him. Mako stepped out of the shrubbery and fixed him with a hard look.

"You are drunk."

"Not anymore," said Ebon, squinting in the sun. "Now I only regret being drunk."

Mako sniffed. "It smells the same. I received your note. What is it?"

Ebon stood from the bench—then swayed for a moment before he could recover himself. He crossed his arms over his chest, a perfect mirror of Mako's stance, and met the man's eyes.

"Did you send a ransom message to Xain?"

Mako blinked. "What in the nine lands do you speak of, boy?"

Ebon sighed, feeling his shoulders droop. Mako was a good liar, mayhap among the best, and so it could be that he only feigned his shock. But the look of surprise on his face was good enough for Ebon, at least in his drunken state. "Never mind. Xain came for me last night, speaking of a ransom note. He thought it came from us."

He was about to sit back down on the bench, but Mako snatched his collar and dragged him to his feet. "What note? What did it say?"

"I did not see it, Mako." Ebon made a halfhearted attempt to remove the bodyguard's hand, but he gave it up almost at once. "Whoever sent it is looking for someone—a woman—and thinks Xain knows where she is. But he said he would never reveal the secret."

Mako's eyes glinted. "Does the woman have a name?"

Ebon frowned. "Not that I know. I told you I did not see the note. Why? Do you know of her?"

A pregnant silence stretched so long that Ebon quite forgot about his headache. But at last Mako released his collar, pushing him ungently away.

"Never you mind, little Ebon. More important than the note itself is Xain's mind concerning it. He says it came from us, and I doubt anything will convince him otherwise. But if the note bore the name of anyone in the family, he would not have come to you; he would have gone straight to the High King."

"I guessed as much myself," said Ebon. "But Xain seemed most certain. Do you think this is something my father could have done?"

Mako frowned. "Once I would have said he would never be so foolish. But he has since proven himself at least that much so. It still does not make sense, though, and for one reason: Shay could never hold Erin without my knowing of it already."

"How, then, do we solve the riddle?" said Ebon. "Someone sent the note, and did so to drive a wedge between us and the dean—or, if they did not intend that, it has happened regardless."

Then Mako's eyes lit, and he snapped his fingers. "They did intend it. It is one more step in their plan. An anonymous ransom note, sent to Xain in the knowledge he would think it was from us. Sent by the one who holds Erin in their clutches."

Ebon frowned, trying to work it out. "Then . . . then Isra sent the note?"

Mako cuffed him on the side of the head, but not, mayhap, as hard as he might have. Still, it made stars dance in Ebon's eyes, and he groaned in pain. "No, little idiot. The ones *behind* Isra. Yerrin. They are the only ones who could keep Isra's hiding place from me this long. If anyone else were hiding her somewhere on the Seat—especially someone like Shay—I should have found her already."

"Do you have a way of finding where Yerrin may be keeping her?" Ebon felt a wave of guilt as he thought of Lilith. Almost he spoke on and told Mako of the conversation with her. But then he thought of Theren's insistence and held his tongue.

"There are many ways of finding out, but I cannot know which will bear fruit," said Mako.

"Then I leave you to it," said Ebon. "Only hurry, because the longer the search continues, the more energetic I think Xain will become, and if it is discovered that Theren holds the amulet of Kekhit, then we are all doomed."

Mako gave him a careful look. "I have spent some thought on that. There is a way to remove the amulet as a threat."

"There is?" said Ebon, frowning. "How?"

"We could let it be known that Theren carries it. The faculty would catch her and imprison her—but you, having revealed the truth, would face no penalty."

Ebon froze. "I . . . but Theren would be . . ."

"My duty does not bind me to protect Theren. Only you."

Rage coursed through Ebon's veins, making him shake where he stood. "You will not do that," said Ebon. "I swear that if you so much as breathe a word of it, to anyone, I will see that you suffer Theren's fate twice over."

Mako cocked his head, and a little smile played at the corner of his mouth. "How very like your father you sound just now. But I take no orders from him, either, little Ebon. My duty countermands your rage, and your threat is shorn of claws or fangs."

"But you do take orders from Halab," said Ebon. He took a step forwards, though he was aware how pathetic it must seem when the bodyguard stood a full head taller. "And if you should betray Theren, I will tell her everything. I will tell her of Matami—yes, mayhap she suspects, and wishes to say nothing, but I will not let the matter lie—and then I will tell her how you made me party to the murder, endangering me before the King's law. And finally, I will return to the Academy and tell Xain all that I have told Halab, and more besides—the truth about Isra, and the amulet, and how you fled just before Isra took his—"

With movements too fast to see, Mako spun him by the shoulder and kicked out the back of his knees. Ebon fell, his head slamming upon the stone bench, where Mako's knobby fingers held him fast. He felt the sharp prick of a dagger on the back of his neck. Even as he gasped in pain, Ebon held perfectly still, terrified to move.

"My duty is to guard you," said Mako. "And to guard Halab. But Halab comes first, always, and you have just threatened to put her in mortal peril. And all for the sake of a girl who is no kin to either of us. Sort out your loyalties, goldshitter."

"They are clear to my mind, if not to yours," said Ebon. "I trust that Halab would emerge from such a mess unscathed. I cannot say the same for you."

He heard a snort behind him, and though he could not see Mako's face, he heard incredulity in the bodyguard's voice. "You would sacrifice yourself for your friend."

"As easy as breathing."

"Be silent. I was not asking—I was seeing a truth for the first time."

The pressure on Ebon's head vanished, as did the dagger's tip behind him.

"Very well, goldshitter. If you wish to live in foolish nobility, it its yours to have. I prefer life, and power, and a purse full of coin."

Slowly Ebon rose. The motion and the impact on the stone had made his headache twice as painful, and he grimaced as he found his feet. But though Mako had thoroughly trounced him, he still felt a small sense of victory.

"Now then. It is of the utmost importance that you find Isra before anyone can discover that Theren holds the amulet."

Mako smirked at him. "I have told you already that I will use my every resource—and I have many of them. We know already that Isra must have used my secret entrance to get into and out of the Academy. I have placed a watch upon it, so that if anyone comes or goes, I will hear of it. Worry not, little Ebon. Your friend will not face the knives of the Mystics. And I will soon remove the problem of Isra from our lives."

He turned and vanished into the hedge. Ebon rubbed at the back of his neck and shuddered as he felt a little drop of blood. It felt very much as though a fox troubled his henhouse, and he had just released a lion to kill the thing. He had little doubt the fox would die—but what might the lion do after?

That night, Theren went to place her mindwyrd on Dasko for the final time. All the afternoon they spent together in the library, she bounced in her armchair. Her leg would not stop twitching back and forth, and a smile played constantly at her lips. Ebon grew irritated after a while, but how could he tell her to stop? She had borne the greatest burden of guilt out of all of them, and she deserved every feeling of elation.

When at last dinner had gone by, she led them out onto the Academy's grounds. Ebon and Kalem kept careful watch for anyone drawing too near as they went. No one did. Theren had little mind for anything or anyone other than Dasko, but Ebon was afraid that fate would play some cruel joke, and that someone would catch them in their crime even as they prepared to stop forever.

But they reached the meeting place without incident, and there they found Dasko waiting for them. He stood as they entered, and while Kalem stood lookout again, Theren went to him.

"After we are done here, you will forget you have seen us, and if asked you will say only that you went out for a walk on the Academy grounds, alone. When I tell you we are finished, you will enter the citadel. You will find Xain, and you will tell him your head is spinning, and that your memory plays tricks on you. You will tell him you saw Isra."

"Yes," said Dasko.

"He should not be so certain," said Ebon quietly. The faculty had to believe that Dasko was under mindwyrd, and therefore his memory needed to be shaky and unclear.

Theren glared at him, but turned back to Dasko after a moment. "You will tell Xain that you think you saw Isra, but you cannot be certain."

"Yes," said Dasko.

Theren released a great heave of breath.

"We are finished."

"Yes." Dasko stepped past her, making for the gap in the hedge. He was almost gone, almost out of sight, when Theren took a half-step after him and called out.

"I am sorry."

"Yes."

Then he was gone.

FOURTEEN

THE NEXT MORNING, EBON FELT HIS HEART IN HIS throat as he approached the dining hall. He found Theren within, already sitting with a plate of food, but Kalem was nowhere to be seen. Theren had great bags under her eyes, and her fingers were twitching. Ebon wondered if she had slept at all the night before. Very soon now, they would learn if the scheme had worked. Quickly he fetched his own food and joined her at table.

"Have you heard anything?" he said.

"Who do you think I speak to, other than you and Kalem?" said Theren irritably. She stabbed her spoon into her oatmeal. Ebon smirked at her words—until he realized how true they were, and how he, too, had precious little conversation within the Academy unless it was with his two closest friends.

It seemed an age before Kalem arrived. When he did, they tried to wave him over to the table, but he only waved back and set off to get food. Theren gave an angry growl and made to go after him, but Ebon urged her to remain seated.

"Let us make no more commotion than we must," he said. "Waiting a little while longer will not change the answer."

At last Kalem joined them at the table. The moment his rear touched the bench, Theren seized his arm to drag him close. "What have you heard?" she said. "Has the rumor flown yet?"

"Let go of me," Kalem groused, pulling himself from her reach. "Am I your only source of news? There are hundreds of students in the Academy."

"Pretend, for a moment, that you are indeed the only one," said Ebon. "Now speak, and quickly."

"Yes, the rumor has flown. They are saying that Dasko was found under the influence of mindwyrd, and suspicion has fallen upon Isra, as it should have."

Theren gave a happy cry, slapping her hand down on the table. Ebon quickly tamped down his own smile, leaning in to hiss at her.

"Be silent. We are trying *not* to draw attention, remember?"

Theren grew quiet, but she could not remove the smile from her face. Nor could Ebon blame her for that. She tore through her breakfast and stood at once, grinning down at them.

"I fancy a walk upon the grounds. Do either of you care to join me?"

Ebon waved her off. "We are still hungry. Go and enjoy yourself."

But just then, Lilith appeared behind Theren. Theren turned to leave and ran straight into her, forcing her to take a step back. Lilith winced and seemed for a moment as if she might fall, but Theren gripped her arms and held her upright.

"Lilith! I am sorry. Forgive me."

"It is nothing," said Lilith, turning aside as her dark cheeks grew darker still. "May I sit with you for a moment?"

Theren gave Kalem and Ebon an awkward look. "Of course. I shall see the two of you in the library."

"Actually, I meant the three of you at once," said Lilith.

"Oh! Oh, of course. Here."

Theren held out an arm, helping Lilith as she settled herself down onto the bench. She leaned forwards, prompting Ebon and Kalem to do the same from the other side of the table.

"I have visited my family—at least those who dwell upon the Seat, and to whom I may speak openly."

"And?" said Ebon. "Does anyone know aught of Isra?"

"No one seemed to," said Lilith. "Of course, I could not interrogate everyone. But if she is being held in some place owned by my kin, some would know about it. And I heard no breath of such a thing, nor saw the downcast eyes of a liar. If indeed someone in our clan is working alongside her, that truth is buried deep. Deeper than I can dig, at any rate."

"Blast," said Kalem. He leaned back, crossing his arms with a pout. "I suppose that would have made things too easy, and fate has no wish to make our lives convenient."

"I am sorry," said Lilith. "I wish I had a different answer, but I do not."

Theren cautiously put a hand on her arm. Lilith stiffened in her seat, but did not pull away. "Thank you, Lilith. You have done us a great service, and more than we should have asked of you in the first place. We will not forget it."

Silence ruled for a moment, until Theren gave Ebon and Kalem a hard look. The two of them quickly murmured their assent.

"It was the least I could do, after Oren," said Lilith. "Good day to all of you."

She stood and left the table, joining Nella, who sat a little distance away.

"That is a disappointment," said Theren.

"Indeed," said Kalem. "I suppose we must rely on Mako now. And on Adara, though I wonder if the lover's guild reaches as far as your family."

"Hm? Oh, yes," said Ebon. In truth he had barely heard them, for he was watching Lilith and Nella. The two of them sat at a table with many other students, but separated from them by a little distance. They were more than alone; they were lonely. Each fixed a somber stare upon their breakfast bowls, and when they raised their eyes to speak, their words were clipped and muted.

They looked nothing like the girls who had tormented Ebon when he first arrived. And that should have seemed like a good thing, but there was no joy in his heart. Instead he felt hollow—but likely only half so much as they did, for they had lost Oren.

He glanced at Kalem and Theren, who had kept on talking despite his distraction. What would it be like, he wondered, trying to carry on with one of them dead? He tried to imagine sitting here, eating his porridge with Kalem, or with Theren, and the third seat empty. Would he ever be able to look away from it? Or would it loom between them, vacant and filled with presence at the same time, as though a spirit sat between them, invisible and silent, watching?

Ebon shuddered, and his thoughts returned to Oren. Despite Lilith's words, he believed Mako: Yerrin had to be behind this. He wondered how a family could be so cruel, concocting schemes that led to the death and torture of their own children. The thought of Isra striking again made him quail, and he imagined her crushing the life from one of his friends as her eyes glowed black.

He could not allow it.

"Magestones," he muttered.

Theren and Kalem jumped in their seats, and both looked quickly all about them.

"Be silent, you idiot," growled Theren. "You should know better by now than to say that word aloud in this place."

"Oh, who cares for that anymore?" said Ebon, leaning forwards. "Xain himself told us all that we cannot keep hiding from the truth about magestones and their effects—though no doubt he would roast me if he heard me saying the word, unjust as it might be. I think Lilith may be able to help us find Isra after all—if she can find where the stones are coming from."

Kalem looked to Theren. "He might be right. If someone is helping her, and they are wise, they will not deal with her closely. They may funnel the stones to someone outside the family, and that person may bring them to Isra."

"I know it is a great thing to ask," said Ebon. "But it could help."

Theren's eyes shifted back and forth, and though she said no word of argument, neither did she rise at first. "She has likely taken a great risk already."

"I think she is clever," said Ebon. Theren's nostrils flared, and he held up a hand. "No, do not misunderstand me. I only mean that I am sure she can ask about such things without endangering herself. Lilith is no fool. And if she does attract some attention, it can be no more dangerous than the peril facing the Academy and all who dwell here."

Theren's jaw clenched. "We should not discuss this here. I will ask her to see us in the library this afternoon."

She rose and went to Lilith's side, leaning down to whisper in her ear. After a moment she straightened and left the dining hall. Lilith looked over her shoulder, giving Ebon a small nod.

FIFTEEN

THAT MORNING IN PERRIN'S CLASS, EBON FOUND himself endlessly distracted by thoughts of Lilith and the family Yerrin. He tried to concentrate, shutting his eyes tight to block out the buzzing of his worries.

"What are you thinking about?" Astrea's words held neither judgement nor much interest. She spoke in the same morose inflection he had come to expect from her recently.

"It is . . . well, it is all the business going on about the Academy these days."

"You mean with Isra. I am no fool."

Ebon frowned. He had not wanted to bring that up. He chose not to answer, instead looking down at the rod in his hand. Turning it from wood to stone was now as easy as blinking. But he had not yet managed to turn it the other way, though at times he felt as if he was close. Some other spells he had grown more proficient in—after the night with Matami, he could shift stone much more easily. But "transmuting up," the colloquial term for turning simple matter more complex, still eluded him.

Now he closed his eyes and took a deep breath. He pressed his fingertips to the rod, peering into it with his mind's eye. The room grew brighter with his magelight. He saw the rod, the simple parts that made up its stone, small and solid and clinging together tightly.

He changed them.

Nothing happened.

He *changed* them.

The rod rippled. A fine sweat broke out on Ebon's brow. His teeth pressed so tight together that his chin began to hurt. A little gasp burst from his mouth, unbidden.

He changed them.

Wood rippled along the rod in an instant, and with a *snap* the magelight died in his eyes.

"Yes!" Ebon crowed, leaping from his bench and holding the rod aloft. Then he froze. The whole classroom had fallen silent around him while every student stared. Near the back of the room, Perrin fixed him with a hard look—though he thought he saw some trace of amusement in her eye.

"Well, Ebon?" she said. "Now that you have all of our attention, what do you mean to do with it?"

"Nothing, Instructor," Ebon stammered. He proffered the wand. "Only I have turned my rod to wood at last."

"That is well done. And what are the rest of you staring at? Get back to your lessons."

Around the room, everyone jerked in their seats and turned their eyes back to the spells on the desks before them. Perrin murmured some final words to the student she was with and then lumbered to the front of the room.

"Well, change it back," she said.

Ebon focused, and in a moment the rod rippled back to stone.

"Good. That comes easily to you now, as it should. And the other way again, so that I can see it."

He took a deep breath, closed his eyes, and concentrated. Then he stared at the rod—no, *glared* at it, every muscle in his body tensing, his knuckles white as he gripped it. It did not take quite so long this time, but still it seemed an eternity before wood rippled down along its length, transforming it.

"Very well done indeed," said Perrin. "It took you mayhap a little longer to learn the spell than it should have, but with your skill at shifting stone, I should say you are right on course to finish this class in a year."

Ebon groaned. "I thought this took no time at all! It has not even been two months yet."

"But this is the easiest of your testing spells. You had better get to work on the next, for it will take you far longer to learn."

He slumped back down onto his bench, dejected. Perrin clapped him gently on the shoulder—gently for her, though Ebon thought she might break his collarbone.

"No need to look so crestfallen. You are a wizard just like any other, Ebon, and that is something remarkable, even if you do not have the strength of some Wizard King."

"Of course, Instructor."

"Do you remember your second test?"

He searched his mind and looked away, embarrassed. "I . . . I confess I have forgotten. I remember I have to change a stone's color, but I think that is the third one."

"Right you are," she said. "Now you must learn to turn a flower to ice without changing its shape. There is a vase of them near the front of the room. Go fetch one."

She left him to help another student while he went to do as she commanded. When he returned, he gave Astrea a rueful look. She returned only a dead-eyed stare.

"There is always another lesson to be learned, I suppose," said Ebon.

"Always," murmured Astrea. She reached out for his wooden rod, which now lay on the desk before her. With a flash of her eyes, she turned it stone—and then, with another flash, she turned it back to wood.

Ebon gawked at her. "What . . . how did you do that?"

The corner of her mouth twitched in a smile, but she crushed it at once. "You have seen me do it before."

"But not so quickly. You did it as easily as flipping a coin."

She frowned and looked about. "It came to me easily. I have said that already."

"Of course, I did not mean offense," Ebon said quickly. But he thought, *How could I not have seen the great strides she has taken in her learning? Am I so poor a friend?* "What else can you do? Have you been practicing other spells?"

Rather than draw her out, that seemed only to make her retreat further into her shell. Her shoulders hunched, and she pushed the rod away so that it rolled down the desk. "No. That one just came easily."

Guilt struck him like a blow to the ribs. He had been so preoccupied with Isra and Lilith the last few days, he had almost forgotten Astrea entirely. The girl she had once viewed as an older sister now ran amok, threatening all who studied at the Academy. How must she be suffering? She needed him now more than ever, but he was off spending his evenings with Adara instead.

"I am sorry I have not come to see you as much," he said in a low voice. "There is no excuse, for I know your heart must be greatly troubled."

"Of course it is." To his surprise, Astrea's voice had gone cold and bitter in an instant. "Everyone is troubled, but I think you are all idiots. I do not believe Isra means to hurt anyone, though it seems clear you think she does."

Ebon frowned. He knew Astrea must be angry about this, but her words were ridiculous. "Why do you think she is here, then?"

"Mayhap she has come to clear her name. Lilith cleared hers when everyone thought she was a villain. Why not Isra?"

"Lilith only had to prove her innocence *because* of Isra," said Ebon. "This is not the same thing."

Astrea gave no answer, but only turned away to hide behind her wild, frizzy hair. Ebon sighed, feeling his quickened pulse gradually slow.

"Isra tried to kill me, Astrea. My friends as well. When we saw her in the kitchen, she tried to destroy us. We only escaped through sheer luck."

She turned on him, her wild eyes sparkling in anger. "You do not know that for certain. No one can. None of you are *trying* to help her. Did you even try talking to her? Or did your friend Theren attack her on sight?"

Ebon went still, mouth open. The first thought that came to his mind was that yes, Astrea was right,

Theren *had* attacked the moment she saw Isra. But that was only after they had fought Isra in Xain's home, where she had made every effort to kill them all, and had placed Theren under mindwyrd. He could not say so, however. And so he had nothing to say at all.

"I thought so," said Astrea. She turned away and buried her face in her arms where they were crossed upon the desk.

Heavy footsteps preceded Perrin's arrival. "Astrea, would you go and help Dorna with her shifting? She is not yet so proficient as you are."

For a moment Astrea only glared up at the instructor. But then she rose and went towards the back of the room, giving no answer aloud. Perrin settled down onto the bench beside Ebon, making it groan and crackle in protest.

"I know you mean well, Ebon. But you must leave off trying to convince Astrea of Isra's evil. Remember, Isra was like a sister to her."

"Yes, but Isra is also an abomination," said Ebon. "Is it not important that she knows that?"

Perrin sighed. "Is it? Imagine yourself in her shoes. Imagine your kin were dark figures who committed dark deeds, and you were but a child—not nearly a man grown, as you are now. Would it help you to know of the evil things they did in the shadows? Or would you be a happier child in ignorance?"

She fixed him with a look, and Ebon felt as though the ground had vanished beneath him. For of course, he *did* come from a dark family, and he *had* been ignorant of it when he was Astrea's age. He tried to imagine knowing the truth about his father, and Mako, and yes, even Halab, and the things she sometimes ordered Mako to do, when he had seen only eleven years. Would it have made him happier?

He knew at once that it would not.

"But . . . but this is different," he said. "I mean, this is not quite what you describe. Isra's darkness is not hidden. She wears her evil like a cloak for all to see."

"You cannot think of it that way. Astrea certainly does not. Remember, she has grown up with tales of Isra's suffering, knowing of the great injustice done to Isra's parents. You have heard the tale."

Ebon stared at his fingers. The way Isra's parents had been killed still made his gorge rise. "I have."

"None would call that anything but a grave evil. That is the Isra that Astrea knows and has heard about since she was a little girl—an even *littler* girl, I mean. And so, naturally, no matter what she hears of Isra now, she will only see this as another great injustice, something suffered but not deserved."

"But it is not," Ebon said helplessly.

"But she is *eleven*," said Perrin. "Do not hold her to the same standards you expect of yourself. Astrea is still a child. It is the job of elders—not just parents—to keep children from the burdens of adulthood, and Astrea is overburdened already."

Perrin pushed back and stood, the bench moaning

in relief. She strode off towards the next student with a hand raised, leaning down to resume another lesson. And Ebon stared at the wooden rod before him, though he did not see it, or anything else at all.

SIXTEEN

THAT AFTERNOON, LILITH CAME TO THEIR PLACE IN THE library. Ebon saw her almost the moment she reached the third floor, for he sat where he could see down the long walkway that led to the stairs. She walked slowly, hesitantly, as though she was afraid of being spotted. When at last she reached them, she stood two paces off, hands fidgeting with each other, looking awkwardly between the three of them.

"Come, sit," said Theren. She stood and waved Lilith into the armchair where she had been sitting and then ran to fetch another.

"Thank you," said Lilith, setting herself carefully down. As Theren found her seat, Lilith looked from Ebon to Kalem. A halfhearted smile stole across her lips. "Never did I think to be sitting and conversing with the three of you here in your own little corner."

Ebon's eyebrows raised. "It is hardly ours."

Lilith waved a hand. "Do not be daft. Nearly everyone in the Academy knows this as your place, and that the three of you may be found here every afternoon."

Kalem's eyes widened, and he looked to Ebon. Ebon was just as surprised to hear they had any sort of reputation in the Academy.

"We will not keep you long," said Theren. "We need to ask you something—something we could not discuss in the dining hall. It has to do with magestones."

Lilith's eyes darkened. She crossed one leg over the other. "What of them? I know very little."

"We think we may use them to find Isra," said Ebon. "You could not find out if anyone in your family is colluding with her. But we know she has magestones. If we can find the movements of the magestones, we may be able to follow them right to her."

That made Lilith think, but after a moment she shrugged. "Mayhap, but again, I know very little. Everyone in the family—and some beyond—know we traffic in them. But details are kept from any who do not need to know them. They are especially kept from any children in the Academy. You three know as well as I do the sort of things they say about magestones in these halls—how evil they are, and how dangerous, and all that sort of talk."

"It is not just 'talk,'" said Kalem, glaring. "They *are* dangerous. Isra should be proof enough of that for you."

Lilith shrugged, and it seemed to Ebon that she barely kept from rolling her eyes. "Yes, yes, of course," she said. "Certainly in untrained hands they can be perilous."

Ebon was about to ask her just what she meant by that, but Theren met his gaze and froze him with a glare. "It seems sensible to me that your family would not let you know of their activities beyond the King's law," she said. "But is there no one who *would* know?"

"A number of people, certainly," said Lilith. "Most would not deign to tell me the hour of the day, but there might be one or two who I can trust well enough to ask for help."

"Not if it will put you in danger," said Theren.

Lilith sighed. "I know I said the same thing when you first approached me, but I have spent much thought upon it since. I decided that I am no safer keeping myself out of things than I would be if I helped you, now that a madwoman runs about the Academy drunk on magestones. At least if my kin should turn on me and kill me, they will do it quicker than the Mystics meant to."

"That is a grim thought," said Ebon. "Though no doubt it is true. How soon will word reach you, once you begin asking questions?"

"I cannot say. I have never done this before. But there is much tumult among my kin just now. You may have heard that some of us were under suspicion for collaborating with the Shades during the attack." She grew grim at that and waited for a long stretch of silence. "It has been all we can do to stave off the High King's justice, and one branch of the family has been cut from the tree. If someone has resumed collaboration with Isra, it can be assumed that they mean also to work with the Shades again, or mayhap with Dulmun. There will be many others who wish to stop such foolishness and punish those responsible. I think answers will come swift."

She stood from her armchair. The rest of them hastened to follow. Theren spoke quickly, holding forth a hand to keep Lilith from leaving. "You could study here, if you wish," she said. "I am not one for reading, myself, but this place is well suited for it. At least Ebon and Kalem lose themselves among pages here for hours on end, so it must be good."

Lilith gave her a little smile that quickly died. "Thank you," she said quietly. "But I will work elsewhere. Mayhap . . . mayhap I will join you all here, one day. I think I might enjoy that." She gave them all a nod and a glance, lingering longest on Theren, and then left.

A long uncomfortable while passed before Lilith came

to them again. Ebon spent his days studying hard and his evenings keeping Astrea company. After their argument in Perrin's class, she did not wish to walk with him at first. But he apologized so earnestly that at last she agreed to speak with him in the common room, and then the next day she walked with him upon the grounds the way she used to. And for his part, Ebon did not try to speak with her when she did not wish it. He spent his time with her in silence, answering every time she asked a question, and occasionally telling her of inconsequential nothings. If she ever wished to speak of Isra again, he would be ready, and in the meantime, he would be her friend.

His latest spell gave him an entirely new difficulty. For the first day he spent all his time in class holding the flower, running his fingers along it, trying to see it in his mind's eye. When his magic flowed through him, he could peer into its substance, but he could not understand it. Its parts were many, and wild, and danced all about each other in an endless buzz of activity. Whenever he tried to change them, he could only manage stone. And if he threw the rose down, frustrated, Perrin would appear at his elbow and lecture him.

"You should not become discouraged so easily," she told him. "No type of substance is more complicated than living matter. Even the most powerful alchemists do not truly understand it, for our bodies, and the bodies of all living things, are made of more things than even the wildest rock laced with crystal and gold.

You have already mastered wood—that is somewhere in between something alive and something made of stone. It is like our bones. Plants are the next step—they are soft and malleable, like flesh and skin. It will take you time to master them."

That did not seem entirely right to Ebon. He knew he could transmute living flesh down to stone—he had done it when he killed Cyrus, though he still shuddered every time he thought of that day. But turning it to ice was another matter. He could not envision ice in the first place, and so he could not make the switch.

To his surprise, after three days it was Astrea who came to his rescue. When Perrin was across the room teaching a lesson to another student, Astrea gave a quick glance over her shoulder and then leaned close to Ebon. "You should learn to master water before you try to turn the flower."

Ebon blinked. "I do not know what that means."

Astrea's mouth twisted. "Here." She took the little wooden box Ebon had been using to practice shifting stone. Then she dipped her finger into the stone, which shifted around her fingertip like water—and then, suddenly, it *was* water. Ebon gaped.

"How did you . . .?"

"I have been practicing outside of class," she said quickly, and then pushed the box into his hands. "Try to turn the water to ice. It may be difficult at first, but you will begin to learn the ways of water, the parts that make it up. They are far simpler than the parts of the flower. We learned this in our first-year class: it is easier to turn a complex substance into a simple one than the reverse. Learn to turn water to ice, and then you will more easily be able to turn the flower into ice as well."

Though he hardly understood her words, he practiced day in and day out, though he had to hide the little box of water. Perrin caught him with it once and pulled it from his hands, insisting that the right way to learn was to work on the flower itself, and that water to ice was far too complicated. Thereafter he practiced on the box beneath the table, or with cups outside his normal study hours. The ice did not come easily, as Astrea had hinted it might not, but he did feel as though he had begun to understand the liquid.

When at last Lilith came to them, they were in the library. Ebon had given up on the tome he was reading—a mammoth book of Idris's early days before it joined the nine kingdoms, and written so dryly that Ebon thought he might fall asleep—and was now resting by playing with the firestriker Halab had given him. Over and over he pinched the crossbars of the ankh, sending little showers of sparks onto his outstretched fingers and making himself wince. Kalem kept giving him nervous looks, clearly frightened that Ebon would light the whole place on fire.

When they saw Lilith, they stood at once. She gave them all a nod—and then she froze for a moment, staring in surprise. Ebon followed her gaze. The chair

Theren had brought for her had remained, for they had not bothered to move it away. Lilith went to it and gingerly took her seat, still smiling as though secretly pleased. Ebon caught a matching smile playing at Theren's lips.

"Good day," said Ebon. "Do you have news?"

"I might," said Lilith. "I wish to take you all with me this evening to see someone."

Ebon tensed. "Do you mean someone in your family?"

"I do. But you need not fear. She is Farah, a cousin of mine, and she is only a bookkeeper, not a warrior."

Kalem's brows furrowed. "A bookkeeper? I think I should rather meet a warrior, for they might know something more useful than one locked in a library all day."

"Not those sorts of books," said Ebon. "She means an accountant. Someone who tracks the flow of coin and goods."

"Still, what good will that do us?" said Kalem.

Theren, too, looked mystified, but Ebon and Lilith gave an exasperated sigh in unison. That made them both start, and they looked at each other uncomfortably for a moment before Lilith finally explained.

"We are not foolish enough to keep track of our magestone dealings in public record. But that does not mean we keep no record at all. That would be madness. Farah is well-placed in the family's dealings, and manages the hidden accounts that we show to no one.

She would know if someone has been moving mage-stones."

"And she wishes to see us?" said Ebon. "Why? How can we trust her?"

"She did not ask to see you, specifically, of course," said Lilith. "But when she heard that I had been poking about after records of magestones, she came to me. I told her my purpose—without revealing too much—and she said she wished to meet those I was working with."

"You did not answer my second question."

Lilith frowned. "I was getting to it. I admit that it is a risk. Farah is my kin, but we have never been especially close. I know, though, that she is an honest sort. I have heard some whispers in the past that she disapproves of our operations outside of the King's law."

"But why must *we* go?" said Kalem. "Why can you not meet with her yourself?"

Theren's glare deepened, and she spoke up quickly. "Because Lilith wanted nothing to do with this in the first place, Kalem. She went searching on our behalf, and now returns with just the sort of thing we hoped she would discover. This is the least we can do, if we hope to catch Isra."

Ebon nodded. "She is right, Kalem. Besides, it is not Lilith who saw Isra. We know more about the girl's dealings. Mayhap our knowledge, combined with the knowledge of this Farah, will be enough to track her down."

Lilith smiled at him in gratitude. "That was precisely my thought. And if it calms your fears, Kalem, know that I will be there with you. If there is any danger, it will be mine as well."

Kalem frowned into his lap, but he remained silent. Ebon looked to Lilith again. "Very well. When can we see her?"

"Tonight," said Lilith. "In fact, we must. She was adamant. Plans too long in the making are more apt to be discovered, and she would rather not be found colluding with Academy students on the subject of magestones. We will go in disguise as well."

That made Ebon afraid for reasons he could not quite identify, and he looked to Theren. "Tonight? That does not give us much time to prepare."

Theren smiled. "Lilith can help us with that. She and I are old hands at this sort of thing."

Just then the Academy's bell rang, signaling the end of the day's studies. "And there is our signal," said Lilith. "What say you? Will you come with me?"

Kalem still looked doubtful, but Ebon squared his shoulders. "We will. Lead on."

They rose and made their way to the library stairs, and then down to the ground floor. As they made for the hallways, they all nodded cordially at Instructor Jia, who gave them a wan smile. She had returned only that day after being tended to by healers. Isra had not had her long under the mindwyrd, and so the aftereffects had been mild. Dasko would be a far longer time in healing, or so it was said.

Lilith took them out upon the streets of the city, and then to an inn a little ways away. It was a small place, tucked down a side street Ebon had often passed but never noticed, and no sign hung over the door. The common room seemed little used, and the innkeeper gave Lilith barely a glance as the group entered, passed through, and ascended the stairs. Kalem looked all about them with curiosity, and Ebon knew he was doing the same. Theren, however, acted as though nothing were out of the ordinary. Clearly she had been here before.

"What is this place?" said Ebon.

Lilith stopped before a door and produced a key from her sleeve to open it. "Why, this is my room."

"Your room?" said Ebon. "Why do you pay for a room here when you live in the Academy?"

Her eyes widened, and she glanced at Theren, who shrugged. "I keep it under rent for just such a purpose as this. Do you not have a room for yourself?"

Ebon flushed, for though he had never thought of such a thing, now it seemed plainly obvious that he should have. "I do not."

Lilith shook her head and led them inside. The room contained nothing remarkable—only a low, wide bed and some other plain furniture. She went to an armoire and threw it open. Within, Ebon saw many dresses and other suits of clothes of every color and make.

"Take what you will," said Lilith. "None have seen use in some time, but they are all laundered."

"I am afraid I am a little too small," said Kalem.

"True, but there is not much we can do about that," said Lilith. "I shall give you the shortest pants I have, and you can tuck them into those high boots you wear."

Theren, meanwhile, went to the rack and shucked off her Academy robes at once. Kalem and Lilith both went beet-red and turned away.

"Theren!" said Kalem.

"Your embarrassment is no concern of mine," said Theren. "And Lilith, you need not act as though this is anything new to you."

"Oh, just get it over with," said Lilith.

Ebon could not help but smirk at Kalem, and even at Lilith. "I may not be a commoner, exactly, but the two of you are too easily flustered, I think. They are only underclothes." He joined Theren in disrobing and looked over the clothes hanging before them. Several thin wooden rods ran from one side of the cabinet to the other, and on these had been hung a variety of outfits. He chose a pair of pants of dark, muted blue, and a light grey tunic under a vest of black. Theren took a dress of yellow that reminded him of his family's colors, much to his surprise.

"Could you . . .?" she muttered, turning. Ebon reached for the strings that tied it at her neck, but they were intricately laced at the back, and his fingers fumbled over them.

"Oh, let me," said Lilith. Theren hesitated only a

moment before turning to let her take them. Ebon saw how Lilith's cheeks darkened still further, and she kept her eyes fixed rigidly on the strings. He could not help a secret grin.

"Mayhap . . . I think I shall wait outside," said Kalem, who sounded ready to die from embarrassment.

"Come off it," said Ebon. "Live like the rest of us, royal son, and get yourself dressed. We do not have all night."

His face was a portrait in discomfort, but Kalem did it—though he made sure to select his entire outfit before he disrobed, and did it as quickly as possible. Lilith acted much the same, and if anything, she seemed more uncomfortable than the boy was. Theren and Ebon stood back, looking at each other with raised eyebrows and little shakes of the head. But while Ebon kept his eyes studiously averted, respecting the others' discomfort, he noticed Theren's eyes continued to wander, and she swallowed hard and often.

SEVENTEEN

ONCE THE BUSINESS WAS DONE, LILITH RUSHED THEM
out of the room. Their Academy robes they left strewn
on the bed. "They will not be disturbed, and we will
return for them," said Lilith.

They went out upon the streets. Lilith had given
them all cloaks of brown—plain, but lined with fur.
They drew their hoods up around their faces, and now
Ebon noticed that they no longer drew the half-curi-
ous looks that Academy students did when walking
about. At last he thought he saw the reason for the
deception.

"No one remarks upon us," he said.

"And why should they?" said Lilith. "We could be anyone—merchants, cobblers, even beggars."

Theren snorted. "You are blinded by your own coin purse if you think any beggar wears clothes this fine," she said. "But they draw the eye less readily, mayhap, than the Academy's black."

Lilith took them north and west and made no attempt to set their trail to winding—she was not, it seemed, afraid of being followed. Ebon began to get a familiar sense, as though he had been in this part of the city before but could not place it. Then it came to him: they were very near to the inn where he had once met an agent of his family's and delivered the uniform of a palace guard. For a heart-stopping moment, he was afraid that they made for the same inn. But then he spotted the street where it lay, and Lilith passed it by. He let out a sigh of relief.

Theren glanced at him. "What is it?"

He shook his head. "Nothing."

At last Lilith stopped them before the black-painted door of a tavern. Here she paused for a moment, looking in every direction from beneath her hood.

"We will enter and move straight to the back," she said. "There is a private room there where Farah is waiting. Do not glance up or meet the eye of anyone else. The fewer who remark upon our arrival, the better."

Ebon heard the sounds of conversation and laughter from within. "It sounds a fair crowd inside. I doubt we need worry of drawing much attention."

"Let us hope you are right," said Lilith, and she pushed the door open.

They all studied their feet as they pressed into the bustling interior. Lilith led the way between the tables, and Ebon was only partially aware of the patrons they passed. Indeed, his guess seemed to be right—as far as he could tell, no one gave them so much as a first glance. Soon they had passed through the crowd and into a short hallway ending in a door. Lilith opened it without knocking and drew them all inside.

At last Ebon looked up and threw back his hood. He found himself in a small room, with every wall showing its bare wood and exposed beams above that looked to form the underside of the building's second floor. They gave the ceiling a little extra height, so that it felt less cramped than it should have considering its small size. Lanterns burned in the corners, filling the place with a warm light. There was also a window in the back wall, and though the curtains were drawn across it, he could feel a slight breeze that told him it was cracked open.

In the middle of the room was a table, and at the table was a woman. She looked similar enough to Lilith—not only the same rich, dark skin, but the pronounced cheekbones and the haughty, discerning brow. But she showed more fat than Lilith, and also she filled out her rich green dress more. She seemed less severe, and more motherly, though that was belied by the sharp glint in her eyes as she took them all in.

"Good eve, I suppose. Sit. Or do not, for it is no matter to me. There is wine."

Ebon bowed. "Well met, Lady—"

"No, no, no," said the woman, clucking her tongue. "You know my name, knew it before you came here. I know yours as well—especially yours." She gave Theren a sharp nod. "So we need not introduce ourselves, for who knows what ears may be lurking? And who knows how little time we have? Sit and take wine if you will, but let us get on with this as quickly as we may."

Kalem gave Ebon a wary look. Ebon shrugged and dragged out a chair to sit across the table from Farah. Kalem sat beside him and Theren to his left, while Lilith took the chair on Theren's other side. Farah leaned forwards and opened her mouth to speak—but paused as Theren reached for the bottle of wine. Theren noticed, and poured the wine far more slowly than she might have. It made Lilith smirk into her cup, while Farah's lips pursed in annoyance. When her cup was full to the brim, Theren turned.

"Do you care for a cup, Ebon?"

"I do," said Ebon. He snatched the bottle from her hand. "Though I will pour it myself. And you may carry on with what you meant to say, Fa—er, my lady."

Farah raised an eyebrow. "A quick study. That is good. I have little to say, but much to hear. Tell me what you have seen of the girl Isra, and what you have not seen but have heard about. The more you know, the better. The less you guess at, the better."

Ebon was about to speak when Theren took her first sip. She slurped at the cup and smacked her lips when she was done. "Mm. You goldbags drink the finest stuff."

At the word *goldbag*, Farah's nostrils flared. Kalem's glared deepened. "Enough, Theren. We all know of your disdain for the wealthy, and if our host did not know it before, she knows it now. Consider your point made."

Theren's eyes widened, and she pressed a hand to her breast. "Me? I am wounded. And besides, our host has been most clear that she wishes for no names to be used—including mine. Please, I ask that you honor her wishes."

"My apologies for my companion," Ebon interjected. "We will tell you what we know and be as thorough as ever we can."

He proceeded to tell her everything they knew of Isra—that is, the "official" version of what they knew of Isra. Of course he told her nothing about Xain's home, nor about the amulet of Kekhit. But he told her about their fight in the kitchens, painting it so that it sounded like Theren managed to catch Isra by surprise.

When he said that, Farah's eyes drew to pinholes. "Very fortunate," she said. It sounded as though she meant to say more, but she did not.

"Fortunate indeed," said Ebon, meeting her eye without flinching. Then he went on to tell her all the rumors that had floated about the Academy since—including a rumor that the faculty were investigating to see if anyone were helping Isra from within. Lilith seemed surprised at that. Of course, that was not truly a rumor, but something they had learned from Dasko.

When they had finished, Farah pursed her lips and steepled her hands. She sat that way for a little while, reaching for her wine cup every so often, her eyes studying Ebon's. Ebon tried not to look uncomfortable, though he was not quite sure he succeeded.

"Our family's particular trade goods have been on the move recently," said Farah, speaking suddenly and from nowhere, in a tone that suggested she was answering a question, though no one had asked. "They were long held in reserve, for no one wished to traffic them after the attack. Now they move again, though slowly, nowhere near so brazenly as they once did."

Theren leaned forwards. "And where are the mage—"

"*No!*" barked Farah, scowling at her. "No, we do not discuss them. They are our family's particular trade goods. That is all they are to me, and to you, or this conversation is over."

"We understand," said Ebon. He fixed Theren with a look. "And we will take that into consideration as we ask our questions."

He could see the visible effort she exerted to keep from rolling her eyes. "And where are your family's particular trade goods being moved to?"

"Here. There. It is never wise for them to move always from one place to another, for that makes them easy to find. Predictable. But someone is moving them, and some are disappearing. Those, I would imagine, are what you seek."

"Where are they disappearing *to?*" said Lilith. "I would not imagine they could simply vanish without repercussion."

"Not unless those who mete out punishment for such things know where they are going, and thus restrain their hand," said Farah. "That, I think, is what goes on here. I spotted it, of course. I saw that the numbers did not add up, that one hundred packets would leave and only ninety-five packets would arrive. But when I told them—the ones who mete out punishment for such things—they thanked me for my diligent work. And then they told me to return to it. And no punishment was meted out."

"Yet you do not know where," said Ebon.

"I do not know where," said Farah. "But that is not the right question. There are five questions, only five and always five, and one leads to the next."

"Where," said Lilith. "When, how, why, and who?"

Farah sniffed.

"Who, then?" said Theren.

"A name," said Farah. "The only name, tonight. A name banished by the family, and then reclaimed. A name that renounced another name to regain favor in the eyes of the King's law. A name that has used that favor to violate the King's law again, thereby putting our clan in danger once more, as though he did not learn the lesson the first time. Gregor."

Lilith sucked in a sharp breath. But to Ebon, the name meant nothing, and looking at Kalem and Theren, he saw they knew nothing more than he did.

"What is it?" said Ebon. "Who is Gregor?"

"She will tell you later, for we draw near the end," said Farah.

"But wait," said Lilith. "I thought he was banished, along with—"

"Only one name, tonight," said Farah. "Only one name, now, that matters."

"Very well, but in any case, he was exiled."

"He returned and threw himself upon the High King's mercy. He told her . . . things. Things that seemed of great value in the coming war. Did he tell her the truth? How can we know, unless we, too, know the truth? But it earned him forgiveness. And now, when I see one hundred become ninety-five, I see also the name of Gregor."

Abruptly she pushed her chair back and stood. "Thank you for your words, and for the meanings behind them. I hope you have found my words as valuable. But now we must leave, and I doubt we shall ever speak again."

Ebon found his feet at once. "Thank you. We will breathe no word of this."

"If I thought you would, I would not have come,"

said Farah. She looked hard at Lilith for a moment. "You did right to come to me. Make sure you never do it again, or both our lives may be forfeit."

She swept past them with the billowing of a green cloak and left them looking at each other around the table. Theren noisily swallowed the last of her cup and moved to pour another.

EIGHTEEN

Lilith led them back to the street and then southeast towards the inn where she kept her room. The moons had risen high now, and the sunlight had almost faded in the west. They walked in a mostly silver light that reflected into their eyes from the snow. They were all silent, staring at the ground, except for Kalem, who looked at the stars. After a time, Ebon raised his head.

"Thank you, Lilith, for helping us."

She shrugged, not meeting his gaze. "It is the least I could do, I suppose. What do you plan to do now, after what you have learned?"

"I have friends who can find Gregor. They were already looking for Isra, but she must be in one of the darker holes upon the Seat. Let us hope Gregor is not so well concealed."

"He most likely is," said Lilith. "Gregor is a man of both means and wit—not the clever kind, but the cunning, ruthless kind, the kind that leaves corpses in its wake. I think he will be much harder to find than some student exiled from the Academy."

"I also have some people of means and wit," said Ebon, a little annoyed.

"Mayhap, but you do not have Gregor." Lilith shivered, though they were tramping doggedly through the snow and their blood was up. "I have heard only a very few tales of him, and yet they paint him as more of a monster than a man. Once he accompanied a caravan through the Spineridge. They were waylaid there by a storm, a freak summer snow that forced them to take refuge in a little town. Somehow, during their stay, the townsfolk discovered the magestones they were transporting. Some curious child poked their nose into the wrong wagon. When word got about, Gregor spoke to the townspeople, promising to pay them to keep their silence. The townsfolk agreed readily enough, for the Yerrin party already paid well for their food and lodging. So for a week the caravan remained in the town. The guards slept in the town's inn and drank in the town's tavern. They likely bedded some of the townsfolk.

"At last the storm abated. Gregor brought all the

folk into the town hall to receive their pay. He waited until they had all arrived, for he had promised them all a gold weight, even the children. First he gave them their money. Then he locked the front door and burned the hall to the ground. He and his men stood watch to make sure no one escaped through the windows. When at last the flames died out, he made his soldiers search through the corpses to recover every bit of gold he had paid out."

Ebon did not remember when they all stopped walking, but at some point they had, and now they stood in a little circle watching Lilith in horrified silence. Now he felt sick, as though he might retch into the gutter, and he knew the chill in his bones was not from the cold air.

"That is monstrous," said Kalem. "It must be false. Surely the High King would not stand for such an act."

"What makes you think word of it ever reached her ears?" said Theren, spitting the words. "Do you think her courtiers let such troubling rumors invade the royal court? It is easier for the merchants and the royals both if they do not discuss such things. And after all, it sounds as if there were no witnesses."

"But that is not the conduct of the wealthy—it is the atrocity of a monster." Kalem sounded indignant, but he could find no sympathy in Theren's face, nor even any understanding. "You cannot think all merchants are that way. Certainly not the royalty."

"Oh, you think the royalty are exempt?" said

Theren. "You know how Isra became an orphan as well as I do."

"But that . . . that is *one* king," said Kalem.

"You are no fool, Kalem, and only a fool thinks any goldbag in Underrealm has entirely clean hands."

Kalem opened his mouth to object again. Ebon spoke first. "Let it be, Kalem."

Kalem gaped at him, astonished. "You cannot say you agree with her. I know your family and Lilith's have reputations, but—"

"I said let it be." Ebon could not meet Theren's eyes, for he could almost feel the fury glowing off her. And when he once would have agreed with Kalem, that her hatred of the rich and the powerful was misguided at best and born of jealousy at the worst, now he could not put fire in such a belief.

"It grows late," said Lilith, rubbing her arms. "We should move on."

They took her advice, pressing on through the light snow that had begun to fall. Theren was the next to speak, after a long silence. The white-hot anger had gone from her voice, but Ebon still heard it smoldering—quelled for the moment, but not gone.

"Why is she waiting? She has more artifacts. We know she took them from Xain's house. Why delay?"

They kept walking in silence, for no one had an answer.

The next morning, Ebon sent a letter to Adara, asking her to search the lovers' guild for news of Gregor. He was not sure what to expect—after all, he had already asked her to seek for Isra, and that had returned nothing yet. But the very next afternoon he received a letter in response, asking him to come and see her at once in her home. It was Sunday, and he had no other demands upon his time, so he fetched his winter cloak and set out into the city. The snow that had been falling for the last few weeks had subsided at last, and though the air was still sharp with winter's chill, the sky above was a deep and pure blue. It stood in stark contrast to the snowy roofs of the city's buildings, and the sun leaped bright from every surface, so that Ebon had to shield his eyes.

Adara answered his knock almost at once and led him upstairs after he stamped his boots free from snow. She had set out a small tray of figs, cheese, and bread, and at first they ate in silence. But soon Adara leaned back in her chair, dabbing at her lips with a napkin.

"I have found your man," she said. "Yet I hesitate to tell you where."

Ebon blinked. "Why? What is wrong?"

She studied him for a moment, lips twitching towards a frown. "Why do you seek Gregor at all?"

"He is the one moving Yerrin's magestones. He is our best chance to find Isra and capture her."

"I have heard many stories of this man, Ebon. He is a fell and grim warrior, prone not only to violence, but to cruelty when he kills. The family Yerrin is known for ruthlessness, but his reputation sets him above even the rest of them."

Ebon shivered. "Well, I mean to set Mako upon him, and so I suppose we will find out who is the more terrible."

Adara shook her head. "Do not pretend that you will be free from danger in this. Why should I put you in harm's way? You are already Isra's enemy. Must you add Gregor's name to the list of those who wish harm upon you?"

That forced a grim laugh from his gut. He spread his hands. "When that list is so long, what is one more entry?"

She sighed. "Very well. He has been seen on the western end of the Seat, going in and out of the sewers that may be found there. Some whisper that the family Yerrin conducts its smuggling through some hidden port, though no one knows exactly where it may be found."

"That is good," said Ebon. "Mako knows the sewers well, and doubtless he will be able to find their hiding place. I am surprised you learned this so quickly when your connections have still been unable to find Isra, wherever she may be lurking."

Adara frowned. "I, too, have been troubled by that. Gregor has all the backing of Yerrin at his disposal, as well as their considerable coin. I cannot think how Isra has concealed herself better than he has, especially after she was spotted within the Academy itself. That should have sent word rippling through the streets, like a stone dropped into a calm lake."

Ebon thought of what Mako had said in the abandoned manor of the family Skard. "Ripples, you say. You are not the first to describe them to me. Yet she moves like a ghost, a specter already dead, and leaves no trace. And, too, she withholds her hand, though we do not know why. It has been a week since she revealed herself—more than enough time, it seems to me, to try again."

"There must be other things afoot, and mayhap Gregor has something to do with them," said Adara. "Wondering about it may do little good. Be grateful instead, and act before it is too late."

"Too much later, you mean," said Ebon. "It is already too late for Oren and Credell, and poor little Vali."

Adara nodded solemnly, and they let the names of the dead linger in silence for a while. Then she stood. "Would you have wine? It is a touch early, but when has that stopped either of us?"

He grinned. "Do you mean to get me drunk again? I am not sure I can survive another night like the last."

She laughed. "No, not that. My head still twinges with pain at that memory." She paused for a moment to look at him. "But I thank you for joining me in that. I know it was an odd request, and had its consequences, yet I do not regret it."

"Nor I," said Ebon. She returned to the table, and he took his goblet. "And I will never forget the words we spoke—nor the promises I made to you."

"I should hope not. I very much intend to hold you to them."

His smile felt somewhat forced. "Yet near the end—the end of the drinking, anyway—I remember you told me something. Something about truth, and how it came hard to you even then."

Her smile grew careful. "Did I? Mayhap my thoughts grew muddled."

The words came easily enough, but he heard the warning behind them. *Let it be. Please.* "Mayhap it was my wits that were addled, not yours," he said lightly. "You told me so many things, after all, that I had never heard before. I was honored to learn them—and would do so again, if you ever wished it."

Recognition dawned in her eyes, an acknowledgement of his unspoken invitation. "Thank you," she whispered. And then she sighed, and straightened, and the moment passed them both by. She ran a finger along the rim of her mug. "I understand you have spent much time in Lilith's company of late. More to the point, I understand Theren has, as well."

Ebon's eyebrows shot up. "And who have you heard that from?"

"The guild carries many whispers, and I do not listen only for the ones you ask me to."

He sighed. "I admit Lilith still makes me uneasy.

Theren seems to trust her utterly—well, better than I do, at any rate. But I do not know how much of that stems from good sense, and how much stems from her feelings."

"She still loves Lilith, then?"

"I asked her that when Lilith was imprisoned, and she said she did not know. Yet her every action tells me that she does. It is not only the trust she places in Lilith. It is the little looks, the smiles and the half-hidden gestures. The way her hand moves towards Lilith's, as though aching to hold her. I can scarcely believe the change in her demeanor, considering how she despised Lilith when I first met her."

"Often love springs forth unbidden," said Adara. "When it does, it is rarely governed by sense."

Ebon smiled. "Do you speak of Theren and Lilith, or of us?"

She kicked him beneath the table, but gently. "I think we are more sensible about things than many. Nor do I doubt Theren's judgement in this. She is a passionate woman, governed more by her heart than by her head, yet she has wit enough to know evil from good. She placed her trust in you quickly, though she had more reason than most to despise a merchant boy. If you are grateful for that trust, return it now. After all, is Lilith not proving herself helpful?"

He frowned. "Helpful enough, I suppose. Yet it is all in the service of catching Isra, whom she hates. And I have bitter memories of her treatment when I first arrived at the Academy."

"Children may be cruel without also being evil."

Ebon mock-glared at her. "She is older than I am. Do you call me a child?"

She returned his frown, though her nose twitched as though she longed to smile. "You *are* newly come to manhood, Ebon, though you had little opportunity to ever be a child in truth."

That brought to mind a question he had never thought to ask, and he cocked his head. "How old are you?"

She smiled. "Do you see wrinkles in my skin? Have you come to regret our tryst? Do you love me only for my beauty? That cannot be, for who could call me more beautiful than any of the fine ladies you must have met throughout your life?"

He stood suddenly, and she yelped as he lifted her from her chair, holding her across his chest while she laced her fingers behind his neck. "I would call you beautiful a thousand times, though the Mystics put me beneath their knives and command me to renounce your grace. But you have not answered my question. Tell me how many summers you have seen, or I may have to draw the truth from you by every means at my disposal."

"Do your worst," she purred.

NINETEEN

THEY SPENT THE DAY DOING LITTLE OF CONSEQUENCE, and it was evening before Ebon left her at last. The sun had almost gone down, and he hurried through torchlight. He had time enough before curfew to return, but he had no wish to remain in the cold a moment longer than necessary.

The streets seemed curiously crowded for a Sunday, when many merchants and crafters chose not to work. The Seat had become flooded with new arrivals recently. There was some vague rumors that the High King soon meant to make her next move in the war.

Ebon soon tired of struggling through crowds and having to halt for every passing carriage or wagon of goods. He broke away from the press, aiming for the yawning mouth of an alley that seemed to head the right direction. But when he reached the end, it turned north rather than south. He grumbled and increased his pace. Soon he saw the alley's end ahead, leading to another street packed even tighter than the last one.

He pushed into the crowds with a sigh, forcing his way across and into another side street. Here at last the way was clear, and it even headed in the right direction for a time. Ebon let loose a breath of relief and slowed.

A boot scuffed on the street behind him. He turned. The street was empty.

His heart began to race, but he scowled and fought the queasy feeling in his stomach. Xain, it seemed, was not done stalking him. He had a chilling thought: had the dean seen him leave Adara's house? But he dismissed that fear at once. No matter what Xain suspected him of, Ebon did not fear the dean would threaten Adara.

Hunching his shoulders, he pushed on through the cold. The side street led him south, but it kept turning the wrong direction as it did so. Soon he had neared the Seat's western edge, where the buildings showed more signs of damage from the fighting and the flames, and there were fewer people about. And then he came upon a street where there were no other passers-by at all.

Three quick footsteps sounded, shockingly close. But when he turned, the street remained empty.

He put his hands to his hips. "Enough of this. I can hear you, Xain, scuttling after me like some pickpocket. If you have received another note, I still know nothing about it. But come out and ask me anyway, if that is your wish, so that we may both go about our evenings in peace."

The person who stepped from the shadows was not Xain.

Ebon froze. He could see no face beneath the green hood, but the person who faced him was a behemoth—nearly as large as Perrin, and clad in mail under their cloak.

There came a *hiss* of drawn steel. A broadsword glinted in the moonslight. Ebon could not drag his gaze from its shine. Thick, heavy boots crunched in the snow, forming holes as deep as Ebon's whole leg.

"I . . . who . . ." Ebon took a step back, almost stumbling in a drift behind him.

The figure reached up to drag its hood back. It was a man, his skin almost as dark as Lilith's, and within his sallet his grey eyes reeked of death. His fist looked big enough to envelop and crush Ebon's skull. Where Ebon had often been awed by the thickness and vigor of Mako's muscular arms, this man now made Mako seem a spindly little boy, a bookish scholar tucked in some dark basement away from the sun, scrawny as Kalem was. Over the chain on the man's chest was a tabard of black leather, and his fists shone with plate.

All this Ebon saw in the scant seconds it took the giant to approach him. They were only two lengthy paces apart now. But then he stopped.

"You have been seeking me." The voice from his barrel-wide chest thrummed in Ebon's lungs, deeper and stronger than Isra's voice even with the strength of magestones. And at the words, knowledge struck Ebon like a mace to the forehead.

"G-Gregor," he stammered. "You are Gregor."

There came no answer, but the man's eyes flashed. And Ebon recalled the story that Lilith had told him. In his mind he saw the hall filled with people, burning, all of them screaming. His throat seized up. He tried to take a backwards step, but his feet would not move.

"Why has your family taken an interest in me?" said Gregor. He took one step forwards, and Ebon wilted.

"I am not . . . I did not . . ."

Gregor shook his head, a single sharp jerk. "No lies. As long as your words interest me, you will live. As long as I hear the truth within them, you will live. You die tonight, but it is up to you how long you have before then."

Like a striking serpent, a hand the size of a boulder shot forth to seize Ebon's robes and haul him up off the ground. Ebon lost control of his bladder, and tears stung his eyes as piss dripped to the snow below him.

"I sought nothing," he whimpered, voice shattering to a sob. "I swear it." *A lie,* he screamed in his mind. *A lie means death.* But he could not help it. His thoughts betrayed him, for he knew now that he would die, here on this street and unseen by anyone.

But then behind Gregor, from the other side of the street, a second shadow detached itself from the darkness between two buildings. Ebon heard a soft *snik-snik,* and saw the silhouette of two daggers. *Mako,* he thought with relief.

He let his gaze linger too long. Gregor caught the look and turned on the spot, faster than such a man should have been able to move. Mako leaped, black cloak fluttering behind him. Gregor caught the daggers on his sword and shoved back with a rumbling grunt. Mako danced, shifting from one foot to the next before striking again. Again Gregor parried the blow, swinging the sword in a wide arc and slicing down with it—but Mako was already gone.

They took a step back, taking each other's measure in the darkness. Ebon wanted to step forwards, to do something, but he knew not what. He was a child in this battle of giants. What good would mists be, if he must draw within Gregor's reach to use them? And he could not help Mako by shifting stone.

Then a hand seized his shoulder to drag him back. Had he not already voided himself, he would surely have soiled his clothes again. "Come, boy," said a woman's voice. "You are of little use here."

He looked back and saw that she was clad just like Mako, and had her hair trimmed close to her scalp. Two steps he took beside her, away from Gregor, before he stopped. "We cannot leave Mako," he gasped.

"That is not Mako," said the woman. "Come."

Ebon peered closer in the darkness—and then he saw that it was the truth. The man standing before Gregor was tall enough, but not quite as broad, and his eyes glinted blue beneath his hood, instead of dark like Mako's.

Now the assassin's knives swept forwards like serpents, striking here, there, and here again in the space of a blink. But though Gregor held no shield, he used his plated arm to block one of the blows, while the others glanced from his chain.

And then his fist swung, faster than when he had seized Ebon, and crushed the Drayden man's face.

The assassin stopped moving all at once, as though a force holding him up had suddenly vanished. He held his feet for a heartbeat, though his nose was pulp and his jaw hung slack on tendons, displaying shattered teeth.

Gregor seized his head, fingers wrapping to the back of the man's skull. With the grip for leverage, he pulled the assassin onto his broadsword. Four hand-breadths of blood-covered steel thrust out of the man's spine, and his legs went limp. Gregor withdrew the sword and smashed the front of his helmet into the man's face. Then he brought the man's head down with a *crunch* against his armored knee.

The Drayden man slumped to the snow, a corpse three times over.

Even as she pulled Ebon away, the woman threw a dagger with a hiss of rage. It struck Gregor in his back, but the chain shirt rebuffed the blade, which fell impotent to the snow. Gregor threw a look over his shoulder—but then Ebon was around the corner of a building and out of sight, still being dragged by the woman.

Now that he no longer beheld the giant, Ebon found he could move again, and he ran, faster even than his rescuer. After they had passed a few streets, she yanked him to face her. He looked into her hard face, wincing at the scar that ran from her upper lip through one ruined eye.

"Back to the Academy," she growled. "Stop for nothing. Look at nothing. Speak to no one. And if you value your life, do not leave again for any reason—not unless Mako is with you."

Ebon wanted to stay a moment longer, to ask her one more question. But even as he hesitated, she seized a shoulder and whirled him around. Then she planted a boot on his back and kicked hard. Ebon went sprawling to the ground, sliding along in the slush with a cry.

"*Leave,* you piss-stained steer!"

He left, scrambling to his feet and barely remaining

upright. Once he started running he could not stop, but could only move his legs faster and faster. Soon he was winded, and his chest screamed at him in pain, but he only sprinted harder. He reached the main road that crossed the island east to west and pressed heedless through the people there. Many of them he struck in his flight, but he did not stop for their angry shouts.

Before long he reached the Academy's front door. Two paces away from it he stopped and doubled over to catch his breath, crying out as that sent lances of pain into his ribs. He looked back down the street. Gregor was nowhere to be seen, nor was any other threat.

The tears that had threatened now spilled forth, and bile leaped to the back of his throat. His mind burned with the image of the Drayden man falling to the ground, of the nauseating way his bones had bent the wrong direction. Falling to hands and knees he vomited. All the wine he had drunk with Adara and all the food he had eaten for supper spilled into the virgin snow.

It was a while before he could force himself to stand. His body groaned in protest when he did, and his legs were clay beneath him. But as soon as he could, he stumbled towards the front door. From the position of the moons in the sky, he had only just made it before curfew, and so he wasted no time before entering.

There in the front hall, to his great surprise, he found Theren and Kalem waiting for him. But if they

saw the state of him, they did not remark upon it—
and once he saw their pale faces and wide, frightened
eyes, he knew that his encounter upon the streets was
not the only thing that had gone terribly wrong.

"What is it?" he said. "What happened?"

"War is declared," said Theren. "Tomorrow, the
armies of the High King march on Dulmun."

TWENTY

For a moment, Ebon could only stand and stare at the news. But then the pain in his side redoubled, and he stumbled.

"Here now," said Kalem, as he and Theren came forwards to take Ebon's arms. "Ebon, what is . . ." Then his nose curled. "Have you . . .?"

Ebon blinked back fresh tears. "I need a bath. Please. Help me."

They cringed, but they helped him, taking an arm each and escorting him to the bathing room, which fortunately was not far away. There he disrobed while

Kalem went to fetch him water. Theren took his soiled robes and put them in a soapy basin to soak.

"What happened?" said Kalem, once Ebon had settled into the water and his friends sat to either side of him.

"Gregor found me." Ebon shuddered at the memory of the man's soulless grey eyes. "Somehow he heard that we were seeking him, and he found me out in the streets."

Theren scowled. "How did you defeat him?"

"I did not," said Ebon. He stopped and closed his eyes, for his voice was dangerously close to breaking. "I did not," he said again when he could speak. "I ran. And I only escaped because two of Mako's fighters came to my rescue."

"Did they . . . is Gregor . . .?" Theren glanced over her shoulder to make sure no one could overhear, but the bathing room was empty.

"They did not kill him," said Ebon. "He killed one of them instead, and mayhap has killed the other by now, for she turned back after she got me to safety. Gregor did not simply kill. He took the man apart. I have never seen anything so terrifying. It was worse than watching Mako put Matami to the question."

"How did he find you?" said Kalem. "What will you do now?"

"I do not know," said Ebon. "The woman who saved me warned me not to leave the Academy again, not for anything, unless it was at Mako's direction and under his guard."

"That seems wise," said Kalem, shivering. Theren glared and remained silent.

"Enough talk of that," said Ebon. "I do not wish to think of it any longer. Now tell me of your news. When did Enalyn declare war?"

They told him all that they had learned so far. That day, while Ebon was with Adara, the High King Enalyn had proclaimed that her host would go to make war upon Dulmun. What fleets she had managed to assemble would set sail from the eastern docks, while a great force of soldiers even now marched east across Feldemar to attack Dulmun's northern lands.

"What of the south?" said Ebon. If the High King's armies meant to march on Dulmun's southern reaches as well, that would take them near to Idris.

"Nothing was said of it," said Kalem. "She may be hesitant to march her armies along the north side of the Spineridge. Or mayhap she means to attack there and is keeping the plan secret, at least for now."

"That brings to mind my chief question," said Theren. "Why would she proclaim any of this? Would it not be better to strike in secret, taking Dulmun by surprise?"

Ebon had thought the same thing, but Kalem shook his head at once. "She does not hope to vanquish Dulmun by means of war. That could be costly in both lives and coin, and we are in the midst of winter. But for months now, ever since the attack, all the nine kingdoms have become mired by indecision.

Only three kingdoms have openly pledged their support to the High King: Selvan, the land from which Enalyn herself came; Hedgemond, my homeland; and Calentin, whose people are so few and so far from the war that their support makes little difference either way, even if they had not sent only a token of their strength, which they have. The other kingdoms hem and haw, neither breaking their oaths nor rushing to fulfill them. By declaring this war openly and putting forth an assault, the High King means to prompt the other kingdoms to action. Now their oaths compel them to lend aid."

"And if they do not?" said Theren.

"They will be branded traitors," said Kalem. "When the war is over and Enalyn has vanquished Dulmun, she will then turn her armies upon the kingdoms that refused to aid her. She will cast their kings down and purge their families—or exile them, if she feels merciful."

"That is a small mercy," said Theren. "But are we even certain she *will* vanquish Dulmun?"

"Of that there is no doubt," said Kalem. "Dorsea will now pledge its full strength; their king is already fearful of Enalyn's wrath, for she nearly executed him after the battle of Wellmont. And Dorsea alone would be enough. Even if the other kingdoms stay their hands—which I doubt—Enalyn will have enough backing to raze Dulmun. She knows it, and Dulmun knows it, and so she hopes they will surrender."

Theren raised her eyebrows. "You seem very certain of all this."

Kalem shrugged. "I have been taught the ways of such things since birth. Where common children learn a trade and merchant children learn to manage coin, royal children are taught the ways of power and war."

"Then Dulmun will surrender, and this war will soon end," said Theren.

"I do not think so," said Kalem sadly. "Bodil of the family Valgun is their king, and she is a warlike woman. Also, she knows that if she surrenders, her life and the lives of her close kin will be forfeit. Therefore she will fight as long as she can, if only to stave off the inevitable. I think that is another part of Enalyn's plan—she hopes to amass as much strength of arms as she can, hoping that either Bodil will surrender, or that one of her kin will rebel against her, depose her from the throne, and surrender in her place. But there shall be much bloodshed before that happens, either way."

They were all silent for a moment. Ebon thought he could almost imagine it: the great legions of soldiers marching across Feldemar, on their way to fight and die upon the soil of Dulmun, and the fleets of ships that would tomorrow speed across the Great Bay to do battle with their foe's mighty fleets. It was a chilling vision, and one not easily dismissed.

"What does the Academy mean to do?" said Ebon.

They both stared at him. "What do you mean?" said Theren. "The Academy means to do nothing, unless it is to keep training its students in the ways of magic. It is a school, not a barracks."

Ebon gaped. "So we are meant to just carry on with our studies? Going to class each day as though a war is not being waged beyond these walls? The Seat is in the middle of this fight—and I do not mean only because the High King dwells here. If Dulmun launches a fresh attack, we will be the first thing in their way."

Again Kalem shook his head. "The Seat is not in danger. It is heavily fortified, and there are many other places along the Great Bay where Dulmun would have an easier time of it. When they attacked it, it was only after luring the High King's armies away with subterfuge. Even then they struck quickly, hoping to win through surprise rather than strength of arms. Now they have lost surprise and will make their war in other ways, as long as they may." He gave a little smile. "If you hoped to escape your lessons for a time, I am afraid to tell you that Perrin will still expect you in your place every morning for your studies."

They sat in silence. It was strange: outwardly, nothing looked to have changed. Yet Ebon felt as though everything was different in some ethereal manner he could not see with his waking eyes. The objects in the room seemed fresh and newly seen, though of course he had beheld them many times before.

"War has come," he said.

"War has been here awhile," said Theren. "Now comes justice."

"I am not so sure," said Kalem. "But now, I think, must come sleep, or we shall all regret it in the morning."

Ebon sat up in the water. "Please, stay. I will be quick, but . . . after tonight, I do not want to be alone."

Kalem lowered his gaze. "Of course. I did not think of that. Forgive me."

And so they stayed, until the water was tepid and Ebon lifted himself out of it, and they all went to bed. But the moment they parted ways at the dormitories, Ebon felt a chill steal over him, and no matter how long he sat before the hearth in the common room, he could not dispel it. He went to bed at last a long time later, drifting off with his thoughts haunted by a pair of soulless grey eyes.

TWENTY-ONE

A HUSH HAD SETTLED OVER THE ACADEMY THE NEXT day. Ebon felt it from the moment he woke, the way no one spoke as they dressed themselves and left the dormitory. The threat of war had hung in the air ever since the attack on the Seat; now the threat was over, for war had arrived. He did not know what they all expected to be different, for they all knew the fighting would take place far away. But he could feel the expectation, in himself as well as the other students, that *something* must happen.

They muddled through their morning classes, but

by the time his lesson finished, Ebon felt the need for fresh air. He pushed against the crowds of students headed for the dining hall and went outside instead.

His steps carried him to the grounds where the alchemy students practiced their spells, and where he had once seen them stop arrows in mid-flight. A rack of weapons, all of them either dull or padded, stood against the wall. He ran his fingers over them, lifting them a bit only to let them *clank* against the rack again. How long would it be before he studied here, learning his own spells of defense? How long until he could defend himself if he landed in a fight, as he had the night before?

He heard only a single footstep on the grass behind him. Then a hand snatched his neck and whirled him around, slamming him into the granite wall of the citadel. It clutched at his throat, stifling his yelp.

"Why must you be such an abominable idiot?" growled Mako.

Ebon slapped futilely at the man's forearm. His breath came in rasps, and only just deep enough to keep stars from dancing in his vision. It was a moment before Mako released him, and Ebon fell gasping to one knee.

"If you die, I will soon follow," said Mako. "I may have no wish to see you dead, but I value my own skin more than yours. Halab is not bloodthirsty—never that—but should I fail to look after you, she will not tolerate my failure. You and I may both thank the sky that I posted guards over you."

"I am thankful," Ebon said, the words rasping from his throat. "And your gratitude seems clear as well." He got slowly to his feet.

Mako pushed him again—harder this time. "Do not be flip with me, boy. Why have you been poking about the family Yerrin? You should leave that to those who are practiced in such things, and will not draw the eye of murderers."

"We think they may lead us to Isra." Ebon paused, unsure of how to proceed. Theren had been adamant that Mako not know they were working with Lilith.

"That is another thing," said Mako. "You should not be bandying about with that Yerrin girl. They are not to be trusted, not even in the smallest of matters. Certainly not in the search for Isra."

Ebon's heart sank. Mako knew, then. It had been foolish to imagine he would not learn of it, when he seemed to know everything Ebon did. But if that knowledge now lay bare, then so be it. "You forget what happened to her," said Ebon. "Isra took control of Lilith and caused her to be thrown to the Mystics' knives. We may have no common ground with the family Yerrin as a whole, but we do with Lilith."

"You can trust no word from a Yerrin, nor can you believe they will keep your confidence. What happens if she tells someone of the amulet your little friend carries?"

That stopped him. Ebon stared at his feet. "We have not told her of the amulet."

To his surprise, Mako grinned. "Well, now. It seems you are not such a fool, little Ebon—not such a complete one, anyway."

"Mighty praise, I suppose," said Ebon. "Now, do you wish to know what we have learned, or not?"

Quickly he laid it out—what Farah had said of Gregor, and what Adara had told him about where the bodyguard had been spotted. Mako's eyes lit when he heard that. "That is something valuable indeed. Sky above, Ebon. You have fumbled your way through this dance of shadows better than I would have given you credit for. Though one of my men died in the process, and that I will not quickly forget."

Ebon lowered his eyes. "Nor will I. I will be forever grateful to his memory. Did . . . did he have a family?"

At first Mako only glared. But after looking into Ebon's eyes for a long moment, the glare softened. "It is wiser not to ask such things. But at the same time, I cannot fault you, for that is the sort of question that Halab might ask."

Ebon tried very hard not to let that compliment, small as it was, go to his head. "Very well. Now that we know where Gregor lurks, we must go after him."

"*We* shall do nothing of the sort—but *I* will, when the time is right."

"That is not good enough," said Ebon. "Every turn of the hourglass is another chance for Isra to strike the Academy, leaving more corpses in her wake."

"Do not worry yourself," said Mako. "Since last she

appeared, my people have been watching every way into the citadel, the passages known and unknown. They will see her if she tries to enter."

"By the time they do, and send word to you, it might already be too late. You must search for Gregor now, without delay."

He wondered if the words sounded as hollow as they felt. They must have, for Mako looked skywards, as though trying to choose the best way to countermand the shrill yapping of an infant. But after a moment he met Ebon's gaze and shrugged.

"Very well. I will begin at once, and search for him on the west end of the Seat."

"Mayhap we should come with you," said Ebon. "Theren and her amulet are your only hope against Isra if you should come upon her."

"No," said Mako, and there was no arguing against his tone. "That would place you in danger, and that is the very thing my duties compel me to prevent."

"But what if Isra is with him, and the strength of magestones behind her?"

Mako was silent for a long moment, gazing into Ebon's eyes. Ebon felt a chill steal across him. Isra had had the strength of magestones the last time Mako had fought her, yet she could not touch the man. Ebon tried not to cringe.

At last the bodyguard spoke. "Look after yourself, and do not fear for my ability to do the same. And do not put yourself in peril chasing after secrets all on your own."

"I will not," Ebon mumbled.

"Good. I will find Gregor, and likely Isra in the same place. The Seat may be the High King's in name, but in another sense it belongs to those like me. I know its dark holes and the bodies within them, the gutters and the blood running through them. But while I busy myself with Gregor, you can make yourself useful as well: keep your eyes and ears open when you are with that Yerrin girl, and see what else you can learn of their deeds upon the Seat."

Ebon frowned. "That is not why we are working with her."

Mako grinned. "Good little Drayden boys can always do more than one thing at once."

He slipped into a nearby hedge and vanished.

Ebon heard nothing from Mako the rest of that day. It troubled him, though he chided himself, for he should not have expected Mako to find anything so soon. When he woke the next day he strode out upon the Academy grounds, even turning his steps towards the secret door in hopes that Mako might find him to report back. But the grounds were empty. Ebon left a scribbled note beneath the alabaster—*Have you found him?*—and went to class.

At his desk, he fiddled with the flower for a time, trying to see the parts of it with his mind's eye. But his thoughts were much occupied with Mako. What if the bodyguard had found Gregor already? What if something had happened to him? Ebon wished he had been able to come along. Even danger would be better than not knowing anything of what transpired beneath the streets. He pictured Mako down in the sewers, just like the night he had killed Matami. Only now the bodyguard was beset on all sides by Yerrin swords, green cloaks covering mail as they pressed him back, back into the darkness.

That made him shudder—and, too, it turned his thoughts to the night before last when he had been attacked. And he thought of the training grounds outside where advanced transmuters practiced their spells.

Ebon turned in his seat and raised his hand until Perrin came towards the front of the room to find him. "What is it?"

"I have been wondering," said Ebon. "Once, when I first came here, I saw other alchem—that is, transmuters, casting spells of defense. I saw a girl stop an arrow in mid-flight, turning it to a puff of smoke."

"Yes?" said Perrin. "What of it?"

"Could I not practice such magic? I have made little progress with my flower, and as you have said before, I might stretch my mind by turning it towards other things."

Perrin chuckled. "Other things, yes, but nothing so advanced. You are a long way off, I am afraid, from such magic. Also, you saw those spells ages ago. Why the sudden interest now?"

"No reason," Ebon said quickly. "Only . . . I have just learned to counter another wizard's magic. I thought I might learn to defend myself against other things, like a fighter with a sword."

Her brows rose. "Have you found yourself pitted against fighters and swords?"

Ebon blanched but tried to appear calm. "Not at all. It is just that, with the attack on the Seat, and now with war in Feldemar . . . it seems the sort of thing that might be useful. I am sure I am not the only one who feels the war hanging over us all."

The classroom had gone curiously quiet. When he looked about, Ebon saw that all the students had stopped in their work and were watching the two of them. Perrin looked at them all, and her stern countenance softened.

"I cannot blame you all for thinking such thoughts," she said. "It is only natural that you do. But I urge you not to worry yourselves overmuch. Every member of the faculty here values your safety above all else, and we will let no harm befall you." Her look returned to Ebon. "That said, I will not hold it against you for wishing to learn spells that can keep you safe. But in ordinary circumstances, you would not even begin to learn them until your third year—if then. Know that the required spells are many, and they must be learned one after the other, and they are not easy."

"Have any of my spells been easy thus far?" said Ebon.

At that she smiled. "I suppose they have not seemed so. Very well. First learn to turn a stone to ice, and then to water. Once you master that, do the same with metal, the more difficult cousin of stone. Then learn to turn it faster and faster. In time you may be able to stop a sword even as it hacks at you. Anyone coming at you with a blade will only find themselves wet. But I say again, you will not learn these spells quickly."

"I know it, Instructor." Ebon bowed his head. "And thank you."

She trundled off towards the back of the room again, and Ebon returned to his flower. Astrea sat beside him, as she usually did. Her eyes were fixed on her own rose, and he wondered if she had paid any attention at all to what had been said. But he did not wonder long, for she spoke after a moment.

"I wonder if I could do it," she muttered. "Turn stone to water, I mean."

Ebon shrugged. "She said it was an advanced third-year trick. It would be a great surprise if you could."

Her gaze rose to the classroom and then turned to him. "I do not mean *now,* of course. I mean if—mayhap I could learn it—oh, never mind."

Ebon frowned, for her tone struck him as odd. Then he saw the flower in her hands. It was ice—crystal clear and beginning to drip on the table.

"Astrea," he said, eyes wide.

She frowned and looked down at her hands. With a cry she leaped up, away from her bench. The rose fell from her fingers and shattered on the surface of the desk.

Thundering footsteps sounded as Perrin ran towards them. "What is it?" she demanded. "What is wrong?" Then she saw the shards of ice on the table, already beginning to melt into droplets. "Astrea, did you turn the flower?"

"I . . . I suppose so," said Astrea. "I was not paying attention. I did not mean to."

"But this is no sorrowful news," said Perrin, beaming. "You are progressing fast—far faster than is normal or expected. Well done. Now fetch yourself another and see if you can do it again."

She put a firm hand on Astrea's shoulder, giving it a little squeeze before she left them again. But Astrea did not go to fetch another flower. She only resumed her seat, splaying her hands out on the desk before her, and Ebon saw that her fingers were shaking.

"Are you all right?" he asked.

"How could I do that without meaning to?" she whispered. "I did not even notice my eyes fill with light."

"It might only have taken you a moment," he said, putting a confidence in his words that he did not feel. "I know the first time I used my magic—the first time I *really* did, anyway, other than the testing spell—it came upon me all in a rush, and I hardly knew what was happening."

"Yes," she said, still in a terrified whisper. "Yes, that must be it. It must have happened in a flash."

She met his look, trying desperately to smile. But Ebon saw the dread within her and felt it mirrored in his own heart.

TWENTY-TWO

THAT DAY, EBON FELT A CREEPING SUSPICION COME across him. Kalem and Theren could see it in him when they sat together in the library, but no matter how often they asked, he only shook his head and held his tongue.

Before he went to dinner, he wrote a letter and placed it beneath the alabaster—where he saw that his note from that morning still waited, untouched by Mako. He took the morning's note away and left the new one, which read:

I fear the threat has entered the Academy again. There are strange happenings afoot. Come and see me as quickly as you may.

He returned to the dormitories and sat long in the common room, brooding as he stared into the fire. Astrea did not act like one under mindwyrd—not exactly. But something strange was happening to her. And the last time Ebon had seen Academy students and faculty acting odd, it had been because of Isra, and then the killing had begun. He could not let that happen again.

The only thing that reassured him was that he did not believe Isra would harm Astrea. Everyone she had controlled before had been used to terrible purpose, and most of them had died in the end. But if Isra did not hold the girl in bond of mindwyrd, then what *was* going on?

Mako did not see him that evening, but Ebon thought he would hear from the bodyguard the next day. It passed, however, without word. And then most of the next day went by, and still there was no sign. Ebon spent most of the day scowling, and his mood was not improved when he went out upon the grounds at lunch and found that his letter was gone from beneath the alabaster. So Mako *had* received his message, and had not come to see him or left any message in reply. That made him irritable during their time in the library. At last Theren snapped her book shut and glared at him.

"Ebon, you are simply insufferable. I never thought I would say this, but if you cannot study in peace, go and take yourself somewhere else so that we may."

Ebon knew he was in the wrong, and so he apologized and promised to be less grim. But that only meant he sat in silence while they read and did not answer when spoken to, and so it was hardly better. The moment the day's last bell rang out, Theren leaped up and threw her book on the table between the three of them.

"I am taking you out," she said. "Let us go to some tavern, where wine and supper may ease your mood."

"We cannot go," said Ebon, aghast. "What if Gregor and his men are lurking outside the citadel?"

"Let him try to hurt you, or any of us," snapped Theren. "I have a mighty need to use my magic upon someone who deserves it in all its strength."

So he let her drag him and Kalem out into the streets, where they made their way to Leven's tavern close by and soon had lost themselves in a bottle of wine. And just as Theren had promised, Ebon soon found his mood improved tremendously. After a time he held his cup aloft, thrusting it towards Theren as if in toast.

"To my good friend Theren," he proclaimed, "who knows me for a happy drunk. And darkness below take Mako, anyway."

"Darkness below," said Theren, raising her own cup.

"That is a bit strong, I fear," said Kalem, joining them in the toast. "But I will drink regardless, for good wine makes up for dark words."

"It depends on the darkness of the words, as well as the strength of the wine," said Mako.

Ebon nearly spit out his drink. The bodyguard had appeared at the head of their table as if by magic. He pushed Ebon hard to make room and then took a seat on the bench. Across the table, Kalem and Theren were staring—and after a moment, Ebon realized why. Mako had a nasty bruise under his left eye, and the black sleeves that now covered his arms had wet spots. They could have been water, Ebon supposed, but a voice in his mind whispered *blood* instead.

"Have you met your match in some barroom brawl, Mako?" said Theren. "That seems no great surprise—you have always been boastful, and such pride often precedes downfall."

"Shut your flapping lips before I gut you," growled Mako. "I am in no mood for jests tonight, especially after you have disobeyed my order and left the Academy."

Theren almost replied, but Ebon silenced her with a stern look. He leaned close and lowered his voice. "What has happened? Have you found . . . him?"

"I have," said Mako.

"And is that what happened to . . . to you?" said Kalem, pointing to his face.

Mako sneered. "No, goldshitter. It is only that I

prefer a very particular sort of lover and have just come from his company."

Kalem blinked. Ebon frowned. "You said you were in no mood for jests. Nor am I. I left you word but have not heard from you."

"I gave you a way to reach me when you had information of value," said Mako, glaring at him. "That does not mean I come to heel at your call. I obey Halab's orders, not yours."

"What have you come for, then?" said Ebon. "What happened when you—"

Mako's hand darted forwards like a snake, closing over Ebon's mouth and lower jaw. "Be. Silent. That is what I have come here to tell you, but you have yammered on like starved puppies since the moment I sat."

"Unhand him," said Theren. A glow sprang into her eyes. "Or I could make you, if you wish."

The bodyguard glared at her for a long moment, and Ebon's pulse thundered in his ears. Then Mako's fingers loosened, and his hand withdrew.

"I found Gregor, indeed," said Mako, in a voice as calm as if nothing had happened. "In the bowels of the sewers, just where your lover said he would be. But Isra is there, too, and we . . ." He scowled. "With her strength added to Gregor's, I need magic to vanquish her. Your magic." He pointed at Theren.

"You need us?" said Theren, arching an eyebrow. "Have the High King declare a holiday, for the impossible has come to pass. Mako has asked for help."

Mako slammed a fist down on the table, so hard that their cups, which were thankfully empty, overturned. "I lost two soldiers tonight," he snarled. "The black-eyed sow killed them. So spare me your smug tone. You have the amulet and can be useful, so useful I will make you."

Theren looked around to ensure no one was close enough to overhear. "I have no wish to use the amulet openly," she said. "We know the faculty are hunting for it. What if we are discovered?"

"We will not be," said Mako. "I mean to set the constables and Mystics upon Yerrin, but not until we have done our business first. Until that happens, Yerrin wishes the presence of the King's law even less than we do."

Theren dropped her gaze to her fidgeting fingers. "Very well," she said with a sigh. "Only let us be quick about it."

Ebon nodded. "Very well. Mako, when can we move?"

"Not we," said Mako. "Or at least, not you."

That made them stop. "What do you mean?" said Ebon. "I am not staying behind."

"You certainly are, you damned fool," said Mako. "How many times must I tell you that my duty compels me to protect you?"

"I will not let my friends—or you—go into danger while I sit here in safety," said Ebon firmly.

Theren shook her head. "I can look after myself

well enough. You will be no great help in a fight, Ebon—forgive me, but it is true."

"I know it, and I know, too, that you are most capable. I will not go because the two of you need me. I will go because it is *my* duty, or at least I call it so—and what else is duty, after all?"

"The same goes for me," said Kalem. "And you cannot tell *me* to stay behind if you bring Ebon, for I might actually be able to help you. Meaning no offense, of course, Ebon."

Ebon waved it off. "It is decided, then. When do we mean to move?"

Mako glared at him—but he must have seen the resolve in Ebon's eyes, for after a moment he sighed. "You will obey my every order, no matter what," he said. "If I tell you to run, you will run, even if you abandon me. If I tell you to hide, you will hide."

"I swear it," said Ebon. "When?"

"Now."

At that they balked, even Ebon. "Now?" he said. "This moment?"

"Yes," said Mako. "I have only just come from a fight with Yerrin soldiers. They will redress their defenses—they may even move their activities to some other dark hole now that we know where they are. If it is not tonight, it will be never. Are you ready?"

Ebon swallowed hard. "We are."

"Very well," said Mako, standing from the table. "Do not make me regret this. Let us go."

TWENTY-THREE

Mako led them down the street and off to a side alley until they encountered a tall gutter where a large gap led into the sewers below. He dropped to the floor and slithered into the opening like a serpent. Ebon felt a moment's trepidation, but Theren followed the bodyguard without pause, and after a moment he did the same. He dropped two paces to the floor and landed easily enough, and then he reached up beside Theren to help Kalem, for the boy's legs did not reach nearly so far into the darkness as theirs.

Though they were beneath the streets, the fading

light of day still did much to illuminate the way before them, for it came through the drain holes and bounced from the light grey stones that formed the walls. Thus they were able to make their way quickly to the west where Gregor had been spotted. Ebon was grateful that this part of the sewers had platforms running along the water. The last time he had gone beneath the streets, there had been no such walkway, and so he and Mako had slogged through the muck. Now he still had to smell it, but he did not have to feel it sinking into his boots.

"How do you know where you are going?" said Kalem.

Mako did not even glance at the boy. "The sewers form a vast and intricate labyrinth—that is how Yerrin could be so busy within them without my knowing it. They are even more vast than the streets of the city itself, for there are many levels built atop one another, and each level stretches as far as the island. But there are different areas, and any who spend much time down here learn to stay close to their own territory. We rule all the levels to the northeast. The Yerrins have claimed the second level to the west. And I know we are going west because of the compasses."

He stopped at an intersection, and Ebon and his friends skidded to a halt behind him. He went to the right-hand passage and stood tall, placing one hand on the top of the tunnel. There Ebon saw an *N* had been drawn. He looked across the way and saw an *S* drawn over the opposite tunnel, and just above him was an

E. The way they were going, a *W* had been scratched. They were dug shallow in the stone, but unmistakable all the same, if one knew to look for them.

"Clever," said Theren, sounding impressed despite herself.

"That is one thing you should always keep in mind, children," said Mako. "Scholars and those who write books often hide knowledge in pretty phrases and dust-covered parchment, for they wish to have it all to themselves and thus earn the worship of common folk. But those who build, and make, and do— they make knowledge as plain as they can and put it in plain sight, hoping to help others who come after. The artisans who built these sewers wanted them to be useful, not mysterious."

"Yet they hold a mystery nonetheless and conceal many dark deeds besides," said Ebon, thinking of Matami.

Mako shrugged, his wide smile growing cruel. "Well, they may have intended one thing for their creation—but they bequeathed it to us, and we have made of it what we wish. Enough philosophy for now. We are moving too slow."

He stalked onwards, and they had to run to keep up with him. Mako did not relax his pace, no matter the distance they covered, and not even when he stopped them and led them down an iron ladder built into the wall. Theren seemed to have no difficulty matching his strides, but soon Ebon and Kalem began to flag, wheezing and huffing as they stumbled along in the now-dark passage.

"Hurry yourselves, goldshitters," said Mako, growling. "Yerrin may have defeated me once, but they will not rest easy this night and have likely already sent for more guards. The longer we take to reach them, the harder the fight we will find waiting for us."

"I am doing my best," said Kalem, who was panting even more heavily than Ebon. "Only I am not used to such exertion."

Theren and Mako snorted in unison and then gave each other an uneasy look before pressing onwards.

It was not so long after that before Mako stopped in his tracks, holding up a hand for the rest of them to do the same. Ebon pressed himself against the wall, as did Kalem, but Theren stepped up beside Mako, body tense, eyes peering eagerly into the darkness.

"Silence your huffing and heaving," Mako whispered. "I am trying to listen."

"Do you want me to stop breathing entirely?" said Kalem between gasps.

Mako glared at him, and Kalem's mouth snapped shut. He and Ebon did their best to still their heaving chests.

At long last Mako stepped forwards again, the tension vanishing from his posture. "It is one of mine. We need not fear—at least not yet." He led them on, and in a moment a shadow detached itself from the wall and came towards them.

"The wagon has pressed on," said a voice from the shadow. Ebon thought it sounded familiar for some reason. He peered closer. Beneath the hood was a woman, the same woman he had encountered on the streets who had saved him from Gregor. She glared at him with her one good eye for a long moment and then frowned at Mako.

"What is he doing here?"

"Do not worry about them," growled Mako. "Only tell me where the wagon has gone."

"West, the same way they were headed," said the woman. "I think the witch left it at some point, but I did not wish to draw too close to make sure."

"Of course not. Well done," said Mako. "Now return to the surface. I will doubtless send you a message soon, and you must act quickly when I do."

"I can stay," she said fiercely. "Let me fight." But suddenly her body gave a shudder, and she slumped against the wall. Ebon saw that one of her hands was pressed tight to her side, and he saw a dark liquid staining her fingers.

"No more battles for you tonight," said Mako. "Do as I say, or I will give you a bruise to go with that scratch."

"Then at least we would match," she said, and grunted out a pained laugh. She held forth a hand, and she and Mako seized wrists before drawing each other close for a one-armed embrace. Before she could go, Ebon took a step forwards.

"Thank you," he said. "For saving me. The other night, I mean."

She glared at him. "A fool's gratitude is of little worth."

Then she stepped into the shadows and vanished.

"Who is she?" said Ebon. "Her name, I mean. I did not get to thank her before—or I did not think of it."

"She is Talib," said Mako, "and has been my pupil for many years. She has saved your skin more times than you know—certainly more than the one time you saw her doing it. Come. We are not far now."

He crept forwards now. Ebon and Kalem no longer had to struggle to keep up. But while his footsteps were quiet as a shadow, and Theren, too, moved muffled and silent, Ebon's and Kalem's steps now seemed horribly loud, and Ebon winced every time his toes caught upon a crack in the stone with a scuffling noise. Mako glared back at him once or twice, and though he said nothing, Ebon's face burned with embarrassment each time.

But then all such thoughts were banished, for ahead they saw the orange glow of a torch, and far off, Ebon could hear the creaking of wagon wheels, a sound as familiar to him as his own breath. Too, there were tramping boots, and they moved quickly, not at some easy walking pace. Whoever accompanied the wagon, they knew they were pursued and were making good time to escape. But not good enough, clearly, for the noise grew louder.

Soon they saw the wagon: it rolled along with a deep rumble, pulled by two Yerrin guards in green cloaks, holding spars that stuck out from the front of it. Three more guards accompanied the cart, walking behind and to either side of it. Two of these held torches, lighting the way forwards.

"Fools," muttered Mako, after he had let them draw a bit ahead and out of sight. "Those torches may show them where they are going, but also serve to make the procession easy to see. And they will not spy us until we are almost upon them."

"What is in that wagon?" said Kalem, eyes wide with fright. "Are they moving magestones?"

"No," said Mako. "Only supplies to feed and care for the crew of a ship that will soon launch from their hidden dock. But upon that ship there *are* magestones, and Yerrin means to send them out across the nine lands. That is not our chief worry tonight, though. Tonight we hunt for Gregor, and mayhap Isra."

"I am more worried about Isra than Gregor," said Ebon.

"Yet you are not in command here, and should not even have come," said Mako, glaring at him. "Therefore your worries are of no consequence."

"Well, what do we mean to do now?" said Theren. "I did not see Gregor among the guards—unless the tales of his size and strength are only exaggeration. And Isra certainly was not there."

"Yet we should stop that wagon all the same," said

Mako. "Anything to disrupt the family Yerrin and their criminal activities is a gift to the High King."

Kalem nodded solemnly, clearly missing the joke; Ebon rolled his eyes at the thought of Mako risking life and limb to uphold the King's law. But Mako was right in any case—to reach Gregor and Isra, they would have to get through the wagon guards. "What do you mean to do?"

Mako grinned at Theren. "Do you wish to show off that magic of yours, girl?"

Theren smiled in return.

In a few heartbeats Mako outlined the plan, and they ran forwards again in the darkness. When they came to the next corner, Ebon and Kalem stopped while Mako and Theren pressed on. They saw a flash of light as Theren's eyes glowed, for she did not bother to hide it with the amulet, and then she burst around the corner beside Mako.

The cart flipped over, slamming to the stone floor upside-down, its contents spilling all over. The wheels flew off, each one striking a guard to either side. They fell with pained cries, their torches falling into the passing flow of water and waste. The guards floundered in the sudden darkness, reaching for blades at their waists—but too slow. Theren struck again, and invisible bands of force picked them up, slamming them into the wall. Their faces were pressed into the stone so that they could not see behind them.

"Boys," growled Mako.

Ebon and Kalem ran forwards at once. The light in the tunnel increased as they reached for their magic, and then together they pressed their fingers to the stone. It flowed out and around the guards, wrapping about their wrists and ankles in bands so that they were held in place. In a moment it was done, and all three of the children released their hold on their magic. The tunnel was plunged into darkness again. They waited for their eyes to adjust to the small shafts of moonslight from above.

"We should destroy their goods," said Mako. "But I would rather not throw them into the water, in case they are carried down to where our enemies await, and they are warned of our presence."

"A moment," said Ebon. He reached into the pocket of his cloak and produced Halab's firestriker. Mako's eyes lit upon it, and he gave Ebon a hard look.

"It was a gift from . . ." Ebon trailed off, looking at the guards on the wall. They could not see, but they could hear. "Well, from family."

Many of the goods were wrapped in cloth, and he tore it up to put in piles at the wagon's corners. With a few touches of the firestriker, the cloth lit, and soon flames licked up to spread along the wagon's lengthy spars.

"That will do it," said Mako.

"And what of them?" said Kalem, pointing to the soldiers pressed to the wall.

"Do what you will to us," said one of the guards,

speaking into the wall, for the stone bands still pressed her tight against it. "You will not find it so easy when you get to the end of the tunnel, wretches."

Mako grinned. "Let her down."

Ebon looked at him, aghast, but Mako only nodded. So Ebon went forwards and shifted stone again, releasing the bands that held her. The moment her boots touched the ground, she turned and reached for his throat. But Mako seized an arm and snapped it against his wrist. Ebon heard the sick *crunch* of a breaking bone, and the woman cried out. Then Mako smashed an elbow into her nose, and she fell to the ground.

"Girl," said Mako. "The amulet. Place her under your spell."

"What? I did not agree to use mindwyrd," said Theren.

"I would not ask you to make her kill herself," said Mako. His voice was soothing, though his hands jerked as he restrained the Yerrin guard, who fought to rise. "I mean to keep magestones out of the hands of rogue wizards. Only that. I promise."

Theren hesitated. But though her eyes did not glow, as she spoke again, her voice was rich with mindwyrd.

"Stop," said Theren.

The Yerrin guard stopped squirming on the floor at once. "Yes," she said, her tone dead and lifeless.

"You will not remember any of our faces," said Theren. "After you have left the sewer, you will forget seeing us, or that you were attacked at all."

"Yes," said the guard.

Theren looked to Mako. "Now what?"

"Have her go to the Mystics," said Mako, smiling. "Have her tell them where we are going and that they should go there in all haste, for they will find a hefty supply of magestones if they do."

"But they will find us," said Theren, taking a step back. "If they learn what I carry . . ."

"We will be quick, and will have vanished by the time they arrive. But they will be there to clean up the mess and deal a grievous blow to the family Yerrin." Mako gave them all a look. "You, more than others, should object to more magestones finding their way into the nine lands. We can do a great deal to stop it, now, tonight."

"Very well," said Theren. She looked at the guard again. "You will find the first Mystic you can. You will tell them of these tunnels, and what paths to follow that will lead them to the rest of your kin. You will tell the Mystics that they will find magestones here, but only if they come into the sewers, now, at once."

"Yes," said the guard.

"Go, then."

The guard turned on her heel and marched away, back down the way Ebon and the others had come. Ebon shivered, and Kalem did the same.

"We have taken longer than we should have," said Mako. "Onwards."

TWENTY-FOUR

IT WAS NOT LONG AFTER THAT THAT THE TUNNEL widened at last, and they came into a vast, open space. Here the walls and floor were hewn from the earth's bones, rather than built by masons, and there were many stone outcroppings all about. Mako ducked behind one of these, and the children hastened to follow.

They had reached some sort of grotto, Ebon saw. He could smell saltwater over the bitter stench of the sewer waste and surmised that this cavern must run out to the Great Bay. They had to be somewhere near the western end of the Seat, he guessed, if not at its very edge.

Where the tunnels emerged into the cavern was a narrow platform, and this joined a raised stone path that ran around the cave's right edge, with many guards posted along it. A fair distance away, the path ended at a wooden dock lined with torches that illuminated a ship.

It was no great vessel, smaller than a schooner but wider, built for capacity more than speed. Two masts it had, though Ebon saw a sail upon only one of them. He guessed it had room for no more than five crew. Two of these walked about the deck, checking lines and stowing cargo, while three managed workers on the dock. There were many crates, barrels and sacks to load, it seemed, and where they were open, Ebon could see that most of them were filled with small packets of brown cloth.

"There," said Mako, pointing at the packets. "Those are magestones, or I am a fool."

"Can it not be both?" said Theren.

Mako snorted—whether in dismissal or in a quickly stifled laugh, Ebon could not tell. "What we see here is worth more than a king's ransom. What do you say? Shall we rob them of it?"

"I do not want to steal magestones," said Kalem quickly.

Mako rolled his eyes. "Loosen your death grip upon your honor, goldshitter. I mean to destroy their cargo, not to take it for ourselves. Magestones are a toxic good to trade, as the family Yerrin is soon to discover."

"We did not come for their magestones," said Theren. "We came for Isra. Where is she?"

"I do not see her or Gregor," said Mako. "Either they have come and gone, or they are still on their way and will arrive soon. If it is the latter, we would be wise to create as much chaos as we can before they come, so that they cannot muster these guards against us. If it is the former, then we have already lost their trail tonight and should do what good we can—by which I mean, chiefly, destroying the cargo Yerrin hopes to escape with."

"Very well," said Ebon. "What shall we do?"

"I tell you again that *we* shall do nothing, and this time I mean it," said Mako. "I have taken you farther already than I should have, and it ends here. You will keep watch. If anyone else should emerge from the tunnel whence we came, you must warn Theren and me so that we are not taken unawares."

Ebon glared, and Kalem did not look entirely pleased either. But they could feel the sand passing through the hourglass—they had little time, for the Mystics would soon be on their way. "Very well. How should I signal you?"

"Squeal like a rabbit, for all I care," said Mako. "Only do not let them see you, and make sure you are not within reach. There is a little rocky shelf up there on the wall—that is where you should wait."

"What will the two of you do?" said Kalem.

"We will make this a night Yerrin remembers and regrets," said Mako. "Come, Theren."

Together he and Theren stole forwards, bent almost double in the shadows, while Ebon and Kalem scrambled onto the shelf. It was just above head-height, with the ceiling pressing down low enough above them that they had to lie down to keep from bumping their skulls.

Ebon thought that Mako and Theren would take the stone path, but Mako turned from it at once. Then Ebon saw that there were other stone shelves like the one he rested on, though not so smooth, so that the Yerrin guards avoided them. But the stone came in levels, and all of them were lower than the stone path, so that Mako and Theren could creep along unseen.

He saw them approach the first guard who stood on the path. They edged forwards until they were as close to the guard as possible, but below him and out of sight. Theren popped her head up and into the torchlight. Ebon froze and almost called out—but then Theren said something he could not hear, and the guard froze.

A few more hasty words she muttered, and then she ducked out of sight again. The guard set off down the path. He approached the next guard, who leaned unaware against the wall. The unwitting target looked only at the last moment—but too late, for the first guard smashed the pommel of his sword into the side of her helmet. She fell to the floor, senseless.

The other guards saw it, and they called out in alarm as they came running to help. There were at least a half dozen of them, and Ebon knew that Theren's mindwyrded guard stood no chance. But just as they approached, Mako and Theren struck.

Mako leaped up on the path, seizing one of the guards and planting a dagger in his throat. He fell from the path and slid down the shelf into the water. Ebon winced. Theren struck with her magic, seizing two of the guards and flinging them from the path. They fell screaming into the water and fought to keep hold of the rock wall as they tugged off their chain mail. Mako nearly killed another, but Theren struck again just in time. Her magic picked up all three guards who still stood and slammed them into the stone wall with the strength of dragon's breath. They fell unconscious to the floor.

"Come!" said Ebon, sliding down off their shelf. He helped Kalem down after him, and they ran forwards to where Mako and Theren stood. Together they ran down the path as quick as they could, for the sense of passing time hung heavy in the air. The ship's crew had abandoned their vessel, fleeing for their lives down a side passage that led in another direction.

"What of the ones who escaped?" said Ebon.

"They could not see our faces in the dim," said Mako. "The ship is all that matters now."

He leaped aboard first, and the children followed more slowly, holding tight to the rope railing of the gangplank. By the time they made the deck, Mako had already gone down a hatch and returned. "The bulk of the stones are down there," he said. "But there are plenty more on the dock. It would be best to destroy them all, but that may take too long."

"I can cast the crates on the dock into the water," said Theren.

"No good. The crates will keep them safe, and those lying in the open will simply float. Yerrin may not be able to recover all of them, but they will recover enough."

"Put them aboard, then," said Ebon. "And we can burn the ship."

Mako scowled. "Idiot. It will take longer to bring the crates aboard than it would to set them ablaze."

Ebon took quite some pleasure in rolling his eyes and gesturing dramatically at Theren. "We have a *mindmage*, Mako."

The bodyguard's eyes widened, and though it looked as though he tried to hide it, a little smirk crept into his lips.

Off to the side, Kalem muttered, "He means mentalist."

It took but a moment. Theren's eyes blazed as she lifted the crates, for she did not need the amulet's power for so simple a task. But the last few still hung in the air when Ebon heard a sharp cry and turned.

There, at the other end of the cavern, two figures stood in the entryway, silhouetted by the torchlight beyond. Gregor—and beside him, Isra.

TWENTY-FIVE

EVEN FROM ACROSS THE CAVERN, EBON SHOOK AT THE sight of Gregor. Images flashed into his mind of the Drayden assassin Gregor had killed. Next to Isra, his size seemed inhuman. The man was at least a head and a half taller than Mako, and it seemed his shoulders were twice as broad. His legs were like ship masts, and his arms as thick as Ebon's torso.

"Drop that crate," Mako told Theren. "I would give both my daggers for a firemage. Boys, find torches and set blazes on the ship. Can you stop her, Theren?"

"I have before," said Theren, her voice filled with steely resolve. "I will do so now, and gladly."

"I hope you are not only boasting."

Mako pounded down the dock towards the path of stone. But Theren did not bother with the dock; she ran to the ship's stern and leaped from it. Ebon's stomach lurched—but then her magic picked her up, and she used it to carry herself to the stone path, reaching it even before Mako did.

Isra gave a scream of rage, and a black glow sprang into her eyes. "Kill the girl!" she cried. Gregor drew his steel and advanced down the stone path. But Mako stepped forth, and the men faced each other across the cave.

"You owe me more than one life," said Mako. "Now I will carve them from you like a boar."

"Try it," said Gregor.

Ebon realized he had been standing and staring too long. He turned to seize Kalem's shoulder. "Enough gawking," he said. "We have our own work to do."

Kalem nodded. "I will fetch one of the torches."

"No, I will see to that. Use your magic upon the ship—break parts of it up into kindling that will catch easier than boards."

As Kalem scuttled to obey, Ebon ran down the gangplank, making for the torches. But a blow struck him just as he neared the first one, a force without sound or sight. It knocked him back, nearly pitching him off the other side of the dock. The torch he had reached for was flung from its mount, falling into the water below with a sharp hiss.

"Ebon!" Kalem came running. Across the cave, Ebon saw Isra staring at him with her black-glowing eyes, and he knew it was her magic that had nearly thrown him into the water. But though her hand was outstretched still, he felt nothing more pulling at him. Theren must have countered the spell.

Kalem reached him and seized his arm, hauling him back up onto the dock. Ebon gave him a grateful smile before they stood together.

"Get another," he said, pointing to the torches.

But Isra gave another great cry. Ebon braced himself for a blow, but none came—except to the torches, which were cast down and into the water of the grotto. Now the dock was nearly pitch-black, and the cavern was only lit by the torches on the stone path. Ebon could try to take one, but it would bring him nearly within arm's reach of Gregor. Isra bared her teeth in triumph. But then Theren redoubled her assault, drawing Isra's focus.

"Darkness take her," said Ebon. "What can we do now?"

"Mayhap the ship has lanterns," said Kalem. "And you have your firestriker. Come! I will search below-decks."

They ran up the gangplank again, and Kalem vanished down a hatch. But Ebon paused, for he had caught sight of Mako. Gregor had pushed the bodyguard well down the path now so that they were less than ten paces from the ship, and Mako was hard-pressed. A new bruise swelled on his face, and he favored his right arm, which was missing its dagger. The other seemed a poor weapon against Gregor's massive sword, and it seemed clear that Mako was no longer attacking—only trying to stay alive.

Ebon looked over the deck around him. There was an open barrel at hand, and within it he saw oranges and apples packed in straw. He seized one of the oranges, gripping it tight in his hands. Light flashed in his eyes as he felt the substance of the fruit, and then he changed it to stone. But then it was almost too heavy to hold, so he shifted some of it away to go dribbling down upon the deck. Now he took the fist-sized ball and, waiting for the right moment, he threw it.

Mako had taken a quick step back, desperate for space, and so the stone came sailing at Gregor at the perfect time. It struck metal, for he wore a helmet, but still it sent his head rocking to the side, and he stumbled. Mako lunged forwards with his dagger.

But Gregor recovered too quickly, and his plated fist smashed Mako in the gut. The bodyguard fell back, landing hard on the stone path. Ebon shouted, turned another orange to stone, and threw it. But Gregor casually batted it away, and took a step towards Mako, who struggled to stand.

Theren grit her teeth and stepped forwards. Isra stumbled against the attack, and the darklight in her eyes flamed up. But Theren broke through, knocking Gregor a pace back from Mako. With a cry she pressed still further, and Ebon saw a rippling in the air. It wrapped itself around Isra in an instant, and the girl screamed as it flung her far out into the cavern, out of the torchlight and into the water with a *splash*.

With her opponent gone at last, Theren sagged and fell to one knee. But she rose almost immediately, pushing Gregor another pace back from Mako. Ebon thought she would fling him into the water as well, but she seemed winded, and fought just to keep her feet.

There came a commotion at the other end of the cave. With shouts and tramping feet, a party of soldiers burst into the cavern, holding torches aloft. They wore mail and carried blades along with the torches, and upon their shoulders were cloaks of red.

"Mystics!" whispered Ebon. But just then Kalem emerged from belowdecks, and in his hand was a lantern. He opened one side of it even as Ebon frantically worked his firestriker, and soon the lantern was ablaze. Close at hand lay a little pile of kindling that Kalem had built. Ebon smashed the lantern down upon it, and its oil spread along the deck.

"It is time to go." Ebon turned to find Mako standing at the gangplank. The bodyguard's face was entirely covered in bruises now, and blood from his split lip dribbled down his chin.

They ran to him, and at the bottom of the gangplank joined Theren. A glance told Ebon that the Mystics were engaged with Gregor, who fended them off with huge, sweeping swings of his broadsword. They should have overwhelmed him already, but the narrow stone path kept them from engaging him more than two at a time.

Mako hurried them towards the other passage, the one the boat crew had used to escape when they first arrived. Just before they ducked within, Ebon glanced back at the ship. It was burning now, burning with a sickly black flame that rose to lick the cavern's roof. The smell of it was foul, a putrid corruption like rotting flesh or a noxious corpse. He nearly retched. Then they had gone around the corner, and the flames were lost from sight.

TWENTY-SIX

THE TUNNEL STRETCHED ON LONG AND DARK AHEAD of them, and they had to slow their pace at first. But then Theren took the lead and, eschewing Kekhit's amulet, she reached for her power. Magelight sprang into her eyes to illuminate the way. It was a poor glow, but better than nothing, and they moved as quickly as they could. Ebon heard no sounds of pursuit, but that could not last forever; eventually the Mystics must overwhelm Gregor, and then they would find this passage.

"How do we know this is not a dead end?" said Kalem.

"Because the Yerrins fled this way," said Mako. "They were afraid for their lives—they would not have trapped themselves here if there was no hope."

Indeed he proved right, for soon they emerged into another cavern. This one was much smaller and opened to the Great Bay almost immediately, letting them see by moonslight. They had come out into a small rocky shore that sloped steeply into the water.

"What now?" said Kalem, looking behind them.

"There were likely boats here," said Theren, pointing. Ebon saw that there was a spike in the rock wall and several lines trailing from it, but nothing was attached to the other end of the lines. "The crew must have taken them all when they fled."

"That means we must swim," said Mako. "Shed anything that will slow you in the water and get in."

"It is the dead of winter!" said Ebon. "We will freeze to death."

Mako scowled at him. "We can reach the shore. Unless I miss my guess, it is just around the mouth of the cave. And if you or I stay here, we will land in a Mystic prison, and the family Drayden may fall."

Ebon looked fearfully at the water. "I am not a very good swimmer."

"Come off it, Ebon," said Theren. She was already shucking off her Academy robes. Soon she stood in her underclothes, but even though she must have been freezing, she did not shiver.

Kalem and Ebon looked at each other for a moment, but Ebon knew they had little choice. They removed their robes, throwing them into the water at Mako's command so that hopefully the Mystics would not find them and learn that Academy students had been present. Their boots they kept, for those would not be a great impediment to swimming, and they would need them to run once they reached land again. Once they had disrobed, both boys hesitated at the edge of the Great Bay's water, which it looked even more frigid now.

"Oh, darkness save us," said Mako. He seized Ebon's shoulders and flung him in.

Ebon sank into the water with a yelp and nearly gasped in lungs of seawater. It was colder than he could believe. A moment later he felt the splashing of another body beside him—Kalem, too, had been thrown in. Together they fought for the surface and hung there paddling, sucking in deep breaths of air that now seemed positively warm.

Theren waded in beside them and struck out for the cave mouth. Mako was just behind her. Ebon and Kalem paddled after them but were soon outpaced.

"Wait!" cried Ebon. Then he took in a mouthful of seawater and lost his words to sputtering. But Mako and Theren glanced back from where they had almost reached the open water.

"Sky above," said Theren, swimming back. She passed Ebon and went to Kalem, who had fallen even farther behind. "Come on, then."

He clung to her back, holding on to her shoulders with a death grip. She struck out again, and though Kalem slowed her down a bit, she still passed Ebon easily. They reached Mako at the cave mouth, and he glared at Ebon as they approached.

"I am not carrying you like a suckling newborn, boy."

"I did not ask you to," said Ebon, though he had meant to, and was now secretly glad he had not.

They broke out into the open water, and Mako's earlier guess proved right. A sandy shore sank into the water a scant thirty paces away. Before they swam for it, though, Mako guided them farther out into open water, for the waves lapped against the stone cliffs of the Seat, and though the sea was somewhat calm, still it could knock them senseless against the rocks. Ebon soon fell behind again. Mako did not carry him the way Theren had Kalem, but he did reach back and seize Ebon's collar, flinging him a little bit farther along every other stroke, so that he was just able to keep up with the rest.

"Darkness take all useless goldshitters," growled Mako.

"I could not agree more," said Theren, who was now fighting against Kalem's weight to keep her head above the waves.

By the time they reached land, Ebon could no longer feel his fingers or his toes. He fell upon the shore, expecting the air to be warmer than the water. But a wind was blowing, and his shivers only redoubled.

"Get up and keep moving," said Mako. "You will not freeze to death unless you try to rest."

"But where?" said Ebon. He fought to gain his feet, but it was hard when he could not feel his limbs.

"There," said Mako. He pointed up the shore, where they could see the glow of the western docks. "There are torches for warmth, and mayhap we can steal some clothes."

So by moonlight they ran on, their steps hampered by the soft sand that grasped for their feet. Mako reached the dock piles first, and by the time they joined him he had popped his head up over the edge of the wooden planks to look.

"There are no guards nearby," he whispered. "And there is a carriage not far off that I think is unoccupied."

"You mean to steal a carriage?" said Kalem.

"No, idiot. If there is a carriage, it is because someone means to take ship. But their things are still in bags atop the carriage, and there we may find clothes. Theren, look after them and keep out of sight—I shall return in a moment."

He slithered up and into the open. Theren poked her head up to look after him, and in a moment Ebon and Kalem did the same. They saw him reach the carriage, climb up top, and pull open a travel sack. He threw it aside before opening another. This one he took up and ran back to them, avoiding torchlight wherever he could.

"Here we are," he said. "Trousers and tunics aplenty. No cloaks, but we will not be in the cold much longer."

The children hastened to don the clothing. Ebon studied Mako as they dressed. The bodyguard stood stock still with no quiver in his limbs, though his clothes still dripped seawater.

"There are clothes enough here for you, too."

Mako sneered, and the clotted blood of his lip burst, sending a crimson rivulet forth to mingle with the saltwater droplets. "I am not some weakling who is troubled by a chill."

Soon they were done. They all had trousers of brown, and Ebon and Theren had found tunics of white. But the only shirt that fit Kalem was flamboyant red with gold trim at the collar and sleeves.

"Well, this does not make me look an utter idiot at all," said Kalem ruefully, holding out his arms and shaking his head.

"Who cares what you look like?" growled Mako. "We have tarried too long. Up on the dock."

And so up they went, and once they had passed the carriage and gone a little distance on, they slowed to a walk, strolling along as though nothing untoward was happening—except for Mako, who still stole from shadow to shadow, eyes roving everywhere to watch for a threat.

"The docks seem curiously empty, do they not?" said Kalem.

"I had noticed the same thing," said Ebon.

"That may be why," said Theren.

She pointed ahead, where a large cluster of people had gathered. There were mayhap two score of them packed in a tight little group, and all facing towards the center, except for some who looked about as though seeking aid.

"Stay away from there," said Mako. "All the better that they will not notice us."

"They will not notice us regardless," said Ebon. "They are looking at whatever is in their midst."

He pressed forwards, away from his friends and towards the crowd, ignoring Mako's frustrated growl behind him. Something was wrong. He could see it in the worried faces of the onlookers, the way they kept looking about, expecting—or hoping—for someone else to arrive, to sort out whatever lay in their midst.

The crowd was packed tight, but he pushed through them, and Theren was at his shoulder. Soon they reached the center, and there they froze. Ebon's breath left him in a rush.

Isra lay there. Dead, clearly, her sightless eyes staring up at the sky. Seawater had turned her skin dark and bloated, and blue veins stuck out in the torchlight. Fish had begun to peck at her cheeks, it seemed, for the skin was open, though the decaying flesh put forth no blood. Only a few scraps of her Academy robes still clung to her corpulent frame.

"She perished, then," Theren whispered. Ebon

heard a grim finality in her voice—no trace of joy, but a steely resolve, a tone like the ending of a tale. "I did not mean to drown her. But neither am I sorry. The nightmare is over."

"Silence," said Ebon quietly. He took her arm, and Kalem's, who had stepped up beside the two of them, and drew them both back through the crowd. They pulled away from the people standing there, where Mako waited with a dark look in his eyes.

"Well?" he said. "What is it?"

"It is Isra," said Ebon. "Dead."

Mako's eyes shot wide, and he pushed past them to dive into the crowd. When he returned, his face was no less grim—in fact his scowl had deepened.

"She must have washed out of the grotto on whatever current was meant to carry that ship," said Theren. "Strange that she should have reached the docks before we did, but then, the sea is wild."

Ebon frowned, but he did not wish to speak. It was Kalem who looked up, fear in his eyes, and met Theren's look.

"No, Theren," he said. "That is impossible. Not just how quickly she came here—but she, herself. She has been dead a long time. Weeks, most likely."

Theren stared at him, uncomprehending. Her gaze shifted to Ebon, who met her eyes, and then to Mako, who was scowling off into the night, chin buried in his fist, lost in thought.

"That is impossible," she said. "We just saw her. It

was less than an hour ago, and she was as alive as you or I."

Ebon shivered as he looked back towards the crowd, all of them still clustered around the body. "Yet it is the truth. I have no more explanation than you do. But Isra is more than a month dead."

TWENTY-SEVEN

THEY DID NOT KNOW WHAT ELSE TO DO, SO THEY MADE their way into the city and back to the Academy. The dock gates stood open, as constables had been summoned to inspect the corpse, and so they entered without trouble. Before they returned to the citadel, Theren took them to the inn where Lilith kept her extra room. Mako waited on the street as they ducked within. At the door to the room, she produced a key from around her neck, hanging on the same chain as Kekhit's amulet.

"I had the key before, you know," she said, looking

embarrassed and refusing to meet the eyes of either Ebon or Kalem. "Before we were estranged. She only recently gave me one again. In case we should need it, for something like this."

"Of course," said Ebon carefully.

She let them in and showed them where Lilith kept extra sets of Academy student robes. Soon they had changed, and Mako led them on through the streets. Curfew was a distant memory, and so he took them around the Academy's east end to the groundskeepers' sheds that housed his secret entrance.

"I must cover your eyes," he said, looking at Theren and Kalem.

Theren scowled. "Why? I can keep a secret as well as the next."

"It is not yours to know, much less to keep," said Mako. "It is bad enough Ebon knows how I get in and out. No others need the knowledge."

He took rags from the sheds and tied them around their eyes, and then he and Ebon led Theren and Kalem into one of the sheds. Inside, Mako had Ebon turn around while he pulled a lever, and the secret way opened before them. The passageway was utterly dark, and Ebon did not know how Mako could see—yet he must have been able to, for soon he opened the door at the other end of it, and they stood upon the Academy grounds.

"I suggest you rest well," said Mako. "Doubtless I shall see you all again soon."

"Thank you, Mako," said Ebon. "Though some things are unclear, it seems at least that this is all over."

Mako gave him a hard look. "I hope you are right, though I doubt it."

He left them. Ebon and his friends made their way into the Academy. It was far too late to be wandering the halls, but they encountered no instructors. Soon they had climbed the stairs to their dormitories. They stopped at Kalem's, where the common room was empty, for the younger children had gone to bed. A fire burned low in the hearth. Ebon threw two more logs on, and then they sat in armchairs around it.

"I cannot fathom all that has happened," said Kalem. "There seems no sense to it."

"Isra is dead, at least," said Theren. "I can worry about the rest of it another day."

"Is she, though?" said Ebon. "That corpse was long decayed from seawater. We all saw it, Theren."

Theren threw her hands towards the ceiling. "What, then, does it mean? Has she been a walking corpse for the last month? We have seen her alive. And tonight we saw her dead. Mayhap you guessed wrong and thought the body more decayed than it was."

"Her clothes were rotten, and fish had begun to eat her," said Ebon.

"Mayhap we are wrong in another sense," said Kalem. "Mayhap the corpse was not her, but only someone who looks like her."

"You do not believe in such a coincidence any more

than I do," said Ebon. "We have seen her, studied beside her, and even fought against her. We know what she looked like—it was her body." But then a thought struck him, and he straightened in his seat. "Unless it was not. It could have been a weremage. Think of it. What if she mindwyrded a weremage to look just like her, then killed them and threw them into the Great Bay? When the body was recovered, it would cast any investigation away from her."

Kalem shook his head. "That is not how therianthropy works. When the wizard dies, they resume their true form." But now it was his turn to look up in realization. "What if the corpse from the Bay was Isra, and a weremage has been impersonating her?"

Theren looked at him with disdain. "She has used mindmagic against us, Kalem. How could she have done that if she was a weremage? No wizard commands more than one branch of magic."

The boy's face fell. "Of course," he mumbled. "I should have thought of that."

Ebon ran the facts through his mind, but he could think of none that made sense—and he knew, too, that he was less able to guess than his friends, for many ways of magic were still strange to him.

Either the corpse was Isra's, or it was not. They could not hope to guess at the truth. But either answer brought another, more urgent question: where was Erin? If Isra was still alive, doubtless she held the boy in captivity. But if Isra was indeed dead . . . was the boy now a captive of the family Yerrin? Or had she left him somewhere else entirely?

Thoughts of Erin brought thoughts of Xain, and his blood went cold.

"One thing is certain," he said at last, speaking quietly against the crackling fire in the hearth. "There will be an investigation now. And we are the only ones who claim to have seen Isra since she disappeared."

They all looked at each other. Then Theren rose from her chair and left without a word, making for the halls. Kalem left a moment later, stepping through the opposite door that led to his dormitory. But Ebon sat there until morning, staring into the fire, exhausted beyond reckoning and yet unable to even think of sleep.

It did not take long for the faculty to redouble their investigation. Ebon guessed that news must have reached the Academy during the night, for the moment he reached Perrin's class she commanded him to visit the dean.

There was no instructor in the hall to walk with him. Ebon stood there for a moment, frozen by indecision. He had a tremendous urge to turn the other way, to make for the Academy's front doors and leave forever, begging for help from Halab and Mako. They could whisk him away to some forgotten kingdom, or even, mayhap, home to Idris, there to be hidden from all knowledge.

But after a time he turned to the right instead and made his slow way towards Xain's study. He had done nothing wrong—or at least, nothing wrong when it came to Isra. He *had* seen her within the Academy. He and his friends had *not* drowned her in the Great Bay weeks ago. He must cling to that, for it was the truth. And only the truth could save him now, because outside of what he had seen with his own eyes, he was not even certain what the truth was.

Xain stood outside his office—but much to Ebon's relief, Jia was also there, as was Dasko. Dasko looked somewhat worse for wear; his face was still gaunt, and his eyes roved all about. But his hands were steady, and Ebon saw no trace of madness in him, the sickness that came over those who had long been under mindwyrd. It had faded in him remarkably fast. Ebon nodded to the instructor and received a brief jerk of the head in return.

"Drayden," said Xain, speaking through gritted teeth. "Come with us."

He stalked off down the hall. Jia and Dasko followed at a somewhat more sedate pace, with Jia holding out an arm to help Dasko along. Ebon decided to match their steps rather than Xain's, and soon the dean was forced to slow.

Ebon had had scant reason to visit the Academy's healing ward before, but that was where they turned their steps now. It lay on the bottom floor of one of the citadel's great wings, the one that stretched northwest, and there were many beds arranged in rows with tall windows that reached from waist-height almost to the ceiling. One of the beds nearest the entrance was covered, and Ebon saw the shape of a body beneath it. He could smell decay mixed with seawater.

Jia paused a respectful distance away, but Xain pushed forwards. Ignoring the healer who stood by to help, he threw back the sheet to reveal Isra's bloated corpse. Removed from the seawater, her skin had turned darker still, and her eyes had swollen into pale, milky globes, the color of which could hardly be discerned. Yet it was still clearly her, as any fool could see. She had been stripped of her clothes and cleaned up. The sight of her almost made Ebon retch.

"How is it possible," said Xain, "that Isra lies dead before us, when you said you saw her just over a week ago?" His words were calm, but Ebon heard the fire burning behind them, hot enough to melt steel.

Ebon swallowed hard, trying to remember to look shocked, as though he was surprised to see Isra dead. It was not difficult, and he thought the paleness of his skin likely helped. "I do not know," he said. "Where . . . where was she? Mayhap she died just after we encountered her."

The healer, a wizened old woman whose hair was drawn up into a tight bun, shook her head. "This corpse has been in the ocean a month at least," she said. "We inspected it most thoroughly."

Xain stalked around the bed to loom over him. "A month. A month ago is about the time she vanished from her classes. And so I ask again—how is it possible that you saw her in the kitchens, Drayden?"

"He is not the only one who saw her," said Jia.

"I am asking the boy, for it is his words that have been called into question. He can speak for himself, or he can speak with the Mystics' encouragement. It matters little to me."

"It is as Jia said," said Ebon, feeling somewhat indignant now. "I have not gone mad. My friends saw her as well."

Xain glanced over his shoulder. "Mayhap. Yet they, too, may prove false."

Ebon heard footsteps behind him and turned to see Kalem and Theren being ushered into the room by an instructor he did not recognize. Both their eyes fixed at once upon the corpse on the bed. Kalem went Elf-white, and Theren did not look much better.

"This is the body of a girl you both said you saw here in the Academy," Xain told them. "Yet she has been dead for weeks. How do you explain this? I cannot read the tale of it, unless someone in this room has been lying."

Kalem tore his eyes away from Isra at last to meet Xain's gaze. "If someone has been lying, it is not I. Not in this. We saw her. Theren fought her."

"Yet I thought you said her eyes were black," said Xain, and his baleful gaze turned to Theren. "How could you resist a wizard with the strength of magestones?"

"It is as I said before," said Theren carefully. "We

surprised her. I tried to flee, but she turned and ran first."

"Clearly there is something at work here," said Jia, her voice calm and measured, and her eyes going too often to Xain. "I am certain the three of you can understand how we would be . . . confused. Concerned, even. After all, the body casts doubt upon this whole affair."

Ebon steeled himself. They stood on the brink of the hearth, now, and it seemed their only choice was to plunge headlong into the flames. "Of course, Instructor. Yet I can offer no better explanation. And after all, *someone* had you under mindwyrd, did they not? And you as well, Instructor Dasko, for longer."

Theren tensed. Xain saw her sudden discomfort, and his eyes locked upon her. "But Isra was not the only mindmage at the Academy," he said.

Feigning surprise, Ebon looked to Theren. "You mean to insinuate that *Theren* had something to do with the mindwyrd? I am only recently acquainted with magic, and nowhere near so mighty in my lore as anyone else present—"

"An understatement if ever there was one," Xain spat.

Ebon's nostrils flared, but he pressed on, though anger now burned in his breast. "—but even I know that mindwyrd is only possible with magestones. And if Theren had been using magestones, her eyes would glow black. Theren, cast a spell."

She looked at him uneasily. But a moment later he saw her reach for her magic. Her eyes glowed white, and a nearby tray lifted into the air.

"There you have it. Theren has eaten no more magestones than I have, or you yourself, Dean," said Ebon, chuckling.

"*You dare to laugh?*" roared Xain. Ebon flinched as the dean stepped up to him. But he did not seize Ebon's robes, nor reach for his magic. He only loomed, his face a finger from Ebon's, until Ebon wanted to wilt and sink into the floor. "My son has been kidnapped—*my son,* you mewling, dung-licking coward—and you dare to laugh? First I am told that this girl, Isra, stole him away. Then you tell me that you saw her but did not stop her before she escaped. Now I see her corpse—and she has been dead, it seems, since she was supposed to have taken him. Laugh again. Laugh, I implore you, for it may very well break me, but I will take you with me when I shatter."

Ebon fought to reply, but pure terror had seized him. It was all he could do not to flee, and suddenly he had a desperate need for the privy. Everyone in the room stood frozen.

But it was Dasko who stepped forwards at last, still shaky on his feet but with a stern look in his eyes. He put a gentle hand on Xain's shoulder.

"Dean Forredar," he said quietly. "No one can begrudge you your wrath, nor your grief, which must be boundless in equal measure. These children are as con-

fused as we are, certainly, and far more frightened—
for to their mind, they have seen a walking corpse.
Ebon was flippant in a moment of foolishness. That
does not mean he is evil."

The instructor's words were gentle, his tone soothing. But Xain did not subside—rather, Ebon saw his
eyes go wide. He took a step back as though he was
regrouping, collecting himself.

"A walking corpse," he whispered. He turned stark
eyes on Isra's body. "A walking corpse."

Ebon knew not what the words meant, what dark
thing Xain thought he had discovered, but it only increased his fear. Jia stepped forwards into the sudden,
awkward silence. "They should return to class, Dean
Forredar, unless we have anything more for them."

Xain did not answer. He only turned back towards
the body upon the bed.

"Out with you," said Jia quickly, brushing them
away. They made for the door. She followed them out
and around the corner, where she stopped them. Ebon
was reminded of the last time she had pulled them
aside to speak privately, when they had been caught
sneaking into the Academy's vaults.

"I tire of repeating myself," she said ruefully. "But
I must ask you to forgive the dean. None of us can
imagine the pain of losing a son."

"Of course, Instructor," said Kalem politely.
Theren only stared off into nothing, while Ebon was
still thinking of Xain's look of dark recognition.

"I know he is angry with you, and anger may not always prompt honesty," Jia went on. "So I will ask you once more—is there anything else you know or have seen that could help? I am afraid there is little hope Erin is still alive, for we have heard nothing from his captors since he was taken. Yet we must cleave to what little hope remains."

That drew Ebon's attention. Jia must not know of the ransom note Xain had received. That meant Xain had not told the rest of the faculty. But he only shook his head and muttered, "Nothing, Instructor. I am sorry." Kalem and Theren gave soft words of agreement.

She sighed. "Very well. Then I have only one more thing to ask. Ebon, please go and see Astrea immediately. I have sent word to Perrin already. She will excuse the two of you. You seem closer to her than most, and so she should hear of this from you."

Ebon balked, looking back towards the healing ward for a moment. "I . . . I have no wish to tell her of Isra's death, Instructor."

Jia's eyes grew mournful. "Nor have I, Ebon. Nor has anyone. But would you rather she hear it from your lips, or as a rumor whispering through the Academy halls?"

He hung his head. "From me, I suppose. But I do not wish for such a duty."

She put a hand on his shoulder. "Thank you, Ebon. Your compassion has never been lacking—and that is why I keep my faith in you."

They left her then, and made their silent way through the halls. Ebon wondered if his friends, too, felt the presence of the corpse behind them, long after the healing ward was out of sight.

TWENTY-EIGHT

EBON'S STEPS GREW HEAVIER THE CLOSER HE DREW to Perrin's classroom, and when at last he reached her door he stopped short. Lifting his hand to turn the latch seemed an impossible task. He very much doubted Astrea even wanted to speak with him just now, as withdrawn as she had become, and he had no wish to speak to her, either, with the news he bore.

Then he thought of her sitting in the dining hall and hearing some whispered word at her elbow. In his mind he saw her turn at the mention of Isra's name and ask a sharp question. He saw the harsh, emotionless mask of her face break down a piece at a time.

Shaking his head, he opened the door.

A few of the students looked up at his return, but Astrea was not one of them. Ebon walked past her and went to Perrin. The instructor looked down at him with sorrow in her eyes.

"Instructor," Ebon murmured. "Jia has asked me to speak with Astrea alone, if I may."

"I think that is best," said Perrin. From the pain in her expression, she must have heard about Isra, and knew how hard Astrea would take the news.

Together they approached her, and when they reached the front table Perrin put a hand on the little girl's shoulder. So great was her size that her hand nearly stretched the width of Astrea's back.

"Astrea," she said quietly. "You are excused for a moment. Please follow Ebon outside upon the grounds. The two of you must speak."

She looked up at Ebon for a moment, her fingers still fidgeting with a flower she held in her hands. Her eyes were emotionless.

"I do not want to."

Ebon shared a look of confusion with Perrin. "Come, Astrea," he said. "It will not take long, but we must speak. I have something I must tell you."

"I do not want to hear it."

"Please, Astrea," said Perrin. "It is good for us to

speak of the things that trouble us, for otherwise they can fester in us like a sickness."

"I know that well enough by now," said Astrea, and grief sounded in her voice for the first time. With a sigh of resignation she pushed herself down the bench and stood, going to Ebon's side with a swish of her robes.

"Take whatever time you need," said Perrin. "And Astrea—if you do not wish to return to class afterwards, you need not."

Astrea shrugged and followed Ebon from the room. He felt suddenly uncertain, even more than he had before. He would have expected fear or grief from Astrea before she heard the actual news, for all tidings had been dark of late. He did not know how to react to this sullen indifference.

"Let us step out upon the grounds," said Ebon. "It is too stuffy in these halls."

She shrugged and followed him out through a white cedar door. Outside, students were practicing their spells in the open air, and he quickly guided her away from them, towards the hedges and the gardens that were free of any onlookers. Above, the sun shone bright in a clear sky, too clear and blue for Ebon's liking. He was exhausted after a night of shadows and death, and now he was the unwilling bearer of grim news.

"Would that I were like Dorren of old, and the skies changed to suit my mood," he said aloud. "Then the day would not be so cheery, as if it meant to mock me."

To his surprise, Astrea nodded. "I have sometimes

wished the same thing. But then we would be firemages, and I am glad to be an alchemist."

"Perrin would tell you to say 'transmuter.' But I am not she."

"You said it anyway," said Astrea. Though the words came out sounding harsh, she glanced up at him from under her wild, frizzy hair and gave a little smirk. It gladdened his heart—but it also pained him, for he knew the words he must say would tear that smirk from her lips and mayhap keep it away for good.

Get it over with, he chided himself.

"Come. Let us sit," he said, waving a hand towards a stone bench. She sat with him, staring at her hands in her lap, though her fingers did not fidget.

"Have you come to tell me that Isra is dead?" she asked suddenly, even as he was taking a deep breath to speak.

Ebon deflated at once, and his mouth worked as he fought for words. She glanced up at him and must have seen the answer in his eyes. "I . . . who told you?" Ebon stammered at last. "They should have let the word come to you from the right lips."

"Who cares where the words came from?" she muttered, looking back down at her hands. "But no, no one told me. I guessed it. Why else would Perrin let you take me from class? It is not as though anyone else could have died. I have no other friends left."

He knew she must break down at that—yet she did not. She only stared into the distance.

"Are you . . . all right?" he said, uncertain of what else to say.

She only shrugged.

"Astrea—"

"What should I say, Ebon?" she snapped. "I have told you I hate it when you ask if I am all right. Do you think I *can* be all right? Isra is my sister."

"Of course I did not mean that," he said quickly. "I only mean . . . I thought you might weep. No one could blame you if you did."

She turned away again. "How will tears help? Mayhap I spilled them all for Credell and Vali. I cannot cry any more."

Ebon leaned over, trying to catch her gaze, but still she would not look at him. He saw the great bags under her eyes, dark and hollow, so like Isra's had been. And he saw how thin and spindly her fingers had become and how gaunt and sallow her cheeks, and he wondered if she was eating enough. Mayhap grief and anger had taken such a toll on her body that no amount of food or rest could repair it.

And then he remembered seeing eyes like hers before, and hands and cheeks as well—but he had seen them in a mirror, and they were his own, and that had been when Momen died. And suddenly he thought he understood her better. He reached out and put a hand on hers, and she did not pull away.

"I had a brother. Did I ever tell you that?" he said. "I do not like to speak of him. He died when I was very young—just your age, in fact. When I heard what had happened I went into my room, where I remained for days while everyone waited for me to stop weeping."

She turned to him, eyes flashing. "I have told you already that I do not need to—"

Quickly he raised his hands in token of surrender. "I do not mean that you should weep. For in truth, I did not. Tears would not come. But that does not mean I did not grieve. I missed him more than I could imagine. It still hurts to speak of him, though I am no closer to crying now."

That gave her pause. Her fingers fidgeted. "You did not feel bad? Because you could not grieve?"

"I felt terrible," he murmured. "Sometimes I still do. But in time I learned that I could not blame myself. We all face loss in our own way. If I could have spent less time in guilt, I would have. I suppose that in the end it was hard for me to believe he was gone. I never even saw his corpse, for he was burned in the distant land where he was killed, and there, too, were his ashes scattered."

Astrea looked down at her shoes. "That is an ill thing."

"We do not always get to say good-bye," said Ebon. "And in truth, I know it does not matter. If I had seen his body or been there when they burned it, he would not have heard my farewell. Sky above, even if I had been there when he passed and we had whispered our parting to each other, nothing would have changed.

He would still be gone, and I would still be here. Yet mayhap the pain would not be so great. I like to believe it would not."

Then he looked at her carefully. "What of you, Astrea? Do you wish to say your farewell? I could ask for it, and I doubt any instructor would refuse you. Not even the dean."

For the first time he saw tears in her eyes, though she was quick to blink them away. She shook her head quickly. "No. You said you wish you could have spent less time in mourning. I want the same thing, and I do not think that seeing Isra would help me. It would only make things worse. You had no choice in the matter—but I do."

He nodded. "Very well. Your words are wise beyond your years—but then, that is no great surprise to those of us who must suffer in class beside you, always overshadowed by your wit."

She glanced at him, and he gave her a sad smile. She did not return it, but her eyes softened, and she shook her head disdainfully.

"Do not be an idiot, Ebon."

"As well tell the sun not to shine—and we know already that that is futile. Will you walk with me?"

"If you want me to," she said. But he could hear the gratitude that lay beneath her words, and she leaped up to follow him with surprising eagerness. And the day's beauty no longer seemed so offensive as they strolled along.

TWENTY-NINE

THE MIDDAY MEAL PASSED SILENTLY FOR EBON AND his friends, for they did not find themselves much in the mood for talking. Together they made their way through the halls towards the library and wordlessly climbed the stairs to their nook on the third level.

As they reached their armchairs, Ebon saw a note resting upon one of them—the one upon which he usually sat. It was only a brief scrawl: *Come to Leven's tavern tonight.*

Ebon looked it over and then met the eyes of his friends. "It must be from Mako."

"Truly? Do you think so?" said Theren in mock surprise, her eyes wide.

Soft footsteps made them fall silent, and they turned to look behind them. Ebon froze where he stood. It was Lilith, hands tucked into her sleeves, eyes shifting uneasily as she tried to avoid their gazes.

"Good day," she said quietly.

For a moment no one answered her, nor even moved. Then Ebon and Theren had the same thought at the same time, and both leaped towards his armchair to turn it about. But they ran into each other instead, and both stepped back awkwardly.

"I will—no, I will fetch another," said Theren quickly.

"Of course. Here," said Ebon, waving Lilith down into the chair.

She took her seat, still not meeting his eyes, while Theren fetched another armchair and placed it beside Lilith's. But she sat in it instead of offering it to Ebon, and so he was forced to take her armchair instead. Kalem had stood in silence, gawking at the proceedings with wide eyes, and it was only after all the other three had seated themselves that he started, as if waking from a dream, and took his own chair.

For a long moment, silence reigned as they all looked at Lilith in the lamplight, and she tried to avoid looking back at them.

"Where is Nella?" said Ebon, desperate to break the stiffness that had settled over them like a sheet of ice.

"We have opposite study schedules," said Lilith.

"Ah."

Again, a long quiet stretched. Ebon's fingers drummed on the arms of his chair.

At last Lilith cleared her throat. "Well," she said quietly. "I suppose there is no use trying to pretend that this is not very strange for all of us."

Theren let out a hysterical bark of laughter, too loud and too high, and then fell silent. Ebon quashed a snicker. Kalem only frowned. "Did you . . . and understand that I do not mean you are not welcome. But did you come to us for any particular purpose?"

Lilith nodded. "I had heard what happened to Isra," she said. "Is it true that the three of you saw her corpse?"

Ebon met eyes with his friends, hoping they all knew better than to say anything of the events that had transpired the night before. "We did," he said.

"Is it true she is long dead?" said Lilith. "That is what the rumors are saying."

"That is true," said Ebon. "Though we are not sure how."

"Because you saw her living, and little more than a week ago," said Lilith, nodding. "How can that be?"

"We have an idea," said Theren, sitting up.

"Theren," said Ebon.

She glared. "Lilith has not betrayed our trust thus far, Ebon. And mayhap she will have an idea for how Isra did it that we have not yet thought of." Lilith leaned forwards to listen, and Theren went on. "I have never heard of magic that could do something of this sort. My first thought was therianthropy, but if the corpse were a weremage it would not look like Isra—"

"—and if it had been a weremage in the kitchens, they would not have had mindmagic to battle you," said Lilith.

Theren slumped in her chair. "That is just what we said."

Lilith frowned, looking into her lap. For a moment Ebon hoped beyond hope that she would, in fact, know how such a feat might be accomplished. But when she lifted her gaze, she only shook her head. "I have no idea how it might have been done. I am sorry."

"It is hardly your fault," said Theren with a small smile. Lilith returned it. Kalem grimaced.

A thought struck Ebon, and he worked it around until he had thought of a question that seemed to pose no danger. "Lilith . . . have you heard aught of Gregor since last we sought him out?"

Lilith's mood darkened, and she shook her head. "I have not—not exactly, anyway. But something happened upon the Seat just last night. A fear has spread throughout my family again, just as it did when the Seat was attacked and the High King suspected us of being complicit. Now our terror is not so great, but it has certainly returned. I will try to reach out to Farah again and see if she knows what happened."

"And we will ask Mako," said Theren, giving Ebon

a meaningful look. He thought he understood—they must keep up appearances that they knew no more than Lilith did.

"Will you see him soon?" said Lilith. "Mayhap I should come. We could pool our knowledge."

"No," said Theren at once.

Lilith frowned. "I do not mean to—"

Theren shook her head. "You are not the one who worries me. Mako would not be pleased to see you. You have been through enough already, and I would not bring you within arm's reach of that man, not for all the gold upon the High King's Seat."

That made Lilith subside, and she gave Theren a wry smile. "Are you certain? I wonder if you know how much gold that would be. It is a large amount. I myself would not hesitate to have a meal with Mako if I could get my hands upon it."

Theren smirked. "You goldbags. Your coffers overflow, and yet always you seek more."

Lilith giggled, and it was a sound so foreign that Ebon froze in amazement. She stood and brushed at her robes.

"I should be going," she said. "I have intruded upon your time long enough."

"It was no intrusion," said Theren. "You could stay if you wish."

"I . . . I have studies," said Lilith, looking down in embarrassment. "Jia requires a dissertation from me. Mayhap another time."

She stepped out between the armchairs—but Theren raised a hand as she did, and Lilith took it on instinct. They held each other only a moment, but their fingers dragged against each other as they parted, as though reluctant to let go.

That night, the streets of the city seemed filled with a heightened tension–or mayhap it was only the fear in the hearts of Ebon and his friends that made it seem so. Oddly, Ebon was calmest of them all. Mayhap it was because he had faced so much danger already that he was growing inured to it.

They breathed a heavy sigh of relief when they caught sight of Leven's tavern. Together they entered as quickly as they could and tramped the snow off their boots in the doorway.

At the bar stood a broad man hidden beneath a black cloak, his hood drawn up. He turned at the sound of their entrance, though no one else seemed to pay them any mind. Ebon saw the flash of Mako's eyes beneath the cowl. He came to join them at their customary table, a bottle of wine in one hand and four cups clutched in the other.

He wasted no time on pleasantries. "Darkness take this mindmage sow," he growled. Theren sat up straighter, but he only sneered. "Not you. I mean Isra. I can find no trace of her."

"No trace but the corpse, you mean," said Kalem.

"Which we already know is not hers," said Mako, growing angrier still. "I can deceive the eye when I wish and remain unseen when I must. But even I cannot conjure my own corpse out of thin air, nor hide from every prying eye upon the Seat. When at last I get my hands on her, I will flay her slow just for the inconvenience she has caused me."

"Is it possible you are jealous?" said Theren lightly. "You seem frankly obsessed with her skill at deception, Mako."

The way the bodyguard's jaw clenched, Ebon feared he might lash out at her. But he only tightened his fist around his cup until Ebon could hear its wood squeaking.

"I find her cunning as troubling as you do, no doubt," said Ebon. "But we have another problem. We told the faculty that we saw her in the kitchens, and so the three of us have fallen under suspicion. I worry what that will mean for us, though of course we are innocent when it comes to Isra."

"Innocent?" said Mako with a cruel grin. "That is an odd word for it, and not one I would choose."

"We did not kill her, is what he means," said Kalem, as Ebon flushed and lowered his gaze.

"Well, only catching her will prove that," said Theren.

Mako pounded a fist on the table. "Yet that seems impossible, though our watch upon the Academy has been ceaseless, except for last night when I summoned my fighters to the sewers—but we know she did not infiltrate the Academy last night, for we saw her below. She is not in any of the Yerrins' usual hiding spots, and she is nowhere else upon the Seat, for I have eyes in every cranny."

"Mayhap she has used mindwyrd to send false tales to you?" said Ebon. "One of your spies might have seen her but been charmed into telling you they had not."

Mako's eyes rolled so far back that Ebon thought the bodyguard might faint. "Oh, how clever of you to think of such a thing, Ebon. If only I had thought of that immediately and taken precautions to prevent it. You should be the family's master of spies, and not I."

Theren leaned over. "I believe he means to say that he has taken precautions against such a ruse."

Ebon scowled into his drink. "It was only a suggestion."

"I do not need your suggestions," said Mako. "I need your lover."

A chill stole up Ebon's spine, freezing him in place. He glared at Mako. "Do not speak of her to me. She has nothing to do with this."

"Not yet," said Mako, glaring right back. "But she must, or we are lost. Go to her. Tell her we need help beyond our own means."

"What are you suggesting?"

"To you? Nothing." Mako threw back his cup of wine and stood. "But the words will carry weight with her. Send them along, little Ebon. Go tomorrow night—I and mine will watch your path along the streets and ensure you come to no harm. Send word to me afterwards as soon as you can."

He walked to the door and vanished into the night. Kalem and Theren stared at Ebon in wonder.

"What was that about?" said Theren.

Ebon said nothing, but only stared into his wine, his heart thundering with fear.

THIRTY

EBON WOKE WITH GUILT ROILING IN HIS GUT.

After seeing Mako, he had wrestled long into the night with his feelings. The last thing he wanted was to involve Adara again. His kin had brought her enough dangers already, and though she always reassured him that her contacts in the guild of lovers would not betray her, still he worried. Though he did not understand the message he was supposed to relay, he did not doubt he would feel even more uncomfortable about it if he did.

His thoughts were in turmoil all morning. But at last, just before the bell rang for breakfast, he fetched parchment and a quill and scribbled a note to Adara, sending it along with Mellie at the front door. Isra's corpse still lay in the Academy, and the investigation would not stop simply because he wished it to. If they did not find Isra, surely it would only be a matter of time before the faculty found out about the amulet, and then they were all lost.

The day's studies went by in a blur. Ebon managed to keep up appearances well enough that Perrin did not bark at him for his wandering attention, and of course Kalem and Theren mostly left him alone in the library, for their thoughts were just as preoccupied. After dinner he set off into the streets for the second day in a row, but this time alone. He looked all about him, hoping to catch a glimpse of a black-clad assassin haunting his steps. But he saw nothing, and wondered if that should make him feel better or worse.

Though the troubles that burdened him seemed crushing in their weight, he still felt a wash of relief the moment he stepped across Adara's threshold. She came to Ebon before he reached the top of the stairs, and he heaved a great sigh as she took him into her arms. The last of his anxiety washed away like soot stains in a downpour.

"My love," she murmured. "I was overjoyed at your message, but now I wonder at its purpose. I can see that a great many things weigh heavily upon you."

"You do not know the half of it," said Ebon, "but I can fix that. Come. There is much to tell."

As quickly as he could, he informed her of all that had transpired since last he had seen her. She listened attentively, stopping him sharply when he left out a detail and threw the tale into confusion. And when he reached the end and told her what Mako had said, he saw her olive skin go a shade lighter.

"He used those words, did he?" she muttered softly. "Darkness take that man."

"What did he mean?" said Ebon. "I hear no special truth in the words, but he seemed to think they held one, and now it seems you feel the same."

"Oh, he does not speak in some code," she said. "Yet he knew that I would know what he meant. How did he learn . . ." She shook her head and stood, going to the cabinet where she kept her wine and her mead. "Never mind that. I need something to wet my throat."

"Do not—that is . . ." Ebon paused, his cheeks flushing with embarrassment. "Might I try some of your mead, instead of wine?"

She arched an eyebrow and gave him a little smirk. "Are you certain? It is an acquired taste. I doubt you will like it."

He raised his hands. "How will I ever acquire it if I do not try?"

Adara studied him for a moment and shrugged before bringing the bottle of mead over to the table. First she poured into his cup, but only a little splash, and then nudged it towards him. "Try it.

I would not waste a whole cup on you if you do not enjoy it."

Ebon lifted it to his lips and took a sniff. It did not smell . . . bad, exactly. But neither did it make his mouth water. He tilted the cup back.

The taste that slid down his tongue and into his throat was both familiar and foreign—like honey without the sweet. Too, there were herbs and spices aplenty; as a Drayden, he could not help but pick some of them out. It was not entirely unpleasant, but neither did it set him at ease the way the first good swig of wine often did.

"Acquired, mayhap," he said. "But not awful at first blush, either."

Adara seemed impressed despite herself. "Indeed? Mayhap I should have expected as much from a man whose tastes are as cultured as yours." She smirked to let him know the words were playful and then filled his cup nearly to the brim before doing the same with her own. Ebon's second sip was better than the first, and made the more pleasant when Adara settled herself sideways across his lap, draping an arm about his shoulders as she met his gaze.

"Now, tell me what hidden meaning I have brought from Mako's lips to your ears," said Ebon. "I do not like that my family's man knows something of you that I do not."

"Oh, but there are so many things you do not know about me, Ebon—and so many more things I look forward to teaching you." Though her words were light, and her tone more so, he could see the concern lurking in her dark eyes. It soon came out in a sigh. "Your man has learned—though I know not how—of a certain . . . friend I have. A friend who owes me a favor."

Ebon's jaw clenched, though he tried to hide it. He inspected his cup carefully, feigning nonchalance. "Is your friend a guest?"

She let out a slow breath through her nose, and he could hear her trying to hide her annoyance just as hard as he had tried to hide his interest. "They are not. In fact they are not interested in lovers at all, for coin or otherwise. But they are . . . well, I did them a favor once, long before I came to this life. I have waited many years for sufficient reason to ask that that favor be returned. But I wonder that I did not think of it before, for certainly I think they could be of help."

"I would not have you waste your one chance on me," said Ebon. "After all, I hardly think they could be more useful in finding Isra than Mako has been."

"You do not know my friend," said Adara, giving him a grim little smile. "You have said before that if anyone can find the girl, Mako can. That is not true. The truth is that if anyone can find the girl, my friend can."

"But that is all the more reason you should not waste such a chance on me," said Ebon. "I may not even need such help."

"Yet you may," said Adara. "And if things go ill for you without such a favor, it could mean your life. That is something I cannot allow."

She rose, leaving Ebon's lap suddenly cool. From a cupboard she drew parchment and a quill, and when she had scribbled a message she sealed it with wax using a seal Ebon had never seen before. But he could not catch a glimpse of its design before she whisked it away and down the steps. He heard her sharp whistle as she flagged down a messenger, and then in a moment she reappeared in the room.

"I must get dressed for a walk," she said. "And so must you."

"Now?" said Ebon. "Surely you cannot mean to see your friend tonight. How can you know your message will find them?"

"It will," she said. "And they will come at once. Have no fear of that. You must not be dressed in Academy robes when we see them. I have some other garments that will do."

She undressed quickly and made Ebon do the same. When his hands wandered towards her, she smirked and slapped them away. She then bundled herself up in winter clothes and gave Ebon an outfit of his own, one that was elegant without drawing much attention. As soon as they had laced up their boots, she went to him and pulled him down for a quick peck on the cheek.

"You must promise that you will not stare overmuch, nor act out of turn," she said. "And you *must not* ask me any questions. Do you understand? Mayhap one day I can explain. But not now."

"Very well," he said.

She caught his cheek and turned him to face her. She stared at him for a long moment. "Promise me."

He frowned. "I promise. Why? What is wrong?"

"Nothing is wrong," she said. "But . . . well, things are about to become very different. For both of us."

With one more kiss, she drew him out and into the snowy night.

The afternoon now wore on, and the days were shorter besides. Adara hurried as she led him along winding streets and alleys, for it would soon be dusk. Every so often he would take her hand—not out of the need for guidance or the fear of losing her in the crowd, but simply so that he could feel the warmth of her skin on his own.

They were making east now, in nearly the same direction where lay the Drayden manor. But after a time they turned off the main road that ran from the western gates to the east. They had long passed the Academy to the south, and the High King's palace loomed close above them when Adara turned aside and led him north a ways, through streets and alleys that grew narrower with every step. Soon they reached a little shop with a large red door, where Adara paused. From its chimney wafted the smell of coals and the sharp, bitter tang of molten metal. But this was no ironsmith—in the windows of the shop were set little trinkets and dishes of silver.

"Around back," Adara murmured. "It would not do for us to be seen entering the front door—and my friend would prefer it that way as well, I think."

To the shop's rear was a small door of plain, unadorned wood. Upon this Adara tapped thrice, and then twice more after a pause. In a moment Ebon heard scuttling footsteps within, and then the door creaked open. Into view came a thin little man, wild grey hair sticking out in all directions. Though the day's light waned, still he blinked at them as though a bright torch had been thrust into his eyes.

"Little Adara," he breathed. "Sky above, girl, but it is good to see you."

"And you, Aurel," said Adara. She bent to give the wizened man a kiss upon the cheek. "Are we expected?"

"I should say so," said Aurel, shaking his head. He stepped inside, waving them after him. "Between this and all the goings-on before the attack, I will be amazed if my heart does not give out before its time."

Adara took Ebon's hand and drew him inside. It took Ebon's eyes a moment to adjust to the dim. When they did, he saw a small sitting room with a stone floor, warmed by a hearth with a metal grate for a screen. Mayhap a pace from the hearth was a low, modest table with three stools. One of the stools was occupied. Aurel glanced at the figure who sat there and then at Adara and Ebon before he withdrew from the room, closing the door behind him with a soft *click*.

The figure rose. He wore a cloak of plain brown, but its unremarkable color could not hide the fine weave of its cloth, nor the work of the expert hands that had sewn its hem. The cloak covered no armor, but there was a sword at his waist—a fine thing, not the plain blade of a soldier. He lifted his hands to throw back his hood. Well-tousled, sandy hair showed a few strands of grey, and his eyes were keen as they took in Adara and Ebon. There was something intensely familiar about him, but at first Ebon could not place it. Then he saw the brooch that pinned the cloak together. It bore the royal seal. *A palace guard,* he thought—but then the truth came to him, and his limbs shook. He fell to one knee and bowed his head.

"Your . . . Your Highness," he gasped, his throat a desert.

Lord Prince Eamin, son of the High King and presumptive heir to the throne, took a step forwards and inclined his head. But Adara did not kneel, only gave a deep curtsey, and to Ebon's shock, Eamin did not seem surprised in the least.

"Well met, son. But come, and treat me no different than you would your friend Adara. Kneeling is all good for the ceremony of a throne room, but it seems a little grandiose for Aurel's little parlor, would you not say?"

Bright teeth flashed in a grin, and Ebon matched it without thinking. His heart stopped when Eamin held forth a hand. They clasped wrists, and the Lord Prince pulled him to his feet. Then, to Ebon's growing wonder, Adara stepped forwards. She kissed one of Eamin's cheeks, and then the other, the way an Idrisian greeted their close friend, or mayhap lover—though she had said that was not the case, he reminded himself.

"Your Highness," she said. "My heart is glad to see you again."

"My own mood is as I said it would be the last time I beheld you," said Eamin. "Though I am pleased to be in your company, my thoughts are solemn, knowing you would not have called except at the utmost end of need. What troubles you, Adara?"

"The same thing that troubles my friend here," said Adara, inclining her head towards Ebon. On instinct, Ebon ducked his head. The Lord Prince could not have gotten a very good look at him beneath his hood, and if Adara did not wish to speak his name, he would not speak it either. He knew nothing of the Lord Prince's politics, but would not be surprised to find that Eamin, like most of Underrealm, held no high opinion of the family Drayden.

"Well? Speak on, son," said Eamin. "We have all three of us wasted enough of a night that might be spent in merriment."

"Of course, Your Highness," said Ebon, bowing still further. His mind raced, wondering where to begin. "I . . . I imagine you know something of the Academy murders?"

Eamin's countenance darkened at once. "I do," he said softly. "Though Her Majesty was quick to send her guards to the citadel, I wish we could have done more, and more quickly. But the killer is dead now, or so they say."

"They say wrong," said Ebon. "She is alive. I do not know how. But she is alive and plotting further evil upon the Seat."

"A corpse was found in the Great Bay," said Eamin, his frown deepening. "How can she be alive if we know where her body lies?"

Ebon quailed, for he could hear impatience in the Lord Prince's voice. But then Eamin put a gentle hand on his shoulder. "Do not quiver so, son. You have not raised my ire—only if what you say is true, it is very troubling, and it has darkened my thoughts."

"It is true," Ebon insisted. "I saw her—I, and some others. It was not long ago. And when the corpse was found, they said it had been dead for weeks. That cannot be. She is out there somewhere and has found a way to deceive us all. But no one will believe us, and so we can find no help to prove it. I only want to ferret her out of hiding before she attacks the Academy again."

Eamin paused, staring into the fire. After a time he met Adara's gaze.

"Please, Your Highness," she said quietly. "Trust him in this."

Eamin looked to Ebon, and Ebon understood at once: Adara was in fact asking him to trust *her*. He thought the weight of her faith in him might press him into the stone floor. Slowly the Lord Prince nodded.

"Very well," he said. "I have some agents who may be relied upon. I will have them search for Isra. If she is upon the Seat, they will find her—wherever she may be."

Hope quailed in Ebon's breast. Mako had been saying much the same thing for weeks. But then he realized that this was not another promise from Mako—this was the Lord Prince.

Then Eamin shook his shoulders as though waking from a deep slumber, and his mood lightened. "But so simple a request is nothing, Adara. You must not consider my debt to you repaid. Do not hesitate to call upon me again."

Adara smiled. "A small deed from a busybody weighs heavier than a great deed from the lazy, they say."

"They are fools if they call you lazy," said Eamin. "And speaking of which, I am sure the two of you have further business to attend tonight, as I do myself. If we may . . .?"

He gestured, and they hastened towards the door together. Once in the alley, Eamin made to go in one direction, while Adara and Ebon headed in the other. But just before they all departed, Eamin stopped them with a raised hand and peered at Ebon beneath his hood.

"It is good to see a Drayden on the side of right," he said softly. "Such a thing is less common than one might hope."

Ebon swallowed hard. So Eamin had recognized him after all. He felt a fool for thinking he could conceal his face so well.

"I hope my conduct may always please Your Highness so," he murmured, and took a knee again.

"Come now, I said there was no need for that," said Eamin. "Stay your course, Drayden. Though not all your kin may feel the same, I think you do your name proud. Prouder than any since . . . he would have been your brother, would he not?"

Everything went still. Ebon could not move a muscle—he even noticed that his mouth hung open, but he could not close it.

"Momen was a good man," said Eamin. "A great one, in fact, and high in the estimation of many across the nine kingdoms. Though I would not guess that your kin have told you so. He deserved better than what he got."

At last Ebon's mouth worked, though just enough to croak, "Thank you, Your Highness. But how did you . . .?"

Eamin smiled sadly. "Another time, I hope. Some tales are not worth telling if they cannot be told properly."

And then he was gone, vanishing through the gently falling snow.

THIRTY-ONE

EBON STAYED AT ADARA'S HOME AS LONG AS HE COULD, but eventually he made his way back to the Academy. The next day he muddled through his classes in a fog, still overawed about the Lord Prince. He half expected some royal messenger to appear at the Academy with news that Isra had been discovered and that the threat was now over. But of course no such message came.

Kalem saw something odd in his demeanor and asked him about it. But Ebon did not wish to tell the story twice, and bid him wait for Theren. They saw no trace of her at breakfast, or at the midday meal. At first

Ebon thought little of it, but when she had not appeared by the beginning of the afternoon's studies he began to grow worried. Together they conducted a quick search for her, looking through the dining hall and the hallways outside, and then even darting upstairs to seek her in the dormitories. But they found no trace of her, and so they went to the library—where they found Theren at last, waiting for them in their alcove. She was shaking, and to their surprise, she sat with Lilith.

"Theren!" said Ebon. "We looked all over for you. What is wrong?"

"I . . . they came for me," said Theren. Lilith looked up in dismay, and Ebon saw that she was clutching one of Theren's hands tightly in both of her own. "The instructors, I mean. I was called to my instructor's office—Nestor, I mean—and there I found the dean, as well as some instructors of the other branches. They sat me down in a chair, and when I tried to resist, they forced me. Then they cast . . . some sort of spell upon me, though I know not what they did. I only saw their eyes glowing and felt the itch on my skin where their magic probed me."

"Why?" said Ebon. "What were they looking for?"

"I have just told you I do not know!" snapped Theren.

But Kalem had blanched, and he sank heavily into one of the armchairs. "I know what they were doing," he said. "They sought the mark of enchantment upon you."

A glance at Theren told Ebon she knew nothing

more of Kalem's words than he did. "What is the mark of enchantment?"

"Do you remember when Theren searched for Lilith's spell-sight within the vaults? It is like that. A sort of trace left upon someone who uses a magical artifact. They sought for a sign that Theren had used an enchanted object."

"But why?" said Ebon. "Why Theren? Of course *we* know she carries the amulet, but how could they?" But then he froze where he stood. His eyes went to Lilith. They had not told her of Kekhit's amulet.

"Do not trouble yourself about that," said Theren. "I have told Lilith about it already."

"You *what?*" said Kalem. He threw his hands up in the air. "Is there anyone left in the Academy who does not know?"

Theren glared at him, and he wilted. "Save us from your dramatics. I trust her. But do you not see? Xain has grown suspicious that I have been using mindwyrd. Ebon showed the instructors that I have no magestone in my blood, but Xain knows that the amulet of Kekhit has been stolen. The faculty may once have thought that the amulet was in Isra's possession, but now Xain suspects it is in mine."

Ebon slumped in his armchair. But then he had another thought, and he straightened once more. "But wait. Kalem, you told us that spell-sight is wildly unreliable, and that no one would take its signature for evidence."

"So I did," said Kalem. "And the mark of enchantment is even more inscrutable. But think, Ebon. Xain is desperate. His *son* is missing. Do you think he would withhold his hand from any method that might recover Erin? It is like we were when we were trying to prove Lilith was the Academy killer—meaning no offense, Lilith."

Lilith arched an eyebrow. "Of course. And you are correct—only Xain is more dangerous now than you were then, because his own blood is in danger, and because he has the power of the office of the dean."

Theren looked at them with fear in her eyes. "But why did they not find the mark? I have—" She cast a quick glance about them to look for eavesdroppers and then went on in a whisper. "I have been using the amulet, after all."

"I do not think the mark lasts for very long," said Kalem. "It is days since we fought Isra in the grotto. The mark must have faded."

"Then I must get rid of it before they try again."

Ebon frowned. "Mayhap you are right. It seems too dangerous now. But what if Isra should reappear?"

"I will be unable to stop her if I am in a Mystic prison with their knives digging into my skin," snapped Theren. Lilith shuddered, and her hands crossed over her chest as she turned her gaze away. "I cannot carry it with me now, in any case. Why should I not be rid of it?"

"What will you do?" said Kalem. "Will you leave it

for the instructors to find? Do you not think that will raise suspicion, that it would reappear *just* after they investigated you?"

"I will throw it into the Great Bay, and good riddance," said Theren.

To Ebon's surprise, Lilith reached out and took Theren's hand. Theren looked over after a moment, and Ebon saw the sadness in Lilith's gaze as their eyes met.

"You must keep it. Only a little longer. It cannot be long before we find her," said Lilith.

Kalem leaned forwards, focusing on Ebon. "To that end—what happened last night, Ebon? Was Adara able to help you?"

For a moment Ebon hesitated, wondering if he should tell them—particularly Lilith—of the Lord Prince. But it seemed there was nothing for it, and soon he had spilled the whole of the tale. As soon as he told them of Eamin, they all went stone-still in their seats, and Ebon could see something very much like worship shining in Kalem's eyes.

"The Lord Prince," he whispered in reverence.

Even Theren's panic seemed to have diminished somewhat. "These are the first glad tidings we have heard since the Academy murders first began."

"How?" said Kalem. "I mean to say, how could Adara . . . it would be impressive enough if she knew him as a guest—that would make her a high courtesan indeed, and worthy of much honor. But outside of her business? What could possibly have brought the two of them together?"

Theren scoffed. "You make it sound as though the Lord Prince is some coward who spends all his days cooped up in the palace. He has walked upon many roads and fought in many battles both great and small. He is one of the few goldbags who even I have some measure of respect for—outside of present company, of course. Adara could have met him anywhere—and if she performed him some service, he would not forget it."

Ebon shrugged. "I do not know. I only know what she told me, and that was precious little."

But in his mind he was wrestling with the same thought that had plagued him since their rendezvous the night before. Yes, it was astounding that Adara knew the Lord Prince, and especially on such terms. But more perturbing still was the fact that Mako knew of their relationship, if so it could be called. How could the bodyguard have learned that secret, if he had only known Adara for a short time?

Mako's ever-growing omniscience had grown beyond the bounds of unsettling and was now close to terrifying. And yet the man still could not locate Isra upon the High King's Seat.

Where can she be?

Lilith loosed a sigh and shifted in her seat. "This is most comforting. If the Lord Prince himself has joined the search, it cannot be very long before Isra is dug out of whatever dark corner she has hidden herself in."

"I am not so sure," said Kalem, scowling as he put his chin on his fist. "After all, she has conjured her own corpse out of thin air. I would once have counted that impossible."

"Many things are impossible until someone of industry carries them out," said Mako.

Ebon leaped out of his chair. Kalem tried to do the same, but tripped over his own feet and went crashing to the ground. Theren leaped up with her eyes aglow, and Lilith fought to stand, but her weakened limbs almost betrayed her. She opened her mouth to scream. Mako thrust one finger at her, and his face twisted in a scowl.

"Keep your silence, and keep your life. Lose one, and lose the other."

"It is all right, Lilith," said Theren quickly. She went to Lilith and put a hand on her arm. "He is no threat. Not now, and not here, at any rate."

"What is he doing in the library?" hissed Lilith. She looked around, and Ebon did the same, for it seemed impossible that no one else could see him. But no other students were in sight, as if by chance—though of course Ebon knew it must be by Mako's design.

"He comes and goes, it seems." Ebon glared at Mako. "What are you doing here, other than frightening us all half to death by appearing from nowhere?"

"The little goldshitter is very flip for one who is sitting and taking council with a Yerrin," growled Mako, who had not taken his furious eyes from Lilith. "But that discussion must be had another time, for matters of true import are afoot. I come with news of Gregor."

Ebon felt the blood drain from his face. Kalem and Theren went very still, and even Lilith gulped before lifting her chin and fixing Mako with a defiant look.

"What of him?" said Ebon. "I thought the Mystics took him."

"They did not," said Mako. "He killed them all. He has not yet managed to flee the Seat, but he is about to. Now, in fact. We must stop him."

"Asking for help again?" said Theren, smirking through her unease. "This is truly a time of wonders."

Mako sneered at her. "The dregs of my resources you may be, but dregs are better than an empty cup. Gregor has killed most of my agents already, and those who remain still bear grievous wounds. Isra is nowhere to be seen, but I need you to contend with a firemage at Gregor's side."

"You mean an elementalist," said Kalem, by reflex. Then he froze.

Slowly, ever so slowly, Mako turned his baleful glare upon the boy. Ebon thought Kalem would die upon the spot, the boy looked so terrified.

"I am sorry," he whimpered. "It was an accident."

Mako ignored him. "Girl," he said, looking at Theren. "Go and fetch your amulet."

"No."

The bodyguard's jaw twitched. "I did not ask you a question."

"Yet I gave you an answer. They are searching for it, and they already suspect me. Besides, you said Isra was not there."

"She was not when I left," said Mako. "That does not mean she has not appeared since, or that Gregor is not making his way to her even now."

"Still I will not bring it," said Theren. "I am no good to any of us if I land in prison—and I value my own skin too highly, besides."

To Ebon's surprise and relief, Mako grinned. "That sentiment, at least, I can sympathize with. Very well—but I hope you are impressive enough without it. Meet me in the gardens as quickly as you can. You know where. Do not bring the Yerrin girl."

Before they could answer, he turned and vanished into the bookshelves.

"'The Yerrin girl,' he says." Lilith snorted. "Darkness take him. I will come if I wish."

"You will not," said Theren at once. "You have not fully recovered from your ordeal, and you have been through too much already on our account. Besides, if you come with us, I do not doubt that Mako will try to slit your throat."

"Let him," said Lilith, raising her chin. "Only a fool threatens a wizard."

"Two wizards, you mean," said Theren. "For I would not let him touch you. Yet still you should not come."

Lilith's mouth twitched, though whether towards a

smile or a frown, Ebon could not say. "Do you think I trust you to look after yourself? You have failed to do so in the past. I will remain here, but I order you to come back whole."

At the word *order*, Ebon tensed, expecting an outburst from Theren. Beside him, Kalem looked between the girls uncertainly.

But Theren's dark cheeks flushed darker for a moment, and she stepped forwards. "Yes, my dear."

And then she kissed her.

Far too much had happened in far too short a time for Ebon to know what to make of this. He stood stock still, heedless of his mouth hanging open, unable to do so much as blink. He was only tangentially aware of Kalem beside him, teeth gleaming in a fool's grin. The moment lasted only a few heartbeats. Then Theren stepped away and hastened off, passing between the boys as she did so. She seized their elbows and dragged them after her.

"If the two of you say so much as a word, I will throw you from the balcony to the library's first floor," she hissed.

"I would not dream of it," said Kalem. But his grin said far more than words ever could.

THIRTY-TWO

THEY SLIPPED THROUGH THE LIBRARY'S FRONT DOORS when Jia was not watching and soon had passed through the garden to the place where they knew Mako's secret entrance waited. At first the space between the hedges looked empty—but then Mako appeared, stepping out from a gap in the plants that looked far too narrow for his broad frame.

"Closer," he said. "Ebon, give me your hand."

Curious, Ebon did so—and then gave an indignant cry as Mako seized his sleeve and tore off several long strips of cloth.

"Cease your mewling," growled Mako. "Now the two of you—turn around."

One by one he used the strips of cloth to blindfold Theren and Kalem, and such was the urgency in his movements that even Theren did not complain. While Ebon turned away, Mako pushed some panel or lever, and they heard the soft sliding of stone upon grass and snow. The air within the passage was cool, cooler even than the wintry air outside. With one hand on each of his friend's shoulders to guide them, Ebon made his way forwards through the dark, and before long Mako had them out on the streets.

"Into the sewers again," said Mako. "But not west this time."

He led them down a gutter and into the stinking passageways beneath the streets. But whether because of the chilled air or because Ebon was growing used to it, the stench was not as noisome as it had been before. Mako set a quick pace, and from the markings on the ceiling, Ebon knew they were heading mostly east.

"Where is Gregor going?" he said.

"He is trying to sail from the Seat and vanish into the nine kingdoms," said Mako. "But the western docks are watched, for the grotto was near them, and so he thinks to have better luck on the other side of the island."

"How did he overpower so many Mystics when they caught him before?" said Kalem.

Mako threw him a quick glance over his shoulder.

"I did not wait around to watch the fight. But you saw his size."

"And how easily he slapped you about," said Theren offhandedly.

The bodyguard said nothing, but Ebon saw his fingers twitch as though they itched to draw his dagger.

They went on in silence for a long while, until Ebon was certain they must have traveled much, much farther than last time. Eventually Mako stopped at the intersection of two tunnels and pressed himself to one of the corners.

"We must proceed cautiously from here," he said. "We might encounter Yerrin guards accompanying Gregor to his boat. But, too, we might find more Mystics, for they have been alerted to Gregor's movements and are coming for him."

"Mystics?" said Kalem. "Then why do we not let them catch the villain, and leave ourselves out of it?"

"Because if they catch him, they are not going to ask after Isra," said Mako. "They believe that Isra is dead, for they have seen her corpse. That is why we must find him first."

"You have thrown us into the middle of a fight between Yerrin and the Mystics?" said Ebon. He straightened and folded his arms. "What happened to the man who went on and on about keeping me out of harm's way? This hardly seems a safe course."

"There are no safe courses left, you goldshitting little idiot," said Mako. "I can let you sit in comfort in the Academy, or you can get your hands dirty and keep Isra from wreaking greater evil. And in the end you will keep her crimes from being blamed on you. What happened to the boy who always wanted to stick his nose in where it did not belong?"

Ebon glared but had no answer.

"I thought so," said Mako. "Come on, then. The sooner we find Gregor, the sooner this is all over with."

But even Mako's caution could not keep them from a fight in the end. He led them around one corner and then the next, but then they had to drop down into a lower level of the sewers. The way seemed clear at first—but the moment their feet touched down in the lower tunnel, they found green-glad warriors just a few paces away. The Yerrin soldiers stopped in their tracks. Their swords came free with a ringing hiss of steel.

"Theren!" growled Mako. He threw himself into the fray.

She hardly needed his urging; two of the guards flew into the air and slammed into the walls on either side. But without the amulet, Theren's spells were not so strong as they might have been. The guards struggled back to their feet. Mako leaped upon one and drove his daggers into the back of the woman's neck. She slumped into the filth that covered the tunnel floor, her body going limp in an instant.

Ebon winced and forced his attention away. He scanned the green cloaks and the open-faced helmets, searching for one who stood above all the rest. But he could see at once that Gregor was not here.

The guards pressed forwards now, and their shock at the sudden appearance of Ebon's group faded with each passing moment. Theren struck and pushed at them each in turn, forcing those in the front back into the others. Mako danced and slashed and stabbed with his knives. Beside Ebon, Kalem's eyes glowed, and he reached into the stone wall of the sewer, pulling forth small handfuls of stone which he turned to iron and flung at the soldiers' heads. But the boy's arms were weak, and his aim was poor.

"Here, give them to me," said Ebon. Kalem gratefully handed one off. Ebon threw it at a guard's head as hard as he could. It clattered off the man's brow, making him stumble, and then Theren's magic lifted him from his feet and cast him back into his comrades. But looking over their heads, Ebon saw still more guards appear around the next bend in the sewer.

"Mako!" he cried. When the bodyguard shot him a look, Ebon pointed. Mako saw the approaching guards, and his mouth set in a grim line.

"Boy," he said, glancing at Kalem. "We must away. Use the floor."

"What is that supposed to mean?" said Kalem, close to panic.

"The *stone,* you idiot," snarled Mako.

Kalem understood at once, and he knelt. Mage-light sprang into his eyes, and he pressed his fingers to the stone floor, ignoring the muck that enveloped his skin. An itch sprang to life on the back of Ebon's neck. Stone rippled under Kalem's fingers, and Ebon could almost see the magic spreading across the floor. It flowed forth like water, turning the stone to liquid, and in a blink it had spread beneath the feet of the Yerrin guards. Then Kalem lifted his hands, and the glow died in his eyes. The stone solidified again at once, and suddenly all the Yerrin guards were encased up to their ankles. They stared at their feet in fear and confusion, nearly falling over.

Mako took a step back, showing Kalem his cruel grin. "Well done, boy. Your head is not completely stuffed with wool, it seems. Come."

He ran off down the tunnel, and Ebon and his friends hastened to follow. Ebon looked back just before they turned the corner and saw the Yerrin guards looking helplessly after them.

THIRTY-THREE

"That was a waste of time," said Theren. "Likely Gregor is already gone by now."

"Let us hope not," said Mako. "But if we do catch him, it will not have been a waste, for he will have fewer swords by his side."

"Were those soldiers coming to reinforce Gregor, or clearing the way for his arrival?" said Ebon. "If they were behind him, he cannot still be there for us to find."

"We will know in a moment," said Mako. "Look ahead."

Ebon did, and saw a pale glow far down the tunnel. The passageway ran straight to it without stopping and with no tunnels branching off in either direction. The way was clear, and no one blocked them from it.

Mako broke into a sprint now, and Theren hastened to keep up. Ebon and Kalem were swiftly left behind, stumbling along on half-dead legs, their breath wheezing out in great gusts that misted upon the air. Mako and Theren burst out into the daylight, and the boys followed a moment later.

Everything was so bright that at first Ebon could only blink, using his hand to shield his eyes from the sun. When at last they adjusted, he searched for the Seat's eastern docks. But the great docks were nowhere to be seen. Instead there were only a few small piles in a row, to which was lashed a small, floating dock.

Everything looked intimately familiar, like a place he had visited many times before, but he could not get his bearings. He looked around, seeing high cliffs rising far above them. The feet of the cliffs ended in the small stone platform where they now stood, stretching around the edge of the Great Bay's water, which was only a few paces away. And across the little cove, steps were carved into the stone, leading up to the tops of the cliffs that stood stark and black against the bright sky above.

Cliffs.

The cliffs on the south of the Seat.

Ebon knew where they were. It was the cove—the cove to which he had followed Cyrus and Adara the day the Seat had been attacked, and where Cyrus had fallen to his death. His sense of familiarity came not from many visits in the flesh, but from the countless times he had visited the place since—in his nightmares.

His legs shook, and he clutched Kalem's shoulder for support. The boy looked up at him, brow furrowing.

"Ebon? What is it?"

Mako heard it, and looked back at them over his shoulder. When he saw Ebon's face, he smiled. "What is wrong, boy? Is this place familiar to you?"

Though Ebon tried to summon an answer, none came—and then all their thought was drawn by Theren's sudden cry. Ebon's gaze followed her outthrust finger, which pointed towards the stone steps on the other side of the cove.

Down the steps came Gregor, moving with measured haste, and beside him were a half-dozen guards. As soon as Theren cried out, he turned and saw them. He wore no helmet now, and so Ebon could see full well how his face twisted to rage, fury smoldering in his eyes.

"There," said Mako. "That is the firemage—the woman behind him." But he need not have warned them, for she stepped forwards just then, and her eyes were aglow. A bolt of flame sprang from her fingers and came screaming towards them. But Theren's own magelight flared in response; the flame died harmlessly upon the air. Theren thrust out a hand, and the firemage stumbled, but she quickly recovered.

"He means to take that boat," said Mako, pulling Ebon's attention back to Gregor and his guards. There was a small rowboat moored at the floating dock, and Gregor was making for it. "We cannot let him escape. Come!"

Around the stone shelf he ran, with Ebon and Kalem trying to keep up. But Ebon did not know what good they would be—Gregor had five other soldiers with him, and he and Kalem were no warriors, nor even wizards of a useful sort for this kind of thing, as Theren was.

But he had underestimated Theren—or he had overestimated Yerrin's firemage. For even as Theren held off the other wizard's spells, she could spare a blast or two of her own. When Gregor and his guards were still only halfway down the stone steps, an unseen forced clutched two of them and cast them over the edge. They fell screaming, not to the stone shelf, where they would surely have died, but into the water. They plunged beneath the surface and came up sputtering, fighting to reach the dock and desperate to remove the armor that suddenly weighed them down. But when Theren tried again, the firemage mustered a desperate defense and held her off.

"Your friend is worth more than she seems," said Mako. "Now is the time to prove your own worth— but stay back where you will not be harmed."

"We are no great wizards, Mako," said Ebon. "How can we help you against swords and armor?"

"Stand at my rear and throw your little handfuls of stone," said Mako. "Let Theren do her work, and do not let them get behind me."

So saying, he approached the foot of the stairs, which Gregor had nearly reached. Two of the guards came forwards first. Like Gregor, they had no shields or armor save a shirt of chain. But they had swords at their waists, and they drew them in unison.

Mako slid his own curved daggers from their sheaths, and then with a flourish he flipped them around to hold them reversed. "Come, my darlings," he said, his tone almost playful. "Come and dance with me."

They did, and for a moment that was all Mako did—he danced. The guards' swords were long and broad, but that also made them heavy, and so Mako could twist and turn around every swing and thrust. Every few moments he would slash with one of his knives—but the slashes were slow and reserved, even to Ebon's eye, meant only to make one of his opponents take a step back. If Gregor had joined the fray, it might have been different—but the stone shelf was narrow, and so he held his ground, but tried to edge around the fight so that he could approach the floating dock where his boat awaited.

Kalem bent and scooped handfuls of stone from the ground at their feet, and when he saw an opportunity, he flung them at the Yerrin guards. But Mako's dance was as erratic as it was savage, and he could rarely find an opening. But then one of the guards' boots slipped into a saltwater pool, and she slipped, and Mako struck at last. Swift as blinking he lunged, slashing the guard's throat open. She fell to her knees, gurgling her last, and Ebon's gut twisted. With one out of the way, Mako easily closed the gap between himself and the other guard, stepping inside his reach and plunging both daggers into the man's gut. To his credit, the second guard grimaced and tried to grasp Mako's throat even in death, but the daggers came out, and they sank into the man's temples. He fell heavily to the ground.

Mako stood looking at the bodies for a moment. Then he shoved his toe beneath the woman and turned her over, so that her corpse sank into the waters of the Great Bay. The man, too, he kicked into the water. Only then did he look up at Gregor.

"With that distraction out of the way—do you care to try and finish what we began the other night?"

The giant's broadsword slid from its sheath with a harsh, rattling rasp. It gleamed in the sunlight, and Gregor held it forth, pointing it at Mako as if the blade were a scepter.

"It shall not go any better for you than it did the last time."

Mako shrugged. "I did not think the last time went so badly. I still have the marks of your love to prove it." With the tip of one dagger he pointed at the bruises on his cheeks. But then he turned the dagger so that it pointed at Gregor instead. "Yet I see that you bear some of my kisses as well—and, mayhap, marks from the embraces of some of our red-cloaked friends, who arrived just at the end of our union?"

Indeed, now that Mako mentioned it, Ebon could see bruises and scrapes all across Gregor's skin. He knew Mako could not have landed all those blows when they fought in the grotto. Gregor must not have had an easy time escaping the Mystics when they arrived. Now the giant's nostrils flared, and he took a step forwards with bared teeth.

"Still your tongue and bare your steel."

"Sky above," said Mako, snickering. "There are children present."

With a roar Gregor charged. Mako danced again, but this time not so easily. Though Gregor was the larger man by far, he was lightning fast. Mako was forced to step nimbly around him, so that Gregor ended up with his back to Ebon and Kalem. They saw it at the same time, and looked at each other.

"Should we . . .?"

Ebon glanced at Gregor's broad back. Would throwing a stone even do any good? They might only anger the man, and then he would come for them. But in the grotto, Gregor had gotten the better of Mako by a wide margin . . .

"It is tempting to let him fight this battle on his own," said Ebon with a sigh. "But no. We must help him. Can you play your trick with the stone floor again?"

Kalem gave Gregor another glance, and he quailed. "I can try."

He crept forwards, hunched almost double so as to avoid Gregor's notice. And Gregor did not notice him—but the firemage on the steps above did. She cried out, and a wall of fire sprang from the stone in Kalem's very face. The boy screamed and fell back, batting at the hem of his robes where the flames had caught. Theren dispelled the fire almost immediately, but the edge of Kalem's robe still burned.

"Hold still!" cried Ebon. He seized Kalem's arm and dragged him towards the edge of the rocky platform. Taking him under the elbows, Ebon threw his legs over the edge and into the water, where the flames died in a hiss.

"There now," said Ebon, pulling him back up. "No harm—"

But Kalem looked over his shoulder, and his eyes shot wide in terror. Ebon did not even turn— he only seized Kalem's shoulder and dove. A rasping hiss sounded as Gregor's sword sliced through the air where his head had been a moment before. Now the giant loomed over them, and they fought to scramble away—but then Mako was there, forcing Gregor to turn around. And across the cove, Theren gave a shout, and her magic struck Gregor a mighty blow. He stumbled away, striking the base of the cliff hard.

The firemage was waiting. As Theren's attention went to Gregor, the woman on the steps let loose a flurry of magic. Fire shot forth, laced with thunder, and a gale behind it all. Theren threw up her arms, holding it back with a wall of pure force. But the winds broke through, and buffeted her, and then an arc of lightning struck her in the chest. She screamed and dropped to the ground.

"Theren!" cried Ebon.

He looked to Mako, hoping the bodyguard could help, though he did not know how. But Mako was not looking at Theren. He had turned towards the steps, and even as Ebon's gaze fell upon him, he threw one of his daggers. It flew through the air, straight as an arrow, and buried itself to the hilt in the firemage's neck.

She stood there slack for a moment. Her fingers probed at the dagger, while her eyes tried to turn in their sockets to see it. Then she tumbled from the edge and landed on the stone shelf with a wet *crack*.

It had taken Mako only a half-moment, but it was long enough. He danced away even as he whirled to face Gregor again, but the giant had already struck, and four fingers of his sword tip plunged into the flesh of Mako's arm before withdrawing almost at once. Mako grimaced, but did not utter a sound, not even a grunt. He sank down on one knee with the pain, and Gregor stepped forwards.

By Ebon's hand lay a sword, dropped by one of the guards Mako had killed. He snatched it up without thinking and leaped. A scream ripped from his throat as he swung it into the back of Gregor's leg. Ebon had thought the man wore only leather pants, but he must have had chain beneath, for the sword rebounded with a rending sound. Still, Gregor stumbled. He turned and sent the back of one boulder-sized fist into Ebon's face. Ebon went crashing into the stone wall.

As he lay there, senseless for a moment, he saw that his little swing had been enough. Mako was up once again, and with a savage kick he knocked the sword from Gregor's hand. It plunged into the Great Bay and vanished. Gregor reached for him, but Mako leaped over his arms and behind him. One massive arm came around, searching, but Mako caught it and wrenched it, and before Ebon could blink he had flung Gregor to the floor. He twisted the hand until Ebon thought it must surely break and put his one remaining dagger to Gregor's throat. Everyone went deathly still.

"Now then, brute," said Mako. "That is enough of your bawling. You have two choices here, and one of them sends your blood flowing into the ocean. But I will let you leave here alive—as long as you tell me where that mindmage whelp is."

"You have your own mindmage," said Gregor through gritted teeth. "Do with her what you will."

Mako sent the tip of the dagger into Gregor's throat—not deep, and almost flat, so that a half-finger of it slid *under* the skin, rather than into it. "Do not give me sass, Gregor. I do you a great honor by offering you your life, for you have killed many of my warriors. Speak now, or die."

Ebon stared at him in wonder. Would Mako really let Gregor sail away from here after all the man had done? But then he saw the hard glint in the bodyguard's eyes. And he remembered in the basement of Xain's home, when Mako had promised to let Isra live and then had tried to kill her anyway. Ebon had stopped him then, but he could not now. Mako had no intention of keeping his word and letting Gregor leave.

But neither, it seemed, did Gregor have any intention of doing as Mako wished. "Drown in your own piss," he spat. "Slit my throat if that is truly your aim, for you will get no truth from me. And you will never find Isra before it is too late."

Mako sighed and opened his mouth as if to speak. But then Ebon heard many voices from above, and Kalem cried, "Watch out!"

Mako dove without thinking, rolling away from Gregor as arrows rained down from the sky. One struck Gregor in the back, but it rebounded from his chain, and he fought to rise to all fours.

Looking up, Ebon saw many soldiers gathered at the cliff's edge, and they were beginning to come down the stairs. They were clad all in the red leather armor of constables, and his heart skipped a beat.

Gregor was up now. Ebon's limbs obeyed him at last, and he scrambled up, expecting the giant to come for them—but instead he turned and ran for the docks. He leaped into the boat there, nimble as a cat, ignoring the cries of the constables. With a dagger from his belt he cut both mooring lines, and then his huge arms pulled at the oars to launch the boat into the Great Bay.

"Time to go," said Mako, teeth bared against the pain of his shoulder. He pulled Ebon along with him, and Kalem hurried after as they ran for the sewer entrance from which they had come. Theren was there, and to Ebon's stark relief, she was up on her knees and looking about, blinking.

"What happened?" she said. "Where is Gregor?"

"Gone," said Ebon, pointing out to sea. He and Kalem took her arms to help her up.

"No!" cried Theren. She reached out, and light sprang into her eyes as she tried to clutch Gregor's boat with magic. But he did not slow, and the magelight winked out almost at once.

"He is gone now," said Kalem. "And we must leave as well." He flinched as an arrow struck the stone by them, though in truth it was not a very close shot.

"No truer words were ever spoken, goldshitter," said Mako. "Into the sewers once more."

THIRTY-FOUR

THEY HAD NOT EVEN ROUNDED THE FIRST CORNER when they heard shouts at the sewer entrance and the tramp of feet behind them.

"I hope you are faster than you have shown yourselves to be, boys," grunted Mako. "Otherwise Theren and I may be forced to leave you behind, for the redbacks will surely catch you."

"You cannot abandon us down here!" cried Kalem.

"He is having a joke," said Ebon. "Though he should save his breath for running."

Mako grinned. "I know my way around these sewers like a wolf in its own den. They will not be able to track us."

But his boasting seemed a lie, for they could always hear their pursuers behind them in the tunnels. When they reached the area they had dropped down before, the Yerrin guards were gone—many ridges in the stone floor thrust through the muck to show where they had been trapped, but the stone was chipped away, and Ebon guessed that they had managed to dig themselves out. Mako helped them up the ladder and into the tunnel above, despite his wounded shoulder. There they felt sure they would lose the constables at last. But in no time they heard their pursuers anew, voices echoing with shouts and cries to halt.

I wonder if anyone ever does, thought Ebon. *Just stops in their tracks and waits to be captured.*

"How do they keep finding us?" said Kalem, voice heavy with fear.

Theren said nothing, but Ebon caught her looking at Mako. He followed her gaze and saw the blood that still flowed steadily from the bodyguard's shoulder. It ran down his arm to his elbow, and from there it splashed to the stone floor every few steps. Some of it sank into the muck in their feet, but much of it showed on the stone.

That was how the constables were tracking them. But what could they do? Ebon would not abandon the man who had saved them all so many times already.

Without warning, Mako skidded to a stop. "Here

we are," he said. "The street above is just outside the Academy. The three of you must climb up and return to the citadel. I will lead the redbacks away."

"You cannot," said Ebon. "You are hurt, and they are tracking you by your blood."

"Do you think I did not spot that?" growled Mako. "Loss of blood has not yet made me a fool. But I was hampered by you and your stumpy little friends. Without you, I can finally lose the constables, as I would have from the beginning if it were not for your useless hides."

Kalem seemed taken aback by that, but Ebon only fixed Mako with a keen stare. "Very well," he said quietly. "Only do not let yourself be captured."

"Do you forget with whom you speak?" said Mako. "You need not worry yourself on my account."

"Who said I was worried for you?" said Ebon, shrugging. "I worry only that if they caught you, it would go ill for the family."

That earned him a smile. "More like a proper Drayden every day. Now shut your fool mouth, for they will be here in a moment."

He lifted them up one by one, and they broke out blinking into the light of the afternoon sun. Then he ran off again with light, springing steps. Ebon and his friends hurried away from the sewer entrance.

"Will he be all right?" said Kalem.

"Of course," said Theren. "And even if not, do you think he would spare any worries for us, if our positions were reversed?" But she could not hide the concern in her eyes as she looked back over her shoulder.

"What time is it?" said Ebon. "If it is still the afternoon study period, we should not enter the front doors."

"The sun is too low," said Kalem, pointing to it. "It must be after the bell."

"If you say so." They ran around the corner into the street just before the Academy. "I know the first place we should go, for I think we all need a bath."

Theren outpaced them for a moment and reached the front doors first. They were shut—and something in the back of Ebon's mind shouted a warning at that fact—but she had them open at once and bounded inside with the boys just behind her.

And there they stopped.

Before them were arranged almost the entire faculty. Ebon saw Jia present, and Perrin, and Dasko—Dasko who looked at them all with smoldering eyes. But Xain was at their head, and Ebon saw a look of fury upon his face—fury, and triumph.

In his hand he held the amulet of Kekhit.

For a moment Ebon and his friends stood rooted, unsure of what to do. Instinct told Ebon to run. Reason told him he would never escape before the instructors there—wizards, all of them—stopped him with spells. Terror told him to throw himself at their feet and beg for mercy, to say it had all been Theren's idea. Pride told him to hold his head high, to demand to know what they were all there for, and to deny any knowledge of the whole affair.

But no emotion won, and so he stood still.

"Drayden," said Xain. His voice was like a serrated blade in a sheath of velvet. "Do you know what I hold in my hand?"

"Dean Forredar," said Kalem. It sounded as though he were trying a diplomatic tone, but his voice cracked, ruining the effect. "The three of us were—"

"Shut up," said Xain. Kalem did. Xain lifted the amulet a little higher. "This is the amulet of Kekhit. An artifact from the Academy vaults. Stolen from them. Stolen by you."

"That is not true, Dean," said Theren. "The three of us—"

"*SILENCE!*" Xain's voice was like a bolt of thunder. The air itself crackled with the force of it. "Silence. The three of you are done talking. You have done too much of that already, and all of it has been lies. You have been behind the mindwyrd from the first. You concocted this story about Isra, when in truth you had killed her long ago and thrown her into the Great Bay. It was you who killed Credell, and Vali, and Oren. You three: a Drayden, and his accomplices."

Theren's shoulders slumped in defeat. She bowed her head, casting her hair into her eyes.

"Now you have my son. My *son*. You cannot know the lengths I have gone to for him already. And now I make you this promise: if he has been harmed in any way, there are no words for the pain I will make you endure."

Slowly Theren turned to her friends. She met Kalem's eyes first, but only for a moment before she looked straight at Ebon.

She gave him a little smile.

"I told you," she whispered. "From the first, I told you. Now run."

Ebon's brow furrowed—and then at once he understood. He lifted a hand. "Theren, do not—"

Magelight sprang into her eyes. Xain's eyes flared in defense—but she did not attack him. With a blast, she threw Kalem and Ebon through the Academy's open front door and into the street.

"Run!" she screamed.

Then with her magic she seized the front doors and flung them shut.

THOOM

Kalem got to his feet and ran for the doors, where they could hear the sounds of blasts and explosions inside. But Ebon seized the back of his collar and dragged him away.

"We cannot leave her!" said Kalem.

"We will help her!" cried Ebon. "Somehow. But we must run. We must."

They did—and every time he heard a spell hammer against the iron doors behind him, Ebon hoped it was not the sound of his friend dying.

THIRTY-FIVE

THEY FLED TO ADARA'S HOME. WHEN HE WOKE THERE the next morning, Ebon could not remember why he chose hers, and not his family's manor. Doubtless Halab would have taken him in. Doubtless she would have protected him. But he could think only of Adara. And by some blessing of the sky, she had been there when they arrived, and had ushered them in without question—though she had many questions once they were safely within.

Ebon told her everything. Kalem added a word or two here or there, but mostly the boy sat in the corner

and wept. And when he thought Ebon was not looking, he glared. How could Ebon blame him? The right
thing to do—the honorable thing—would have been
to return to the Academy and throw their lot in with
Theren. But Ebon knew that they would never convince the faculty of their innocence—especially not
Xain, who had hated him from the first. And mayhap
outside the Academy they could come to some solution.

Adara left once they had finished their tale, but
only to put word out through the lover's guild. By
the next morning they learned that Theren was not
dead, but was in the custody of the Mystics. Ebon
knew full well what that meant. His mind filled with
visions of Lilith when he had visited her before, when
she had languished under torture for days. To imagine
that pain being visited upon Theren . . . his stomach
clenched when he thought of it.

After that first night, Ebon fully expected he would
have to find another hiding place. But the moment he
mentioned it, Adara shook her head and insisted that
he and Kalem remain with her.

"I will not turn you out," she said. "And I may be
of help to you."

"So might Mako, or others in my family," said
Ebon. "I should return to the manor. I should have
gone there from the first."

Adara arched an eyebrow. "That would have been
your death," she said. "Do you not think that that is

the first place the constables and Mystics would have gone to search for you? Doubtless they have agents posted in the streets around it even now."

Ebon frowned, for indeed he had not thought of that. "But still, I only put you in danger by remaining here," he said. "Mako knew of us, and he cannot be the only one."

"He very well could be," said Adara. "Think of it— even the Lord Prince did not know until you appeared by my side, and he has his eyes and ears in every corner of the Seat."

Kalem straightened where he sat on the floor. "The Lord Prince! He must know that the constables seek for you. He could expose us."

"I have sent word. He will not intervene, though he is not happy about it," said Adara flatly. "But while he will not act to harm us, for he believes me when I say that you are innocent, neither will he help us. He will only keep trying to find Isra before she wreaks more havoc. For that is still what is most important, Ebon. Even with Theren's peril, you cannot forget that. Isra means to kill again."

"Aye, and she means to kill goldbags," said Ebon, folding his arms and slumping in his chair. "All of them, if she can. And now none of us are there to stop her, and the faculty do not even believe she is alive."

"What do you mean to do about it?" said Kalem, a strong current of annoyance in his voice.

"We must flee the Seat," said Ebon. Kalem gave

an angry snort, and Adara looked at him in surprise. Ebon spread his hands. "It is the only way. What else is there? We can never prove our innocence now—not until Isra acts, and that may not be for a long while, until all this furor has died away."

"You mean to flee?" said Kalem, rising to his feet. "You would leave Theren here, suffering as the Mystics put her to the question? Often I defend your name to others, Ebon, but this is just in line with the dark tales your family seems to attract."

"Of *course* we will get Theren first," said Ebon. He felt the heat of his blood rising in his ears. "Do you think I am so faithless? Stop looking for evil in my heart, Kalem. You are as bad as Xain."

Kalem glowered, but he lowered his eyes. "How do you mean to get her out?"

"I do not know," said Ebon quietly. "We need someone who . . . can do that sort of thing. We might tunnel up from beneath the Mystics' holding cells, but it is risky, and I would not know how to get there in the sewers. I hope that Mako shows himself soon, though that is one thing I never thought to hear myself say."

"You mean to abandon the Academy, then?" said Adara. "You will let Isra kill the other children of merchants and royalty within it?"

Ebon could not meet her gaze. "I do not know what else to do," he said softly. "If we try to stop her, we will only be caught and killed ourselves. Of course I will try to help them, if we can think of a way to do it."

She rose from the table. "I will not say if this counsel is good or bad," she said. "But I urge you to think on it. We have little else to do, for a while at least."

By their third day of hiding, Ebon began to feel as if he was going mad. Adara's home was no hovel, but it was no mansion either. He could only stand so much of her four walls and coarse wood floor and Kalem's sullen glares. And of course Kalem's presence made time alone with Adara impossible, so there was not even that outlet for relief.

"You are *certain* no one will find us here?" he said, not because he was dissatisfied with her answers the previous times he had asked, but because there was nothing else to say or to do.

Adara fixed him with a look that told him she was growing annoyed. "Yes," she said. "Only the others in the guild of lovers know of our arrangement, and they will never breathe a word of it. And even if someone did, there is a hiding place beneath the floor. I will stow you there if Mystics should come knocking—or mayhap I will stow you there now and leave it locked for a while."

"I am sorry," said Ebon, and he meant it. "I only wish there was something we could do."

"I have sent word to your family as you asked, but they are . . . inscrutable. It will take time for my note to reach them."

Then, from across the room, Kalem shot up from the floor. "Alchemy!" he cried, his eyes wild.

Ebon stared at him. "What?"

"Alchemy," said Kalem, quieter this time. "That is how she did it. Isra, I mean. How she provided the corpse. She found some alchemist—and it must have been a powerful one—who took a corpse and turned it so that it looked like Isra's corpse instead. She must have done it almost the moment she kidnapped Erin."

"So long ago?" said Adara. "That shows incredible foresight. Isra may be devious, but she is only a girl."

"Likely Gregor had her do it," said Ebon, glaring at the floor. "Or whoever else in the family Yerrin commands Gregor."

"At least now we know," said Kalem. "That is one mystery solved."

"Can you prove it?" said Ebon, heart racing. "Is there some trace of her magic on the corpse that we can show to another alchemist, and thus establish our innocence?"

"Well, no," said Kalem. "But we have an answer."

"Knowledge without a course of action is useless," said Ebon, scowling. But when Kalem's hopeful expression fell, he felt guilty and tried to ease his tone. "But you are right, in that at least we have an answer. I am sorry. It is only that I am grown irritable with inaction."

"Think nothing of it," said Kalem with a sigh. "I feel much the same."

Adara stood. "It is time I was going, for the guild

will need me tonight. Do not get into trouble before I return—at least not more trouble than you can get yourself out of."

Ebon rose to see her out. "We will not. Kalem, if you are still bashful about such things, turn away; I have been an annoyance to the love of my heart, and I must kiss her well to make up for it."

Kalem did indeed turn away, and Adara gave Ebon a wry smile. "What makes you think I want a kiss now? You have not bathed since you arrived." But she showed her words to be a lie by gripping the front of his robes and pulling him in. For a long moment they held each other. She put her lips to his ear and whispered, "We will solve this. Together. We share it, as in all things. Even peril."

"Even peril," he whispered back. "Thank you."

Then she was gone.

That left them alone for some hours. To distract himself, Ebon drank, and Kalem joined him at the table and in his cups. Ebon had tried to withhold himself from wine since he arrived; though Adara offered it to him often and insisted it was no bother, he had no wish to drain her cabinet, which he knew he might do if he gave himself free rein. And besides, who would want to sit drunk in the home of their lover for hours?

But now he and Kalem let themselves relax into one of Adara's fine vintages. When the bottle was nearly done, Kalem concocted a plan to rescue Theren that involved melting the front door of the Mystics' station, and Ebon nodded sagely that it was a brilliant idea. Then Ebon, in turn, decided that it would be better to recruit a firemage, some sellsword wizard, and have them burn the place to the ground. Somehow they would get Theren out before the flames and the smoke killed everyone inside.

He knew their ideas were beyond foolish, and he knew that Kalem knew it as well. But after two days of sitting and reflecting on their own hopeless situation, it felt good to speculate upon the ridiculous. Somehow they drank another bottle, though Ebon did not remember getting up to open it—mayhap, he reflected in the back of his mind, Kalem had done it, though he did not remember the boy rising from the table, either.

Much time passed this way before Adara returned. Ebon and Kalem were giggling when they heard the front door's latch turn, and they both stifled themselves while shushing each other heavily. But when Adara reached the top of the stairs, she was not alone; Lilith stood beside her.

"Lilith," said Ebon. He shot to his feet, but too quickly—he had to put a hand on the table to steady himself. The sight of her had a sobering effect on him, but not enough, for his head began to spin as soon as he stood. "What are you doing here?"

"She found me," said Adara quietly. "Theren told her you might be with me."

"Theren?" cried Kalem. He stood as well, but he handled himself even worse than Ebon had and very nearly fell to the floor. Adara took his arm to steady him. Kalem hardly seemed to notice. "You saw her? Could you speak with her? Is she well?"

Lilith glowered, and even Ebon winced at the words. "Well? She is far worse off than you two are, sitting here and getting drunk on your lover's wine."

"We did not mean for her to be caught," said Ebon, slowly, so that he could be sure to say each word clearly. "She sacrificed herself to save us."

If he thought Lilith would soften at that, he was wrong. "And do you mean to do the same for her?" she said, voice rising. "Or do you mean to sit here until you rot? It has been days since she was taken—three days, Ebon. You know what the Mystics are doing to her. You saw them do it to me. And now they are even more eager for the truth. Xain is urging them on, desperate to find his son. So how do you mean to fix it?"

Kalem looked doubtfully at Ebon, who avoided Lilith's gaze. "We . . . er . . . we have been trying to think of a way to get her out."

Lilith folded her arms, and Ebon thought she likely knew just how productive their thoughts on the matter had been. "I hope you have concocted some brilliant strategy. Because no one else will solve this unless it is us—the people in this room, and no others."

"Mako will find us soon," said Ebon. "With his help, we will find a way."

"Theren thought he would cast my life aside easily to protect yours," said Lilith. "Do you think he views her more tenderly? He did not strike me as that sort of man."

"He might surprise you," said Ebon. "In any case, I will make him help us rescue Theren—and then he will find Isra for me. If she has not fled the Seat, anyway. She might have, the same as Gregor."

"No." Lilith shook her head. "Gregor left to save his own skin. Isra has never cared to do that before, or she would have fled in the first place. She only wants to destroy the goldbags. And I know how she means to do it. The Goldbag Society she began—that she had *me* begin"—she paused as a shiver ran up her body— "they are having a secret gathering. An assembly. It is in less than a week. They are keeping it secret from all but their own members."

"How did you hear of it, then?" said Kalem. "I thought you no longer trucked with their sort."

"Nella told me. She was worried, though she did not know why. I urged her not to go, and urged her besides to dissuade others from going. But I fear my words, or hers, will have little effect. Isra means to gather them all together, and then she will destroy them. It will be the perfect chance."

Ebon met Kalem's eyes. "It must be what she has been waiting for," he said. "She wanted to strike them down in one fell swoop. We stopped her when she tried to do it using Jia. But that only gave her more time to ensure that *all* the goldbags will be together."

"And we are going to stop her," said Lilith. "All our

efforts to find her thus far have failed, but we *know* she will be there—and we know when."

"But we cannot re-enter the Academy," said Kalem. "We will be caught and killed."

"I know you have a secret way in," said Lilith. "Or at least your bodyguard does. Find it and come. Three days hence."

Ebon met her gaze. "Very well," he said. "We will. Though Isra has magestones, and mayhap we will perish in the end. But it is the best chance we will ever have, and I will not let it go by."

Her eyes softened, and she nodded slowly. "Thank you. I told Theren, too, when I saw her. I asked her— no, I *commanded* her, to hold on until then. Because after that . . . well, one way or another, Theren's innocence will be proven."

"The same way yours was," said Ebon heavily. "Though I wish you need not have suffered as you did before then."

"I survived it," said Lilith, her voice toneless. "Theren will do the same, for she has always been stronger than I am."

She turned and made for the stairs leading out. But she paused on the top step, her hand on the bannister. "I will expect you, Drayden. Let us right the many wrongs that have been done in recent weeks."

"As you say, Yerrin," said Ebon. "And if we fall in doing so, let that right the wrongs that we could not."

Lilith gave him a final nod and left.

THIRTY-SIX

THAT NIGHT, MAKO APPEARED AT LAST.

They had gone to bed, Ebon and Adara together (but chaste) in the bed, and Kalem wrapped in blankets on the floor. Ebon thought his sleep had been deep—until he heard pounding at the door and shot awake at once. He went to rouse Kalem, but the boy was already up. His wide eyes showed their terror in the moonslight that came in through the slats over the windows.

"Into the floor, quickly," said Adara. She lifted the panel for them, and they climbed in. The space was not large, and very nearly stifled them when she put the panel back down, but they managed to still the sound of their breath.

They heard footsteps as Adara went down the stairs, and then the sound of the door opening. Almost at once, heavy boots came tramping up—but only one set. That made Ebon frown. Then he heard a growling voice from the room just above them: "Come out from hiding, boys. I may be more dangerous than the Mystics, but I am not after your blood. Not yet, anyway."

"Mako," said Ebon in relief. He pushed the panel up and emerged into the open. The bodyguard's eyes flashed as he beheld Ebon, though he did not smile. Adara had closed the front door, and soon appeared atop the stairs again, pulling her robes a bit tighter around her and cinching the sash at her waist.

"Apologies, my lady, for the lateness of the hour," Mako told her, turning and bowing low, the way he had when first they met. But then, as before, he turned to Ebon and scowled. "And what have you been doing the past few days? No doubt sitting around getting drunk, with no plan to save yourself."

Ebon lifted his chin, though Mako's words were not far from the truth. "I have had little to do, it seems to me. I was waiting for you to arrive."

"If everyone waited to be saved, the nine kingdoms would be nothing but graveyards," said Mako. "Yet here I am after all, and with a scheme. You must ready yourself, Ebon, for soon you will leave the Seat."

That made Ebon balk. "What? You have secured passage?"

"Not just yet," said Mako. "It is a tricky thing. We cannot send you in one of our own caravans, for those will be ruthlessly searched. It shall have to be with someone else. Fortunately, many of the lesser merchant families owe us favors, and I have called upon some of them to collect."

"Thank you, Mako," said Ebon. "But I cannot take that passage. Theren still rots in a Mystic prison, and we finally have a plan to stop Isra."

Mako's brows drew together. He folded his arms and said, "What plan?"

Ebon told him what Lilith had said about the gathering in the Academy and the opportunity to stop Isra. Mako listened silently, and when Ebon had finished he shook his head.

"You mean to fight her on her own terms, when she is prepared for it," he said. "The only safe course would be to find her before then and attack when she does not expect it. Yet I cannot find her, despite my best efforts—and those efforts are very good indeed." He paused and looked to Adara. "I imagine, my lady, that even your special friend has had no luck, or else I should have heard of it by now."

Adara met his gaze, her eyes betraying nothing. "If he has had any more success than you, he has not told me of it."

Mako waved a hand in her direction as though he

presented a platter of sweetmeats. "And there you have it."

"We could still take her unawares," said Kalem, surprising Ebon with his vehemence. He stepped up beside Ebon and fixed Mako with a glare. "You could, if you meant to. But you do not even care if she kills students within the Academy. Nor do you care about Theren's torture."

To Ebon's surprise, Mako's scowl softened slightly. "I would not see your friend die under the knives of the Mystics," he said. "She has proven herself most . . . resourceful. Useful, even. But you *will* leave the Seat, Ebon. I will force you if I must, for I have orders from Halab."

That stopped Ebon cold. "Halab?" He had almost forgotten about her in his worries over Theren and the Academy.

"Yes," said Mako. "She is worried sick about you—terrified, even. She has not sent word home to your parents, for she fears your mother would go mad with grief and fear. Normally I keep details from her for her own safety, but she ordered me to tell her everything that has happened to you. I have never seen her this distraught. To ease her mind, there is nothing I would not do. Even kidnap you from here, if I must. But I would rather not. Ready yourself to go."

For a moment Ebon hesitated. Always Halab had been strong before him: strong and benevolent, as when she arranged for him to attend the Academy; or strong and wrathful, as when she had struck Matami down for threatening him. The thought of that strength now reduced to weakness, the steel in her eyes reduced to terror and tears . . . it struck him to the heart, making him sick.

And Mako said he would take care of it. He would stop Isra, and if she was exposed, then Theren would be pardoned.

But he thought of Theren. And he thought of how Lilith had looked when he had visited her. And he remembered Mako's words to Gregor in the cove, when he had promised to let the man live—the same way he had promised Ebon that he would not kill Isra.

He squared his shoulders. "No."

Mako's eyes narrowed. "Say again, boy?"

"No. I will not go with you. I will save my friend. And I will stop Isra before she kills anyone else. The family may be more important to you than anything, Mako—and for Halab's sake, I am grateful for that. But I have spent too long worrying after my own safety and disregarding the consequences to everyone else. Theren would not be in prison if it were not for me. And Isra . . . well, her deeds are not my fault, yet no one else will stop her now, if I do not."

If Mako's face had indeed softened for a moment, now it hardened again, and he grew angrier than before. When he spoke it was through gritted teeth. "You are boastful, boy. I have told you I will take you from here if I must. That is no idle promise. Ready yourself or not, as you will—two days hence, you leave the

Seat. And do not think to try and flee. I will know if you do, and I will track you down."

He went to the top of the stairs, but then he paused. One last time he turned and gave Adara the same deep bow as when he had arrived. "My lady."

Then he was gone.

They spent a restless day with uneasy thoughts—and then the very next evening, another knock came at Adara's door. Once again they looked at each other, and once again Ebon felt a ball of fear forming in the pit of his stomach. When she had stowed the boys under the panel in her floor, Adara answered it—but she returned almost immediately and called them out of hiding.

"It was only a messenger," she said. In her hand was a letter, the seal of which she had already broken—but Ebon saw the royal insignia upon it. "It is from the Lord Prince. He says he has exhausted all resources to hand and has found no trace of Isra. If she appears he will be notified, but for now he has done all that he can. She is not on the Seat."

Ebon sat down heavily on the bed, putting his face in his hands. "She must be. She *must* be. Darkness take her," he muttered. "How? How is it possible that she could be so invisible?"

"Still, we know where she will be," said Kalem. "We can stop her."

"Yes, but we cannot remain here in the meanwhile," said Ebon. "Mako will return here tomorrow night, and he will try to take me before we have a chance at stopping Isra."

"I can find us another place to hide," said Adara. "But Mako said he would mark our passing."

"Can you not command him to leave you alone, Ebon?" said Kalem. "No servant of my family would dare to disobey my order."

"Your family is not the family Drayden," said Ebon, shaking his head. "Halab could command him to leave me be, and he would obey her—but he will not heed my word over hers. And I have no way to send her a message and ask for her help."

Ebon gave a frustrated growl and stood to pace. He ran his fingers through his hair and then gripped it to tug at it. "None of this would have happened without me. Theren is in danger because of me. I am even the reason Isra is free, for Mako would have killed her if I had not prevented it. Mayhap that would be no happy ending, but at least the Academy would not still be in danger. And in all the time since, we have failed to find her. Where could she hide herself that no one, not even Mako—sky above, not even the Lord Prince!—can track her down?"

"It must be some magic," muttered Kalem, shaking his head. "Some dark magic, a spell unknown to us. Mayhap it is some ability granted to her by one of the artifacts she stole. I should have thought of that.

Mayhap we could have searched the vault logbooks for a clue, but that chance has passed us by."

Ebon froze where he stood.

"Dark magic," he whispered.

Kalem arched an eyebrow. "Ebon? What is it?"

"Darkness take me. Kalem, I have been an idiot. We all have. And we must go. Now."

"Now?" said Kalem, incredulous. "Where?"

"To the Academy." Ebon gripped his shoulders and gave him a little shake. "Kalem, she is in the vaults. Isra is in the vaults."

Kalem's eyes shot wide. "Sky above," he whispered. Then he stammered, "We—we should summon Mako, or—or, I do not know, we should find help. Somewhere. We cannot go alone."

"When next we see Mako it will be tomorrow night, and he will try to take me from the Seat," said Ebon. "Tomorrow during the day, we cannot sneak in and find her. We can only do it now, when most of the students and faculty will be abed."

"I . . . er . . ." Ebon could see the fear in the boy's eyes.

"Think of Theren, Kalem," said Ebon quietly. "If we stop Isra—*now*—we can save Theren. Mayhap even tonight."

Kalem's eyes hardened, and he gulped. "Very well," he said, quiet but firm. "Let us go."

Ebon nodded and went to Adara. He took her by the shoulders and kissed her. "I promise I will return," he said.

She gave the barest of nods, her jaw set in a firm line. "Do not make promises you cannot keep," she said. "Promise me instead that you will be careful, for that is something I can believe."

"I promise it, then," he said. "I love you."

"And I you."

He took Kalem's arm and fled out the door with him into the night.

THIRTY-SEVEN

EBON WAS THANKFUL FOR THE LATENESS OF THE HOUR as they ran through the streets of the city. He and Kalem were in regular clothing given to them by Ada-ra, and not in their Academy robes. But he was still wary of being recognized, and had pulled his hood as low over his face as he could. That, combined with the shadows that filled the streets, would hopefully hide his face from any curious constables or Mystics.

The cold night had driven most people indoors, and so Ebon and Kalem found the streets almost clear as they went. Soon they had reached the Academy—

but Ebon passed the front door by and ran around to the side, where the scorched groundskeepers' sheds sat against the wall. He entered the one where he knew Mako's hidden entrance lay, and once Kalem had followed him inside, he closed the door behind them both.

"We must use Mako's passageway," he said. "Though I do not know how to open it, I know it is through this wall. Let us shift the stone and open the way."

Together they put their hands against the wall, where Ebon knew the door would open up for them. Ebon reached for his power, and the shed brightened as a glow sprang into his eyes. He saw the glow in Kalem's face as well, and together they pushed at the granite of the wall.

But nothing happened.

Ebon strained, trying to *see* into the stone. There it was, just as any stone or other substance he had ever shifted. Yet when he tried to command it with his magic, it would not move. And furthermore, he felt the connection to his magic slipping away. Soon the glow faded from his eyes, and he loosed a breath he had not known he was holding.

"I cannot move it," he said. "Why?"

"Enchantments," said Kalem. "Of course. The Academy is protected by many spells. Otherwise any transmutation student could slip in and out at will."

"We must find the regular way to open it, then," said Ebon. "Mayhap it is a stone to be pushed . . ."

They ran their hands along the stones, pushing on each in turn. But none moved. The wall remained solid. Ebon gave a frustrated growl and slapped the granite.

"A fine start to this adventure," said Kalem. "Should we try to sneak in through the front door?"

"No," said Ebon. "We will be spotted at once. Give me a moment to think." Then he snapped his fingers. "When you place your magic upon an object, you can see it, can you not? What if you extend your magic *into* the object? Can you search for a secret latch, or a lever, that way?"

"I can try," said Kalem doubtfully.

Magelight glowed in his eyes again, and he ran his fingers along the wall. His lips pursed, and his brow furrowed.

"Is that . . . here."

His fingers slipped into a seam between two stones, and Ebon heard a *click.* Silently, the door swung out towards them.

"Ha!" whispered Ebon. "Mako will spit with fury if he ever learns that we know his secret."

"For that to happen, we would have to survive," said Kalem with a sigh. "I am not optimistic."

"Still your tongue, doomsayer," said Ebon. "My plan has been forming all the way here. Now keep your hand on the wall to our left and probe it with your magic. We must follow the passage until we find the other door."

It was utterly dark within the wall except for the pale glow of Kalem's eyes. Fortunately there was nothing there to run into, but it was still an unnervingly tight passage. They walked on, Ebon studying the stone to their left, hoping the lever or latch would be easier to see here on the inside.

After a while he was certain they had gone too far and had missed the door, and would be lost in the passage forever. But then Kalem breathed a sigh of relief—Ebon, it seemed, was not the only one who had been frightened—and said, "Here it is."

Again his fingers found a seam in the stone, and again the wall swung open silently. A wave of fresh air washed across their faces, and Ebon drank it in deep.

They were in the Academy grounds, the same place where they had met Mako only a few days before. No one else was in sight, which Ebon was grateful for, as he could not entirely muffle the *crunch* of his footsteps in the fresh snow.

Suddenly he realized that they had made a grave error. "Darkness take me," he muttered. "We should have brought our Academy robes after all." In the clothing they now wore, they would attract as much attention as if they had set themselves on fire.

"We can take spares from the supply room," said Kalem. "Let us hope Mellie is not on duty and guarding it, or she will catch us for certain."

They found a white cedar door and slipped inside. The halls were nearly as deserted as the grounds had been, and so they were able to move quickly towards the front hall. Once or twice they heard approaching footsteps, and they quickly ducked out of sight around a corner until the way was clear again.

At last the passage reached the entry hall, and they poked their heads out around the corner. In unison they breathed a sigh of relief; Mellie was not on duty. It was some other wizened woman with salt-and-pepper hair. But she sat in her chair by the front door, and her head nodded towards her chest with sleep.

They snuck past her and into the supply room. Inside they found robes of the right size and quickly shed their street clothes to don them. Then, throwing up their cowls, they entered the halls again and made for the stairs.

"We will need Lilith's help," he whispered to Kalem as they made their way up towards the dormitories. "We will be nearly helpless against Isra on our own. And Lilith may not fare any better against magestones, but if we gain the element of surprise, she could end the fight quickly."

"You are placing an awful amount of faith in Lilith," said Kalem.

"She has placed faith in us as well," said Ebon. "And she found us in Adara's home and did not reveal us afterwards. I am willing to wager that she will not reveal us now."

Another student came down the stairs towards them. They went silent and ducked their heads at once, hiding beneath their hoods. The other student passed without comment. Soon they were outside Lilith's common room—and Ebon's. It seemed many lifetimes had passed since he had laid his head upon his pillow here, though in truth it had only been a few days.

The common room was empty, for which he was grateful, and soon they were in Lilith's dormitory. In between the rows of beds they stepped, peering through the dim light of the moons from the windows.

But before they found her, another student sat up in their bed and saw them. Her eyes met Ebon's, and they widened. It was Nella.

Her mouth opened to shout, but he leaped forwards and covered it with his hand. He put a finger to his lips, pleading with his eyes for her to keep quiet. "Please," he said. "For Oren—please, do not shout. We are not here to harm anyone."

At Oren's name she froze. He took that for a good sign and pressed on. "We know where Isra is, and we mean to stop her. Now, tonight. But we need Lilith's help to do it."

Nella's eyes widened. Slowly, Ebon took his hand from her mouth. "Please, Nella. Where is Lilith?"

Slowly she raised a hand, pointing to a bed in the other row. Looking over, Ebon saw Lilith's dark frizzled hair poking out from the covers. He met Nella's gaze and gave her a grateful nod. "Thank you."

"Wait!" she said. She stood from her bed and

reached for her robe, throwing it on over her under-clothes. "I can help."

Ebon and Kalem looked to each other. Kalem shrugged. "If you are willing to ask Lilith for help, I do not know how we can refuse Nella."

Nella glared at him, but Ebon raised his hands to calm her. "He only means that we did not begin on the best of terms. But thank you, Nella. I, for one, am glad for your help."

They went to Lilith and woke her with a hand over her mouth. The moment she saw Ebon she sat up, awake at once, and wordlessly dressed herself. They crept out into the common room again, where Ebon spoke to them in hasty whispers.

"Isra is in the vaults," he said. "It is the only place she can be. The only place where no one could find her—not even Mako, or . . . well, anyone else who aided us in the search."

"Sky above," whispered Lilith. "Of course. We must alert the faculty."

Ebon shook his head at once. "No. Even if they believed us—which I doubt—many could be hurt if Xain charged in there with flame and battle. But if we sneak in on our own, we may be able to stop her before she knows we are coming."

"We may be able to kill her, you mean," said Lilith. "She must die, Ebon. After all she has done, there is no other way."

Ebon could not muster an argument. But still he

frowned, and his gut twisted, for the faces of Cyrus and Matami came to him. "If that must be, then it must be," he said quietly. "I do not think I could bring myself to do it, but I will not stay your hand."

"As if you even could," said Lilith. But her tone was not as fiery as her words.

"You know the vaults better than we do," said Ebon. "Will we be able to enter them?"

"There is one guard posted, but they can be subdued," said Lilith. "And I know where Egil keeps the key to the main door."

"Let us go, then," said Ebon.

They ran through the halls, ducking out of sight whenever they heard footsteps approaching. But that was rarely, and soon they had reached the vault's front door.

"The guard is inside the front office," said Lilith. "Nella, you should deal with them. Mindmagic is better for knocking someone senseless without killing them. I have no wish to catch them in a blaze."

"Very well," said Nella. She cracked her knuckles. "Open the door for me."

Ebon took a firm grip on the handle. He threw it open at Nella's nod, and she leaped inside. There was a single sharp cry, and then a *crack*. Ebon heard a body slump to the stone floor. They stole in behind Nella to find a member of the faculty—some instructor Ebon did not recognize—slumped against the far wall. She was unconscious, but her chest still rose and fell.

"I hope you are right about this, Drayden," said Nella. "I hate to think of the punishment I will receive otherwise."

"I hope I am right, too," said Ebon. When she looked at him in horror, he mustered a small smile.

"But wait," said Kalem, frowning. "If the vaults have been guarded, how could Isra have come in and out, as we know she has done?"

"Mindwyrd," said Lilith. "She still has magestones. And you would do well to remember that, or you will find yourself her unwitting slave. That is not an experience I, for one, care to repeat."

That threw a somber mood across them all. Silently Ebon opened the second door, and they entered the vaults.

THIRTY-EIGHT

ALMOST AT ONCE, EBON FELT THE CREEPING SENSATION of magic upon his skin. He remembered it well from when he, Theren, and Kalem broke into the vaults for the first time. Enchantments beyond number guarded this place, making him feel as though small creatures crawled over him, their thin and spindly legs tickling his spine.

The place was utterly dark. They were in the very bowels of the Academy and had no windows to allow moonslight. Lilith's eyes glowed as she whispered, and a small ball of flame sparked to life above her palm. It painted the place in blood, from the arched doorways to the ceiling that seemed oppressively close. Wordlessly the four of them drew closer together, eyes roving uneasily.

"Need we disable the spells?" whispered Ebon. "Jia told us there were enchantments to warn the faculty if anyone came here."

"That is a spell of mentalism," said Nella. "Isra will have disabled such magic, or else she could not come and go as she pleases."

"Should we light a torch?" said Kalem.

"My flame will do," said Lilith. "It will be easier to douse at need. We do not want her to see us coming."

Kalem nodded. For a long moment they stood there, peering into the looming blackness of the tunnel.

"Well," said Ebon.

He took the first step. The second one came easier. The others followed after a moment. Their footsteps echoed from the stone walls and mingled with the low murmur of Lilith's flame. Surely Isra could hear them, wherever she was. She must be able to. They were a chorus, an army marching with thunder.

But nothing came to greet them.

They reached a place where the hallway split. Lilith turned right. Ebon paused. "Where are you going?"

"The room where the first artifact was stolen. Its enchantments are gone. It would make sense for Isra to stay there. Anywhere else, she would have to remove the enchantments all over again."

Ebon swallowed and nodded. He had forgotten that Lilith once worked in these vaults, as Theren did. "That is sensible. Lead on."

Lilith turned them again a few paces later. But as they approached the next intersection, Kalem stopped in his tracks. He stepped away from them and went to a corner, stooping to pick something up. When he turned back, he held a cheese rind for them to see.

"Well," he whispered, his voice croaking. "If we doubted she was down here, this seems to prove it."

"Do not forget her magestones," said Lilith. "If she sees us first, we are lost. She can overpower Nella and me faster than blinking. We must surprise her."

Just then they heard the sound of leather shifting against stone down the hall.

Kalem squeaked. Lilith doused her flame. Ebon ran for the wall and pressed himself against a door, behind the stone lip of its frame. A small body struck him in the stomach, and he almost screamed in panic. But it was only Kalem.

The hallway went deathly still. No sound came to them—none but their own heavy, terrified breathing. Ebon wanted to ask Lilith for a light, but he dared not speak.

He stuck his head out. There was a glow. It was faint, just at the end of the hallway. It came from around the corner to the right. He did not know the vaults, but he would have wagered that it was the last corner before they reached the room they were looking for.

The glow was so small, he thought it must come from a candle. He tried to let his eyes adjust to it, but it was not bright enough. He could not even see Kalem pressed to the door beside him.

When he lifted a foot, its scrape sounded like a thunderclap, and Kalem went rigid. Ebon still could not see Lilith or Nella. He put the foot down again and then took another step. Bit by bit, one hand pressed to the wall, he crept forwards.

He reached the corner safely. The glow was brighter now, almost bright enough to see. When he stepped around into the next hallway, he would be able to see its source. He closed his eyes.

Sky above, protect me. And if not, then look after Albi when I am gone, and Halab, and especially Adara.

Ebon stepped around the corner.

As he had guessed, there was a candle. But the candle did not catch Ebon's eye so much as did the figure lying on the floor next to it. A small figure, partially blocking the candle's glow. Their head was laid upon the stone, and their shoulders shifted slightly moment to moment with breathing.

A hand gripped his shoulder, and he nearly died of fright. But then he heard Lilith's whisper. "It is her. Stand back. I will end this."

"No!" Ebon stuck out an arm to restrain her. "That is not Isra."

And indeed, he could see clearly that it was not. The figure was too small. And after looking a moment longer, his heart sank. Even in silhouette, he recognized the wild hair.

Astrea. Sky above.

The poor girl must be under Isra's control, left here as a guard as the older girl slept. Who knew how long she had been under Isra's command? Now Astrea's worsening complexion made sense, her increasing weariness and the heavy bags under her eyes. Ebon imagined it: Astrea returning to the vaults each night, receiving Isra's commands, and sitting in sleepless vigil in case anyone should come to capture her. Likely she only slept now because her body had given out, casting her into slumber despite all the power of Isra's magic.

"It is mindwyrd," said Ebon. Lilith looked at him. Her eyes narrowed for a moment, and then went wide as she nodded. She understood.

Kalem and Nella had approached and stood just behind them. Together they all moved forwards once more. Soon they reached the open door; Ebon recognized it from when they had come with Theren. The frame still stood bare, for no one had replaced the door after Isra had blasted it from its hinges.

Within the vault were two sleeping figures. One, nearer the back, was Isra. But there was a second, smaller figure, its shaggy dark hair sticking out in all directions, clearly unwashed.

Ebon gasped. "It is Erin!"

The dean's son lay on his back, his hands folded over his chest. For a moment Ebon feared the worst, but then he saw the boy's chest rise and fall. Quickly he stole forwards to put a hand on the boy's shoulder—and then, thinking better of that, he put his hand over Erin's mouth before shaking the boy. But he might as well have shaken a log. Erin's eyes remained closed.

"She could have commanded him to sleep," said Lilith. She whispered with her lips almost pressed to Ebon's ear, watching Isra warily. "If she did, he will not rouse until she commands him to or until the mindwyrd wears off. You must carry him out of here."

"After we . . . deal with Isra," said Ebon.

But Lilith shook her head. "No. In her death throes, she may lash out. Mayhap Nella and I can protect ourselves, but not all of you. Get the children away, and we will finish it."

Ebon nodded and motioned Kalem over. He came at once and stooped to lift Erin into his arms. Fortunately the boy was slight, and Kalem could bear the weight with only a little struggle. He trundled off down the hallway with jerky, staggering steps.

Next Ebon went to Astrea. Her mouth was slightly open, and a little drool had come out of the corner of her mouth. He hesitated. Surely she was not mindwyrded to sleep—Isra would have left her on guard. She would rouse when he tried to wake her. If she attacked Ebon with magic, could he stop her? He was not nearly as advanced in alchemy as she, but he had countered her spells before.

He gave a nervous glance over his shoulder. Lilith

and Nella stood there, magelight in their eyes, looking at him. He must hasten, or Isra might wake, and then all would be lost.

Mayhap the mindwyrd had worn off already. He would have to risk it, and if not, then he must hope he was able to stop her magic. He should have kept Kalem around to help, but the boy was already out of sight around the first turn in the hallway.

Ebon slapped a hand over Astrea's mouth. Her eyes shot open. They flew about the hall wildly as she blinked in the light of the candle.

"Shh, shh," said Ebon, placing a finger to her lips. "It is me, Astrea."

She focused on him at last. Her brows drew together. But she did not lift her hands, and he saw no glow of magic in her eyes.

"That is right," he said. "It is Ebon. Are you under Isra's command?"

At first she only stared at him. His heart sank. But then, slowly, she shook her head.

Relief washed through him. "Good. Then come with me. I am getting you out of here."

He took away his hand and stood, reaching down to help her up.

Panic filled her eyes, and she screamed, *"They are here!"*

A blast of power shook the walls as Isra came awake.

THIRTY-NINE

THE CANDLE DIED—A SPELL OF LILITH'S—AND THE
hallway was plunged into darkness. Then a hand
gripped Ebon's arm and dragged him down the hall.
He screamed and tried to fight it off, but then he heard
a growl in his ear.

"Shut up, Drayden, and run."

It was Nella. Ebon gained command of his limbs
again and followed her, though he could see nothing.
She jerked left, turning the corner down another hall.
The instant they reached it, Lilith threw up a ball of
flame.

"We cannot let her see us," cried Lilith. "If she can see us, she can kill us." Mentalism relied upon line of sight, Ebon knew—even with magestones, Isra could not harm them if they were hidden from her view.

They heard Isra's enraged screaming behind them, and Lilith doused the light again just a few paces from the next corner in the halls. They stumbled forwards blind, and then when they turned the corner Lilith lit the way once more.

"Astrea!" said Ebon. "We have left her behind!"

"Isra had her under command," said Lilith. "She will not be harmed."

Ebon glanced back, uncertain. But what could he do, other than throw himself into Isra's wrath and surely perish?

Soon they reached the vault entrance and burst into the Academy halls. Now the place was well-lit by torches, and Ebon felt his heart in his throat. If Isra caught sight of them for so much as a second, they were lost. He saw that Nella had taken Erin from Kalem's arms and was panting heavily as she ran. Kalem was barely keeping up with them. The boy wept in fear, his breath wheezing from his near-bursting lungs.

Now they could not worry about being discovered. Indeed, Ebon hoped someone would spot them, because then they could give warning of Isra's presence. But there was no one in the halls. No instructors, no other faculty. They would have to survive on their own.

Just as they turned a corner, making for the front

hall, there came a *crack* of shattering stone. Shards of granite flew through the air. One struck Ebon in the arm, forcing a cry of pain. Isra must have just caught a glimpse of them as they fled around a corner. He thanked the sky that she had not seen them in full view. But then he saw Nella and Kalem. Their pace flagged more and more with each step—Kalem from weariness, and Nella from carrying the dean's son.

Without warning he shoved them off down the next side hallway they passed. "Go!" he cried. "Get Erin to safety and get help. She will not kill all of us, at least." Then he took Lilith's arm and ran on with her. Nella cried out in protest, but she did not come after them, and soon he heard the sound of her footsteps hurrying off beside Kalem's.

Ebon and Lilith reached the end of the hall, and he pulled her to a stop before they turned the corner. Together they faced the way they had come, ready to dive out of sight the moment Isra came into view. Lilith glanced at him. "That was bravely done, Drayden," she said.

"The least I could do," muttered Ebon.

Isra rounded the corner at the other end of the hall. She was so surprised to see them standing there, facing her without running, that she skidded to a stop and nearly fell over. For half a moment she paused, too shocked even to use her magic against them.

In that half-moment, Ebon took her in. Her hair was all dishevelment, sticking out in many directions. Her clothes were filthy from collar to hem, and grime covered every bit of her skin. Hiding in the vaults had given her little opportunity to bathe, it seemed.

"Run!" he cried, and dove out of view with Lilith. Too late, a black glow sprang into Isra's eyes, and stones in the wall behind them shattered as she struck.

"She will chase us now, I think," said Ebon, breaking into a sprint.

"What wonderful news," said Lilith. They shared a grim smile.

They reached the next corner half a moment too late. Just as Ebon thought he was about to pass it safely, an invisible force picked him up and slammed him into a wall. For one moment he floated there, feeling Isra's magic crush him. But Lilith turned back, and with magelight in her eyes she struck. A blast of wind slammed into Isra. She fell to the floor, surprised by the attack. Ebon slumped, and Lilith dragged him up after her.

"It is only a matter of time before she catches us," said Ebon. Then he cried out, screaming as loud as his burning lungs would let him. "Help! Help! An enemy within the halls!"

Lilith seized his sleeve and slapped him, then shoved him on to run again. "Be silent, you fool! You will only bring more into the fray—more for Isra to kill. And I have an idea."

They were near the front hall now, but Lilith turned from it. Soon after, she skidded to a stop before a door Ebon recognized. It was the entrance to the bell tower.

He balked. "Here? But atop the tower, we will be trapped."

"Not if we can throw her from it," said Lilith. "It is the only thing I can think of." Light sprang into her eyes, and a massive ball of flame erupted from her fingers. The door exploded with a heavy *BOOM,* falling inwards as smoldering kindling.

They ran to the stairs and up, and now Ebon's lungs screamed in earnest. His pace flagged, but then he heard Isra's shrieks of rage beneath them, and fright lent his legs new strength. The stairs behind them crumpled, and one piece of railing after another exploded into splinters. Ebon raised his arm to shield himself as they pounded up the stairway. But it blocked them from Isra's view, and she could only lash out at the space around them, not ensnare them in her mindwyrd.

When at last they reached the top of the tower, Ebon fell to all fours. He forced himself to crawl forwards, heedless of Lilith when she seized his shoulder and dragged him on. Fighting to his feet seemed like the hardest thing he had ever done.

"I will hide in one corner, and you another," she said. "Whoever she finds first, the other will be behind her. If it is you, you must strike. You cannot stay your hand. Do you hear me?"

He nodded, too breathless to speak. She shoved him behind many coils of rope piled high and then ran to the same place she had hidden when he first saw her in the tower.

The place went silent. Ebon gasped and gulped, trying to control his breath, fearful that Isra would be able to hear him.

Then he heard footsteps coming up the stairs. He clapped his hand over his mouth.

Each step made the stairs creak and groan. The wood was old already, and Isra's assault had battered it so that it was now even more unsteady. But then she reached the top, and the sound of her footsteps vanished. Ebon froze, trying to press himself deeper into the coils of rope.

When a few moments had passed without a sound or sight of her, he dared to poke his head out to peer with one eye around the rope coils.

Isra came into view. The black glow raged in her eyes. She held both hands raised, ready to strike. Her frame was nearly skeletal. Her hair seemed somehow thinner than he remembered. Skin clung to her bones so that her face was little more than a skull.

A noise came from the crates where Lilith was hiding. Isra whirled. Ebon looked desperately around. There was a large metal hook on the ground, as big as both his hands. He stooped and lifted it. With a cry he jumped out of the ropes, swinging the hook at her.

She turned too quickly, and a wall of force met him in midair. It pitched him back against the ropes, which scattered in all directions. He slumped to the ground and fought to rise again. But behind Isra, he saw Lilith step out of hiding. Magelight was in her eyes, and she screamed a word of power. Isra turned and held up a hand. Lilith's magelight died. Isra seized her and threw her sideways with terrible force.

Lilith struck the stone floor ten paces away, slid under the railing, and vanished screaming over the edge.

"No!" cried Ebon, leaping up. He swung the hook again. This time Isra did not strike him, but seized him with her magic and lifted him into the air. Invisible fingers clutched at his throat, and it felt like two steel plates pressed his body flat. He struggled for breath, but could not even raise his hands to clutch at his neck. An image flashed into his mind of his battle against Cyrus on the southern cliffs of the Seat. But now Adara was not here to save him.

"Drayden," hissed Isra. "The goldshitter whose shit is most golden of all. I wish I had killed you in the kitchens, but it will be sweeter after waiting for so long."

Ebon tried to answer her, but he could only wheeze.

"You will not speak except to answer my questions," said Isra. She tightened her fingers closer to a fist, and Ebon cried out in pain. "Now tell me: who was the man with you in the basement of Xain's house?"

Spots danced at the edge of his vision, and for a moment Ebon could not understand her words. Snarling, she let her hand relax a bit, and the pressure on his chest relented. "Mako," he gasped. "His name is Mako. He works for my family."

"How did he withstand me?" said Isra. "I had the

amulet. Even if he was a wizard, he should not have been able to stop me."

"He is no wizard," said Ebon. "I do not know why your magic was powerless against him."

She gave a frustrated shout and clenched her fist. Ebon tried to scream, but could only choke. He felt his spit catch in his windpipe, but he could not even cough it up. He began to suffocate.

The black glow increased in Isra's eyes, and her nostrils flared. "Tell me how he withstood my magic," she said. Her voice was suddenly thick and rich with power.

Ebon felt something close over his mind. It was like a fist gripped his thoughts with a force just as powerful as that which held his body. She had used her mindwyrd upon him. His muscles went slack, and he stopped his struggling. He could no longer force his vacant eyes to focus. In his mind he screamed, but his mouth made no sound. He was watching his body act now, and all thought of control had gone.

"I do not know how he withstood your magic," he said, his voice toneless. He had not summoned the words.

"You are under my command!" cried Isra. "Tell me how he did it!"

"I do not know," said Ebon. "I cannot tell you."

She bared her teeth. Trapped within his own mind, Ebon knew he was about to die. He could not give her any answers. And without answers he was of no value to her. He braced himself and readied to be crushed or thrown from the tower's edge.

But the glow in Isra's eye faltered. She shuddered, and the force clutching Ebon vanished all at once. He came crashing to the ground as Isra sank to one knee.

At once she fumbled in her robes, reaching for something in one of her pockets. "I am so close now," she muttered. "You will not stop me. You cannot stop me."

For a moment Ebon was stunned, too surprised to act. But he recovered just in time, just as she pulled forth a brown cloth packet. Just as she pulled a black, translucent stone from within it, he bore her to the ground. The cloth packet spilled from her grip, and the stones scattered on the floor.

Isra scrabbled for them, fighting him with the strength of a madwoman. But her limbs were thin and wasted, and Ebon forced her hands away. One of his hands went to cover her eyes so that she could not use her magic against him. The other went to her throat. Almost unbidden, he felt his power flow into him, and the tower grew brighter as his eyes began to glow.

He *saw* her. All the tiny parts of her that made up her skin, and the flesh beneath, and the blood that flowed through it all.

Almost, he changed it. Almost, he turned it to stone. But he froze at the last second.

He saw Cyrus plunging into the Great Bay. And he heard Matami's screams in the sewers beneath the city.

She will kill you, he thought. He remembered Lilith pitching over the tower's edge, and his jaw clenched.

He *changed*—

A glow flooded Isra's eyes, and she flung him off with desperate strength. He flew back, landing flat on his back on the stone, and all his breath left him. Even as he gasped, he saw Isra scoop one of the black stones off the floor and shove it between her lips. Her whole body spasmed, back arching and then curling in on itself. She screamed, but the scream turned into a laugh, terrible and long and cruel. The black glow returned to her eyes, and she rose to her feet on the strength of her magic alone. Once more her teeth showed in a skull's smile.

"Now die, you Drayden shit," she growled.

Ebon flinched—and then flames erupted all over her body, and she fell to the ground, screaming.

He looked past her. There, beyond all hope, was Xain. The dean stood at the head of the stairs, and a mighty glow was in his eyes. His teeth were bared in a grimace just as terrible as Isra's, and he screamed dark words as the flames leaped higher on Isra's skin.

But Isra had the strength of magestones, and she recovered herself before he could press the advantage. She snarled, and the flames upon her skin winked out in an instant. Still smoking and smoldering, she turned and battered him with spells. Xain tried to fend them off, but she overpowered him and he fell back, landing hard on the stone floor. Still he raised a hand, warding off a blow that might have crushed his head to a pulp.

Somehow Ebon found the strength to rise. He tackled Isra from behind, and again he covered her eyes with his hand. Crying out, he tried to press harder, digging into her eyelids. But her fingers gripped his, and with terrible strength she began to pry off his grip.

"Ebon! Get away from her!" cried a voice.

The shout dragged up his gaze. Lilith knelt at the tower's edge. Fury was in her eyes, and her lips spasmed in anger.

He rolled off and away. Almost before he was clear, Lilith sent forth a bolt of lightning. It flew straight and true, and struck Isra straight in the eyes.

Isra screamed, a scream so terrible that Ebon feared his eardrums might burst, and her head struck the stone as she flew back. She thrashed back and forth, clawing at her eyes, but between her fingers Ebon could see the damage: beneath her brow was a ruined pulp, a mix of burned and melted flesh and flowing blood.

Lilith stepped forwards, lifting her hands again. Her screams matched Isra's own, as full of fury as the mindmage's were of pain. Flames sprang to life on Isra's body again, white-hot, so that Ebon had to shield his face from them. He scrambled away from the roasting fires and the sudden sounds of melting, popping, sizzling flesh. Lilith did not relent. The flames grew in strength, rising higher and higher. Even when Isra stopped moving at last, Lilith kept the fires blazing, kept screaming, tears streaming from her glowing eyes as the corpse turned to slag upon the floor.

FORTY

The tower faded to silence. The only sounds were the crackling of the flames on Isra's remains and Lilith's ragged, heavy breathing. Her hands began to shake. She looked at them, fear dawning in her eyes. Quickly she shoved them into her sleeves and huddled her arms against herself as if for warmth—and indeed, now that the terror had begun to leach away, Ebon was again aware of how cold the air was. Outside the tower, a light snow had begun to fall, and it skittered in little eddies around the belfry.

Behind Lilith there came a groan, and Xain struggled groggily to his feet. Ebon's heart skipped a beat as the dean straightened and looked at him. When Xain walked towards him, Ebon fought to crawl away—but Xain only reached down a hand to help him up. Ebon stared at it a moment before reaching up to take it. They clasped wrists, and in a moment Ebon was on his feet.

"Are you all right?" said Xain gruffly.

Ebon tried to speak, but did not know what to say. In the end he shook his head.

Xain snorted. "Fairly said."

Lilith was now shaking where she stood. Ebon stepped past Xain and went to her. Just before he reached her, her knees gave way—and to his surprise, she clutched his shoulders and held him in a sort of embrace. His hands hovered in the air, unsure of what to do, before he gingerly placed them on her back. It lasted only a moment, and then she stepped away, refusing to meet his eyes. But she left a hand on his arm, gripping him tight for support.

"She threw you from the tower," said Ebon.

Lilith's brow furrowed. She pointed to the edge over which she had been thrown, and together they went to it. Just below the edge, Ebon saw one of the great hanging banners with the Academy's sigil upon it.

"I caught hold of the banner," said Lilith. "If I had not, I would be dead."

They turned to see Xain staring at both of them. Ebon could read nothing in his expression.

"You found her in the vaults," said the dean. There was no question in his voice. "How?"

Ebon shook his head. "Ever since we saw her in the kitchens, my friends and I have been searching for her—and my family as well. Even when the corpse was found. But our best efforts turned up nothing, and we thought she must not be on the Seat. It was only tonight I realized that the vaults were the one place on the island she could hide where no one would find so much as a trace of her."

But thought of the vaults reminded him of Astrea. His eyes went wide. "In the vaults, hiding with her, we found—"

Xain raised a hand to stop him. "Astrea. She is in the healing ward now, and under Jia's care. My son is with them."

His voice grew thick at that, and he blinked hard as he looked away. It was a moment before he went on.

"Kalem found me almost at once, for I had been roused by the sound of your flight. Then I followed the trail of destruction here to the belfry."

His eyes fell upon Isra's corpse—or what remained of it. Ebon did not even wish to look at the body, it was so twisted by the flames. Xain recoiled, though Ebon saw it was not from the sight of melted flesh. He had focused instead on the black stones scattered upon the ground.

"The magestones," he said. "Gather them."

Ebon glanced at Lilith. She nodded and released

his arm. Ebon went to do as he was bid, scooping the magestones up into the brown cloth packet from which they had fallen. Some had been caught in the flames that had consumed Isra, but Ebon saw that they had not been burned.

"Destroy them," said Xain, once Ebon had gathered them all up.

Ebon raised them before his eyes. "Should I . . . should I crush them?"

Xain shook his head at once. "No. Not here. Not where we can . . . not here."

"Shall I throw them from the tower, then?"

"*No,* you fool," snapped Xain. "Some student will find them and go mad, or worse, someone *else* will find them, and then all the Academy will be purged as abominations."

Annoyed now, Ebon thrust the packet forwards. "Fine, then. Destroy them yourself."

Xain recoiled as though Ebon had thrown an adder in his face. "No! Get them away from me. Fire. Only fire will do it."

Ebon pointed to Isra's corpse. "They were caught already in the flames. It did not harm them."

"Not magical fire," said Xain. "True fire."

The belfry's torches were all cold. Ebon thought for a moment, and then with a flash of realization, he reached into his pocket. His fingers closed around Halab's firestriker. With a few quick squeezes, he cast a flurry of sparks upon the brown cloth packet. It caught like parchment, blazing with surprising heat and forcing him to step back—but the flames were dark and twisted, and seemed to reach for him.

Xain quivered, his whole body shaking as a long and ragged breath slipped from him. He closed his eyes for a moment, and Ebon thought he saw the dean sniff. When his eyes opened again, they were clear, and fixed upon Ebon's.

"Thank you," he said quietly. "Now, the two of you should come with me. We must fetch your friend Theren from prison, where she should never have been in the first place."

Ebon's heart thundered in his chest. "We are pardoned, then? I thought you might not, for we held the amulet in secret."

Xain fixed him with a look. "Because you knew you would need it against Isra," he said quietly. "And because you knew she held my son. Words will be had—with the King's law, as well as between us. You are not free from all penalty, Drayden. But I will not let the mindmage girl suffer any longer when she only tried to save my own blood. Come."

Lilith took Ebon's arm again, and he felt her hands trembling. He helped her make her shaky way down the bell tower steps after Xain.

FORTY-ONE

THE REST OF THAT NIGHT PASSED LIKE SOME NIGHT-mare, a memory in reverse of when Ebon had gone with Theren to fetch Lilith from the hands of the Mystics. Only this time Theren had not suffered so greatly, for she had not suffered under mindwyrd as Lilith had.

They all returned to the Academy, and there Lilith helped Theren to bed. But Xain took Ebon aside and brought him to his office, demanding to know everything.

For the first time, Ebon spoke freely of Isra. He told Xain what had happened in the dean's home and how Erin had been stolen away in the first place. He told Xain of how Theren had used the amulet of Kekhit upon Dasko, and repeated the tale of how they had seen Isra in the kitchens, and now Xain believed him. He said nothing of Mako, of course, nor his uncle Matami, nor anything to do with the family, for some secrets were not his to tell. Neither did he mention Adara, but when he came to that portion of the tale, he only spoke of going into hiding somewhere in the city. Though Xain's eyes flashed with interest, he held his peace. And at last Ebon told him how he guessed where Isra must be hiding, and came to find her.

When he had finished, Xain stared into the candle on his desk for a long while. In the end he said only, "I see."

Ebon's brows raised. He tried to hold his tongue, but as another silence stretched he felt compelled to speak. "Is that all?"

Xain's mouth worked as though he were chewing upon his own thoughts. "I understand what you have done, Drayden. I even understand why you did it, and your motives were nowhere near so dark as I thought. Yet you have committed crimes—crimes that can carry with them grave punishments."

Ebon tried to hold his head high, but he could feel himself shaking, and knew Xain must see it. "Will those punishments be meted out?"

Xain shook his head, and Ebon's heart leaped—

but when the dean spoke, his hopes were dashed. "I cannot say. At least not now. This is a matter for the morning."

He stood and bid Ebon to return to his dormitory and sleep. Ebon obeyed—or tried to. He lay awake for hours before giving up and going to the common room, where he stared at the flames until morning light showed through the windows. The moment they did, he rose and traversed the Academy's halls, making for the western wards.

Jia sat in a chair outside the door to the healing ward when he arrived. She sagged in her seat, her head drooping, but the moment she spotted him coming she straightened and stood.

"Ebon," she said, nodding stiffly. "I am glad to see you well."

He stopped before her, lifting his chin and giving her a formal half-bow. "And you, Instructor. I much prefer our meetings when you are not trying to throw me before the King's law."

Jia's nostrils flared. "I prefer it when you and your friends are not holding a member of the faculty under mindwyrd."

His face fell, and his mouth worked for a moment as he fought for words to say. In the end, the only thing he could muster was a strangled "I spoke only in jest."

She softened, but only a little. "I know why you did it, Ebon. But sky above . . . what were you thinking? How could you be so foolish? Do you have any idea what it did to Dasko?"

Tears sprang into his eyes as he turned from her. "I do," he said. "I wish I had not . . . that I had not asked Theren to . . ." He stopped before his voice broke.

Jia let the silence rest for a moment. "We can reflect on what we might have done," she said at last. "But that is of limited use. Look to your future instead. You must be better from here on. If you are truly sorry, then you must never be so foolish again. And you must do what you can, now, to make it right."

He swiped his sleeve against his eyes. "I will, Instructor," he whispered. "I promise."

She waited until he met her gaze, and he saw that her eyes shone as well. "I believe you."

Then the door to the healing ward opened, and by unspoken agreement they looked away from each other. A plump older woman stepped out into the hallway and fixed Ebon with a look.

"You are the transmutation student, I imagine?" she said, frowning.

"I am," he said. "Is she all right? I have come to see her."

The healer's eyes widened. "Not likely. She needs rest and time. The madness of mindwyrd was set deep within her, for she wished to believe the lies she was fed. She will not be ready for visitors for a while yet."

Ebon frowned—but over the healer's shoulder, he saw Jia trying to catch his eye. As soon as he looked at her, she nodded and took the healer by the shoulder. "Freya," she said. "I have been working on a poultice that I wanted your opinion on. Could you come and take a look at it for me?"

Freya turned to Ebon a final time and said, "Come back once a week has passed, hm? We will see if she is ready to see anyone then."

"Oh, yes, ma'am," said Ebon, nodding quickly. He meandered off down the hall in the other direction, but slowly, while Jia led Freya away. Once the two of them were out of sight, he stole back towards the healing ward's door and slipped inside.

He saw Astrea at once, for all the other beds in the ward were empty. She glanced at him as he came in. If she was surprised to see him, she did not show it. Indeed, her face did not show any emotion at all. And when Ebon approached her bed, she turned away towards the tall windows that covered the far wall. The pink light of morning painted her face in its glow.

"Hello," said Ebon quietly. "How are you feeling?"

She gave him no answer.

Ebon sighed. "You . . . you have heard what happened by now, I suppose. Or you can guess it."

"Isra is dead," said Astrea. "You killed her."

"I did not—" But Ebon stopped himself and bowed his head. "Yes. I did, in part. I beg you to believe me when I say that she would have killed me if we had not stopped her."

"You do not know that," whispered Astrea.

Again he wanted to answer, but again he held his tongue. Instead he asked another question. It had run through his mind endlessly in the common room as he stared into the flames.

"When I saw you in the vaults," he said. "I asked you if you were under her mindwyrd. You said you were not. That was not a lie, was it?"

Slowly she turned until their eyes met. The silence between them stretched into a chasm.

Ebon's eyes fell away first. "I do not blame you," he said softly. "I have wanted so badly to believe in people before. It is not your fault, what Isra did. It is *not*. Do you understand?"

"She did nothing wrong," said Astrea.

Ebon let that hang there for a moment. Then he said the other thing on his mind. "An alchemist created Isra's corpse," he said. "The one they found in the Great Bay. That alchemist was you."

Astrea's nostrils flared, and for the first time her eyes filled with fear. "Yes," she whispered.

"How?" said Ebon. "How could you do it? You are only a second-year student. Kalem said he did not even know of an alchemist in the Academy who could accomplish such a feat."

Astrea shrugged. "I . . . Isra helped me. There was a black glow in her eyes, and she . . . she *told* me to. And I did. I could. I obeyed her without even knowing how."

Ebon shivered, though he tried to hide it. But just

then, the door to the healing ward creaked open. Ebon shot to his feet, expecting a tongue-lashing from Freya. But instead, Xain appeared in the doorway. Ebon's stomach did a somersault.

"I . . . I am sorry for sneaking in," he said. "I only wanted to see—"

Xain cut him off with a wave. "Stay your fear, Drayden. I am not here about that. But a matter needs tending to."

Something in his tone made Ebon quail. "What matter?"

To his surprise, Xain grew solemn. "The matter of punishment," he said quietly. "Come."

Ebon's feet seemed suddenly to be made of lead. He turned back to Astrea upon the bed. "I will come and visit again," he said. "As soon as I can. Be well, and rest."

She turned away once more and gave him no answer. He forced his limbs to move, and followed Xain out the door.

Xain led him through the halls and towards his office. Ebon wanted to ask him what this was all about, but he also feared to speak, and that fear kept him silent.

When Xain opened the door, Ebon's heart sank still further. Within the room were Kalem, Theren, and Lilith. But there, too, was Instructor Dasko. The man sat in a chair, leaning heavily upon the armrest, his chin buried in his fist. He looked up as the door opened, and his eyes fixed on Ebon, and narrowed.

After he had ushered Ebon in, Xain moved around behind his desk and sat. Ebon took his place beside Theren. She was seated in the other chair and had her arms clutched about herself. She had been cleaned up considerably after Ebon had seen her the night before, but bruises still stood out angrily on her cheeks, and she pulled her sleeves low to hide the cuts and scars on her arms. Lilith stood on Theren's other side, her hands folded as she studied the floor. Kalem was looking all about the room, licking his lips nervously. Theren's eyes stared straight ahead—not at Dasko, nor at Xain, but somewhere in between them, and seeing nothing.

"Now then," said Xain. "In accordance with my duty as the dean, a matter of punishment must now be resolved. I speak of crimes committed by students in this room, against a member of the Academy's faculty also present."

Silence stretched. If Xain expected Dasko to say anything, he was disappointed, for the instructor only kept his eyes on Theren. Upon the arm of the chair, his fingers had begun to twitch.

Xain cleared his throat. "For a period of many days, you, Theren, held Instructor Dasko under mindwyrd. You forced him to obey your commands, and through him you spied upon the Academy's investigations into Isra. You did this to hide your own involvement in the events that took place in my home, in which Isra stole many artifacts that were under the care of the Academy. Those artifacts are yet to be recovered, and are likely lost. Ebon, Kalem, and Lilith—you all knew of the mindwyrd, though Lilith learned later than the rest. You are complicit in the crime, though your punishment, if there is one, will be less."

"If there is one?" said Theren, her voice a weak croak.

"Yes," said Xain. "Your knowledge of the stolen artifacts is an Academy matter, and therefore under my judgement. In light of the punishment you, Theren, have already received, and your aid in rescuing my son from Isra's clutches, I have decided to pardon those crimes. But your use of mindwyrd is another matter. Instructor Dasko was your victim, and so it is for him to decide whether you will be punished for using it against him."

Ebon's breath seeped from him in a quiet sigh. But then he saw Dasko's eyes. The Instructor regarded him with cold scorn. Now he sat straighter in his chair, like a king about to pronounce judgement from his throne.

"I do not pardon them," he said. "They will be punished. All of them."

"What?" said Ebon. "Instructor, you cannot."

"I cannot?" said Dasko. His hand shook where it gripped the arms of his chair. "Do you even know what your schemes have done to me, Ebon? She was inside my mind. My memory is in shambles. Sometimes I forget where I am—I have forgotten *who* I am, on occasion. I will never remember all the times the three of you dragged me into the garden, when you wiped away my very thoughts, where you took away my will. *My mind is not my own,* even now. And you tell me that I cannot?"

Ebon could say nothing. He tried to plead with his eyes, but Dasko's own were hard and vicious. Silent tears leaked from Theren.

Xain's jaw clenched. "Mindwyrd can carry the penalty of death," he said softly. "Withholding knowledge of it may bring banishment. Do you wish to press for these punishments?"

The office fell utterly silent for a moment. Ebon's heart stopped. *He will do it. He will sentence Theren to death.*

But though his mouth twisted, Dasko grated out. "No. She need not die for this. But she will be banished from the Academy. They all will."

Ebon felt as though a hammer had struck him between the eyes, casting him out of his own body so that he was watching events take place from afar. He could not feel his skin. He could not feel the breath in his chest. Theren's tears dried at once, as though she had moved to a place beyond grief. But Kalem took her place, casting his gaze into his hands and weeping openly. Even Lilith's dark skin had gone a shade paler.

This meant least to her, Ebon knew. She would return to her family, almost a full-fledged wizard already. Kalem had many more years of schooling ahead of him, but he, too, would return to a family who would welcome him, and mayhap they would even find him a private tutor to continue his training. If not, he had gotten far enough in the Academy that he could continue practicing, and mayhap come to the height of his power in time.

But Theren. Ebon wanted to weep as he saw her there, trying so hard to sit straight in her chair, trying so hard not to let the pain shine through in her eyes. Theren would suffer more than any of them. She would be forced to go home to a patron she hated and who disdained her, and would make her perform mind-numbing toil in court for the rest of her days.

"No," said Ebon, softly.

Dasko's eyes snapped to him. "You think to countermand me?" he said, voice nearing a shout. "You think that after—"

Quickly Ebon shook his head. "I did not mean that, Instructor," he said, his words growing in strength. "I know your anger is justified. But I beg you: do not turn it into punishment against the rest of them. Your mindwyrd was my idea. From the very first. Every day, Kalem argued against it. I had to drag him from Xain's house the first time we took control. Theren begged me—*begged* me, Instructor—to stop, to throw the amulet into the Great Bay. She did not suffer as you have suffered, but she suffered enough. And now the Mystics have had days to play their knives across her skin. I put the plan into motion, and I ordered it to continue.

Banish me. Punish me even further than that, if you want. But spare the others."

That stunned the room to silence. Theren did not look at him, but Kalem did, and Ebon saw tears shining in the boy's eyes. Lilith showed her gratitude in a small nod, while Xain leaned back as if appraising him. But Ebon's heart sank as the fury in Dasko's face only doubled.

"I believe you," said Dasko quietly. "I believe you, and I call myself a fool for not seeing it earlier. I came to you before because I thought you might be like your brother. He was a good man, and sought to escape the darkness of your family name. But now I see that he was alone in that. You are a schemer, a trickster, and vile as any of your kin. If the headsman's axe hovered over your neck instead, I would jump upon it with both feet. But I will not spare your accomplices. Let them learn what it means to follow the will of an evil man."

Before Ebon could reply, Theren spoke up. "Followers we might have been, but not equal in sharing the blame," said Theren. "It was I who controlled you, Dasko. I will vouch for the truth in Ebon's words—Kalem urged countless times for us to stop, until even I wearied of it. And Lilith has known of it for all of a few days. Punish Ebon, and punish me. The mastermind, and the lackey who did the deed. Spare the others."

Dasko's nostrils flared. He studied her for a long

moment, until Ebon was sure he would refuse. At last he shot to his feet and sniffed.

"Very well," he said. "The boy and the Yerrin girl may stay. But I hope never to lay eyes upon the other two again."

Dasko swept from the room, even as a high whine sprang up at the edge of Ebon's hearing, like a scream in his mind.

He was banished.

He was banished from the Academy.

FORTY-TWO

No one in the office moved for a long while. Theren was the first to stir. She fought to gain her feet, and Lilith quickly came forwards to help her. Ebon, too, took an arm. When at last she had risen, she met his eyes.

"I am sorry," he said. "This only happened to you because of me."

Theren pursed her lips, and then shrugged. "I could not have long remained in any case. But you are right, it would not have happened if not for you."

She took a halting, lurching step, aided by Lilith.

Ebon held her as best he could, though she did not put much weight upon him. "I am sorry, Theren. Please. There must be something I can do. Mayhap my family . . ."

He trailed off as she shook her head slowly. "No. No, let your family be. This is not their doing—not for the most part, anyway." He knew she was thinking of Mako. "Only be better in the future, Ebon. Remember this, and remember that the false path never leads to a good end."

Ebon drew back. But she softened her words by taking his arm, and pulling him close for an embrace. "I do not hate you, Ebon. And I am not leaving tomorrow. We will have time to speak again. But now I must rest."

Lilith helped her hobble out the door. Kalem stared at it for a moment. Then he burst into tears and fled into the halls. Ebon meant to go after him, but Xain raised a hand and spoke.

"A moment, Drayden. I am sure your friends need tending to, but you and I must speak first."

"I . . ." Ebon looked to the door. He considered ignoring Xain's words and running after Kalem.

"Give them time," said Xain, but gently, as if he had heard the thought in Ebon's mind. "Come."

Xain rose and guided Ebon out of the office. He led the way through the halls and out a white cedar door onto the Academy grounds. The hour was still early, and their breath misted in the air. Ebon rubbed his arms against the chill.

"Allow me," said Xain. He whispered as his eyes glowed, and a small ball of flame sprang up before them and between them. Ebon held his fingers out towards it.

"Thank you," he said softly.

Xain nodded. Then he sighed, as though preparing himself for a most unpleasant task. "I am not skilled in such things, and so I will be brief: I was wrong to think so poorly of you simply because of your family name. I treated you worse than I ought, and that was my error. It does not excuse what you did, but mayhap my own ire made things worse than they might have been."

"Worse than you ought?" said Ebon, arching an eyebrow.

Xain's jaw clenched. "*Much* worse, I suppose."

But Ebon only shrugged. "In all honestly, I am rather used to such treatment by now."

His words earned another sigh. "I suppose you are right. Many of us, it seems, are accused of crimes these days in which we were blameless."

Ebon gave him a look. "You mean what happened between you and Drystan, and Cyrus as well," he said.

Xain's easy look darkened: not, Ebon felt, out of anger at him, but rather at a memory. "I suppose everyone here knows something of that, do they not? I do not know if you had any love for Cyrus, but I—"

"I killed him."

Xain went very still. He stared at Ebon for a long moment. "Say that again."

"I killed Cyrus," said Ebon. "It was the day the

Seat was attacked. I saw him sneaking off through the streets. I followed him to the cliffs on the south of the island, and there he attacked me. I turned his feet to stone, and then I cast him into the water, where he drowned." Tears stung his eyes, and his breath came short in his chest.

"If that is true, why would you not tell the King's law?" said Xain. "If you defended yourself—"

"I do not fear the King's law," said Ebon. "But do you think my family would feel the same?"

The dean's lips twitched. "You should not be telling me this. Why would you?"

"Because I need you to understand," said Ebon, his voice cracking. "I could have stopped Isra when we fought her in your basement. And I could have stopped her last night, before you arrived. Only . . . only every time she was at my mercy, and I could have taken her life, or allowed it to be taken by another—I saw Cyrus, I heard his screaming, the way I do in my dreams, over and over again—"

He broke off, for his voice would not last much longer, and he turned away so that Xain could not see the tears in his eyes.

Now you have done it, you fool, he told himself. *Now Xain will reveal you, and your life will be forfeit.*

Let it.

"It was my fault your son was taken," he whispered. "I thank the sky that he survived, but he might not have. Because of me."

He still faced away from Xain. But behind him, he heard the dean sigh.

"It is no ignoble thing to stay the hand from killing," said Xain softly. "I have taken my share of lives. My share and more. Yet someone wiser than I am reminded me in recent days that it is not for the living to lightly mete out death."

When Ebon looked again, Xain's eyes were far away. "Then you will reveal my crime to the constables? I would not blame you."

Xain snorted. "Your murder of Cyrus? Hardly. I knew the man—likely better than you did. I am not so reckless about killing as I once was, mayhap, but I will not mourn his passing."

Shaking, Ebon let loose a long sigh. "I am . . . relieved to hear it."

"I imagine you are," said Xain, fixing him with a stern glare. "But your relief may not last long. For I heard what Theren said to you, and I agree with her. If you seek redemption for what you have done, you cannot look to your past, but to the future. And not just your future—but the future of all of Underrealm."

The air had grown thick with tension, so thick that Ebon found his breath coming shallow. "What do you mean?" he said.

"You must leave the Academy, yet I do not think you wish to return to your home of Idris," said Xain. "What if I could arrange for you to stay here upon the Seat? I could even arrange for you to have a private tutor—an instructor who would continue your training in magic."

Ebon's heart thundered in his chest. "You would do that?" he said, managing little more than a whisper.

"Yes. But not for free."

"What, then? I would pay a hefty price for such a gift."

Xain shook his head. "I do not want your coin. Rather, I want what your coin has secured: your family's influence and power across the nine kingdoms."

Ebon blinked. "I do not understand. What do you mean?"

Xain hesitated. "I only share this with you because you have proven yourself to be . . . something nobler than your kin. I know the Drayden name and the darkness that surrounds it, and you do as well. Yet as a Drayden, you have access to resources I could never hope to muster on my own."

"I thought you were favored by the High King herself."

"So I am, and we work together in this," said Xain. "Yet the High King Enalyn walks in the light of her own laws. The Draydens often dip into the darkness beyond those laws. That is where I think you might help me. All sanctioned by the High King. You will face no blame for any help you give us."

Fear thrummed in Ebon's chest, and he felt himself standing on the edge of a precipice. "You do not make this sound like any light matter, Dean."

"Nor is it. You are about to learn something known only to a handful of people across Underrealm. You are going to help me find the Necromancer."

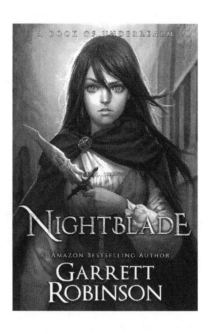

KEEP READING

You've finished The Firemage's Vengeance, the third book of the Academy Journals.

More books are on their way. But while Ebon struggles to uncover the secrets lurking on the Seat, another young champion hounds a traitorous merchant across the nine lands.

That tale is told in the Nightblade Epic, another series of novels set in Underrealm—and in their pages, you can discover how Xain Forredar became the Dean of the Academy.

Take your next step into the world of Underrealm. Visit:

Underrealm.net/Nightblade

ACKNOWLEDGEMENTS

Well. I hope you're pleased with yourself.

Really, in general, I hope you're pleased with yourself. You're awesome. And I appreciate you.

But on a more immediate note, I hope you're pleased with this book.

If you are, it's because of several people who are not me. And they deserve their moment of your attention, because they really went above and beyond.

First and last, my wife. This book was written during a tremendously tumultuous period for both of us. My business partnership dissolved, and she stepped in to fill the gap. As I tap out these pages, we are moving our family from one state to the next, and she's handling the lion's share of that planning. And through it all she's remained my confidante and best friend.

My children, by remaining blissfully oblivious to the unbelievable stress their parents are under right now, have been a constant escape I can always rely on. When my work gets overwhelming, I spend time with them and pretend the world is as carefree as they believe it to be.

Karen Conlin, my editor, is as stalwart as my wife (though in a very different way, of course, at least as far as our personal relationship is concerned). I have never been as confident in the work I produce as I am now that she runs her keen eyes across it.

With this book, my beta readers have rendered

their greatest service since the almost-apocalypse that was *Darkfire*. Thank you, Jess, for revealing this book's fundamental flaw before it went to the presses, and especial thanks to the "new kid," Joe. Thanks as well to Erad, Karl, and Kristen.

To my advance readers—you people are the best. You made last book's release epic, and I can't wait to see what we do with this one (and all the ones to come).

Thank you to the Vloganovel crew, too many to name, but all appreciated. So many writers shudder in horror at the thought of writing with an audience. I recoil, instead, at the thought of going on these journeys alone, without you by my side.

And last as she is first, my wife again. Just hold on, Meg. We're al . . . most . . . there.

Garrett Robinson
June 2016

CONNECT ONLINE

FACEBOOK

Want to hang out with other fans of the Underrealm books? There's a Facebook group where you can do just that. Join the Nine Lands group on Facebook and share your favorite moments and fan theories from the books. I also post regular behind-the-scenes content, including information about the world you can't find anywhere else. Visit the link to be taken to the Facebook group:

Underrealm.net/nine-lands

YOUTUBE

Catch up with me daily (when I'm not directing a film or having a baby). You can watch my daily YouTube channel where I talk about art, science, life, my books, and the world.
But not cats.
Never cats.

GarrettBRobinson.com/yt

THE BOOKS OF UNDERREALM

THE NIGHTBLADE EPIC
NIGHTBLADE
MYSTIC
DARKFIRE
SHADEBORN
WEREMAGE
YERRIN

THE ACADEMY JOURNALS
THE ALCHEMIST'S TOUCH
THE MINDMAGE'S WRATH
THE FIREMAGE'S VENGEANCE

CHRONOLOGICAL ORDER
NIGHTBLADE
MYSTIC
DARKFIRE
SHADEBORN
THE ALCHEMIST'S TOUCH
THE MINDMAGE'S WRATH
WEREMAGE
THE FIREMAGE'S VENGEANCE
YERRIN

ABOUT THE AUTHOR

Garrett Robinson was born and raised in Los Angeles. The son of an author/painter father and a violinist/singer mother, no one was surprised when he grew up to be an artist.

After blooding himself in the independent film industry, he self-published his first book in 2012 and swiftly followed it with a stream of others, publishing more than two million words by 2014. Within months he topped numerous Amazon bestseller lists. Now he spends his time writing books and directing films.

A passionate fantasy author, his most popular books are the novels of Underrealm, including The Nightblade Epic and The Academy Journals series.

However, he has delved into many other genres. Some works are for adult audiences only, such as *Non Zombie* and *Hit Girls,* but he has also published popular books for younger readers, including The Realm Keepers series and *The Ninjabread Man*, co-authored with Z.C. Bolger.

Garrett lives in Oregon with his wife Meghan, his children Dawn, Luke, and Desmond, and his dog Chewbacca.

Garrett can be found on:

BLOG: garrettbrobinson.com/blog
EMAIL: garrett@garrettbrobinson.com
TWITTER: twitter.com/garrettauthor
FACEBOOK: facebook.com/garrettbrobinson

EPILOGUE

Halab looked up from her wine as Mako opened the door. He stepped into the drawing room and then stood aside, holding the door open.

Nella stepped into the room. Her gaze flew everywhere, and Halab could see at once how the girl was overwhelmed by the finery. Not a merchant child, though Halab had heard she was friendly with the Yerrin girl.

Mako closed the door with a soft *click*. "Tell her what you told me," he said gently.

The girl looked up in fear, meeting Halab's eyes for

the first time. Halab smiled at her. Nella gave a little smile back, seeming to draw some comfort from the gesture.

"I . . . I told him about the day the Seat was attacked. I saw Ebon slip away from the other students."

"This has reached my ears already," said Halab. "Did he not run off trying to help a student who had become lost, only to discover she was a handmaiden from the palace?"

"That is what he told everyone when he came back," said Nella, nodding. "But it is not the truth. He and I were fighting together. We battled those— the grey-and-blue clad warriors, the ones they call Shades. So when he ran off, I ran after him a pace or two before I turned back. And I saw where he really went."

Halab took a sip of wine. Then she shook her head. "Sky above, forgive me, girl. My manners have fled me. Would you like a cup of wine?"

Nella swallowed hard. "I might. I can finish the story first, if it pleases my lady."

"Oh, I am no woman of nobility," said Halab, smiling graciously. "And there is no hurry. Mako, pour her a cup. You may take the chair beside me, girl."

The girl nodded and came forwards to sit in the chair. Mako had a cup in her hand in the space of a heartbeat, and she sipped at it. Her eyes widened, and she took another, deeper sip.

"That is the best wine I have ever tasted," she said.

Halab's smile grew. "We keep fine vintages on hand. Now, please continue."

"Well—and now, understand, I only glimpsed them for a moment—I saw Cyrus. Cyrus of the family—well, your kin. He was the dean before the new one, that man Xain with the dark eyes."

The room went quiet. Halab looked from Nella's face over to Mako. The bodyguard's expression betrayed nothing.

Nella felt the tension in the room, clearly, for her next sip of wine was timid. "That . . . that is who Ebon went after. Not some palace woman. He went after Cyrus. What happened to them both after that, I do not know."

Halab had not taken her gaze from Mako. "Does this mean what it sounds like it means?"

Mako shrugged. "Mayhap. Cyrus is dead; that much we know. If he were not, I would have found him. Ebon might have killed him."

Pursing her lips, Halab stared into her cup. She took another sip. Beside her, Nella's eyes had gone saucer-wide. She drank a heavy gulp of her own cup.

"Halab." Mako's tone had become worried, reluctant. "This throws everything into disarray. Cyrus should have died in the fighting, so that others would think he perished heroically upon the Seat. The fact that everyone thinks he fled has been a serious blow to our standing, and now, to learn that Ebon might have killed him . . ."

She flung her glass goblet into the fireplace. The glass smashed, and the wine hissed in the flames. "Do not lecture me about what this means," she snapped.

"Of course," said Mako, bowing his head.

"How could this happen?" she shouted, letting the fury show in her voice. It was rare that she let it out, for she had learned long ago that rarity gave it strength. "How could we not have learned this already? It is your job to know such things."

"I learn what I learn in just this way," said Mako quietly. "From the right questions put to the right people. I could not have known that I should have asked this exact girl this exact question. Meaning no disrespect, of course." He inclined his head towards Nella.

Nella still sat frozen in her seat, looking afraid to move. At Mako's words, she shook her head quickly.

"If Cyrus knew of our involvement with the Shades . . ." said Halab.

"He did not," said Mako at once.

"Pardon me if I do not put complete faith in your word just now," spat Halab. "What if he did, Mako? What if he told Ebon?"

Another long moment of silence passed. Mako sighed. "I can . . . I can remove the danger of this situation."

Halab glared at him sharply. "We have already had to kill one of Shay's sons. We will not kill the other. We *will not*. Do you understand me? Ebon may yet be molded. And I love him, Mako. He is not Matami. Am I completely understood?"

Mako bowed again. "Of course, Halab."

Now Nella's face was covered in sweat, though she still feared to move. It was as though she thought that, if she only remained still, they would forget she was there. But as the silence now stretched for longer than ever before, she at last mustered a small, squeaking voice. "Should I remove myself?"

Halab sighed and put her hand over the girl's. "Child, no one must know about what we have spoken of here. You understand that."

Nella's eyes filled with tears. "Of course I understand that. I will never breathe a word of it."

Slowly, sadly, Halab shook her head. "We both know that that is not what I meant."

Mako drew his dagger across the girl's throat. Halab withdrew her hand before the blood could splash upon her fingers.